FROSTED KISSES

Also by Heather Hepler

The Cupcake Queen

Love? Maybe.

FROSTED KISSES

HEATHER HEPLER

Point

Library of Congress Cataloging-in-Publication Data

Hepler, Heather, author.
Frosted kisses / Heather Hepler.—First edition.
pages cm
Sequel to: The cupcake queen.
Summary: After her parents' separation Penny and her mother moved from New York City to Hog's Hollow—now, six months later, Penny is still coping with the dynamics of her new situation, including possible boyfriends, enemies at school, and getting swept up in her best friend Tally's campaign to raise money to save the local animal shelter.
ISBN 978-0-545-79055-0
1. Money-making projects for children—Juvenile fiction. 2. Animal shelters—Juvenile fiction. 3. Best friends—Juvenile fiction. 4. Mothers and daughters—Juvenile fiction. 5. Dating (Social customs)—Juvenile fiction. 6. Schools—Juvenile fiction. [1. Fund raising—Fiction. 2. Animal shelters—Fiction. 3. Best friends—Fiction. 4. Friendship—Fiction. 5. Divorce—Fiction. 6. Dating (Social customs)—Fiction. 7. Schools—Fiction.] I. Title.
PZ7.H4127Fr 2015
813.6—dc23
[Fic]
2015001396

10 9 8 7 6 5 4 3 2 1   15 16 17 18 19

Printed in the U.S.A.   23
First edition, November 2015

Book design by Ellen Duda

FOR HARRISON

Chapter One

When your best friend tells you she needs your help, you say yes. But if your best friend is Tally Greene, who has orange-and-red streaked hair (to match the autumn leaves); loves all animals to the point of obsession (even a prima donna albino vulture); and will do anything for a friend (including pretend to eat lard sandwiches), you might want to ask a few questions *before* saying yes.

Blake is quick to point out my mistake as he hands us our masks, goggles, and gloves. "Penny, this is Tally. You *always* ask more questions."

"I can hear you, you know," she says.

Blake smiles at her. "I know. All I'm saying is that not everyone is quite as willing to go to the lengths you do for the things you believe in."

Tally frowns at him. "Since when is yard work *lengths*?"

"Tally," I say, pulling on my gloves. "I don't think you usually have to wear hazmat gear for yard work."

Tally nods. Then she looks a little sheepish. "Are you mad?" she asks.

"Of course not," I say. "Whatever it is, I'm in."

For some reason, Blake finds this hysterical. "Oh, you'll be *in* all right," he says. He leads us around to the back of the barn.

"Well," he says. "There you go." He points toward a giant mound of deep brown soil.

We walk a little closer and I realize it's not soil. It's compost. Fresh, ripe compost. The brown dirt is marbled with clumps of manure and studded with bits and pieces of kitchen leftovers. Eggshells, lemon rinds, strawberry hulls, and lettuce leaves all peek out from between the clumps.

Tally makes a face. "I thought we were raking leaves."

"There are leaves," Blake says. "And there will be raking." He grabs a couple of rakes leaning against the fence. "Mask up, ladies."

I'd put my mask on as soon as I saw the pile. I might be a city girl, but I know manure when I smell it. I pull my goggles over my eyes and make sure my gloves are secure before taking the rake from Blake. Tally gives Blake one more dirty look before donning her protective gear. Blake quickly explains that we're supposed to mix the piles of leaves and grass clippings into the big pile of compost.

"Got it," Tally says.

"You have to really mix it well," Blake says. "Otherwise the methane gas will build up and there could be an explosion."

"That would be bad," Tally says.

"That would be bad," Blake confirms. "All right, then," he says, nodding toward the pile. "You're burning daylight."

"Okay, bossy," Tally says. She grabs her rake and stomps over to the pile. I start to tell her that stomping in fresh compost probably isn't the best idea, but I'm too late. She hits a grapefruit rind with her heel and sends it rocketing to where Blake is standing. It smacks him in the chest. Even with the mask on, I can tell she's grinning.

Blake smirks and shakes his head. "I'll be back in a while to check on your progress." He starts walking away from us.

"Wait!" Tally calls. "Aren't you going to help us?"

"Nope," Blake says. "I have my own chores." He disappears around the end of the barn, leaving Tally and me and a giant pile of compost all alone.

"Guess we'd better—" Tally lifts one of her feet and examines the bottom of her borrowed boot. When she puts her foot down, it squelches. She looks at me. "Sorry," she says.

"It's fine," I say. "What's a little poop?" I lift a forkful of leaves and toss it onto the pile. "Besides," I say. "It's for a good cause."

Tally's latest big idea was to hire ourselves out to do odd jobs so that we can raise money for the ARK animal shelter. Monica, the ARK's director, wants to buy a backup generator for the exotics building. Without it, one power outage and the lizards and tropical birds could freeze to death. Even with the big discount Lancaster Hardware is giving her, a good generator is easily over three thousand dollars.

"You're a good friend, Penny Lane," Tally says, turning over a forkful of compost. (Yes, Penny Lane—my dad is a hardcore Beatles fan. I guess I'm just lucky he didn't name me Ringo.)

"I am a good friend. Aren't I?"

"And very humble," she says.

"Humility when you're as awesome as I am is very important," I say. This makes Tally laugh.

"Hey!" Blake calls from the corner of the barn. "Get to work!" This makes Tally laugh even more, but we do as he instructs and get to work.

I've only lived in Hog's Hollow for a few months—ever since my parents separated and my dad stayed in Manhattan and my mom and I moved here to live in the town where she grew up. In the short time I've been here, I've learned that Hog's Hollow has to be one of the weirdest places on the planet. Just a few weeks ago, I walked an albino vulture in the Hog Days parade behind a trailer carrying the Hog Queen and her court. The parade route wound right through downtown, past the bank and the antique stores and The Cupcake Queen, my mom's bakery.

I tried to ignore the dirty looks the Hog Queen was giving me. Charity Wharton, aka The Meanest Girl in the Known Universe, had, in spite of Tally's best efforts, been picked as queen. Charity's hated me from the start. At first it was just because my mom had been chosen over her mom for Hog Queen every year they were in high school together. Then it was because I was the cause of a cupcake tsunami at her birthday party. Then she hated me because Marcus, her longtime crush, ended up liking me more than her. Of course the fact that I walked in the parade with Marcus probably didn't help any. But I'd stopped noticing her dirty looks when he'd started holding my hand.

After a while, Tally says, "I think we should take a break."

"I agree," I say. We've been raking and mixing and flipping for close to an hour. And it is hot. Tally and I walk over to one of the apple trees behind Blake's house and sit in the shade. I slide my hands free of my gloves and pull off my mask and goggles. The cool breeze on my face feels good. Tally takes her gear off and lies back in the grass.

"Are you working on Saturn tonight with Marcus?" she asks.

I nod and lean back against the tree. Marcus and his dad are building a stunning to-scale model of the solar system to memorialize Marcus's mother, who passed away almost two years ago. Saturn is the last of the planets to be built, but it is proving to be the most difficult, so Marcus called me this morning and asked if I would help. Building something that beautiful to honor Marcus's mom is one of the most amazing things I've ever heard of. The planets, peeking through the trees, are massive. Saturn's rings are over thirty feet in diameter and Jupiter stands over eighteen feet tall. At night if there's a full moon, you can see the light glinting off of the copper stripes of Jupiter or the red iron of Mars.

"What are you doing tonight?" I ask Tally.

Tally shrugs. "Blake said something about a movie."

"That sounds fun," I say, wishing that Marcus had asked me to go to a movie. I mean, I like helping him and his dad, but other than the Hog's Hollow dance after the parade, we've never actually gone on anything resembling a date.

"Blake will obviously want to see *The Flaming Skull of Death*," she says.

"That's a movie?" I ask.

"Probably," Tally says, smiling. She closes her eyes. "Maybe you should ask him to the movies," she says.

"Blake?" I ask, teasing her. Tally kicks my foot. We've had this discussion before. Tally thinks I should just ask Marcus to the movies. (Or to do anything, really.) But that's Tally. That's not me. We are about as different as we can be. Half of the clothes Tally wears are Tally Originals. I wear jeans and T-shirts and hoodies. Tally dyes her hair all the colors of the rainbow. Mine is brown. Tally is outspoken. I'm quiet.

"Besides, I barely have time to work on Saturn. I promised my mom I'd help this weekend at the bakery, and if I don't learn the irregular French verbs, I'm doomed."

"You could ask Charity to help you," Tally says. Charity, in addition to being fluent in meanness, is also fluent in French.

"Yeah," I say. "That's not going to happen."

"Hey! What are you two doing?" Blake is at the back of the barn holding bottles of water. "I come all the way out here, thinking how hard you must be working and how thirsty you must be, and you two are sandbagging."

"We're done," Tally says.

Blake looks at the pile of compost and nods. "Nice job, ladies." He walks over to us and hands us the bottles of water. I take a long drink.

"Would you stop calling us that?" Tally asks.

"What?" Blake asks.

"Ladies," Tally says.

"Fine," Blake says. "Nice job, dudes." Tally rolls her eyes. It's then that I notice his T-shirt. The front of his shirt reads WITHOUT ME. I frown, wondering what I'm missing. "Well, as soon as you *dudes* are ready, we can move on to the chicken coop."

"Chicken coop?" I ask.

"No problem," Tally says with confidence. I raise my eyebrow at her. I'm not, in general, a fan of chickens. Beady eyes. Pointy beaks. I take another long drink of water, draining my bottle. Tally does the same. Then we hand our empty water bottles back to Blake, pick up our gear, and stand. We walk with Blake toward the gate, where I can already see the chickens milling about. He grabs our rakes on the way.

"You sure about this, Tally?" I whisper.

"We got this," Tally says to me. I wonder how much of that she believes and how much of it is not wanting to show weakness in front of Blake. They are the most competitive non-couple I've ever met. Blake opens the gate and shoos the chickens out of the way. He motions for us to follow.

Six months ago, the only chickens I'd ever seen were photos of hens on the labels of the organic eggs my mom always bought. Now, a dozen or more chickens swirl around me as I follow Tally into the yard. Blake shuts the gate behind us and heads toward the chicken coop. I quickly find out why they call it playing chicken. The hens think it's crazy fun to freak out the city girl by sprinting under my feet, moving just before my boot clips them.

"You might want to put your gear back on," he says.

Tally and I both don our gloves, masks, and goggles again. Blake leans the rakes against the side of the coop, then he pulls the door of the coop open. The smell of ammonia makes my eyes water in spite of the goggles.

"You sure about this, Tal?" Blake asks. I want to say, *No! I'm not sure*, but Tally has a different take on the situation.

"No problem," she says. "Peaches and gravy."

"Don't you mean peaches and cream?" Blake asks. Tally shrugs. We stand in front of the open door for several moments. "Go ahead," Blake says.

Tally glances over at him. "Aren't you coming?" she asks. Suddenly all of her bravado is gone.

"Nope," Blake says. "This is all yours." He turns and heads toward the greenhouse. I see the back of his shirt as he's walking away. On the front: WITHOUT ME. On the back: IT'S JUST AWESO.

Tally sees me reading his shirt. "He got a grab bag from some T-shirt Web site. A dozen shirts for ten dollars or something ridiculous. He won't let me see them until he wears them. Just think. Eleven more to go." She tries to look pained, but I can see through it. Tally adores Blake's weirdness. Just as much as he adores hers. They keep not talking about their relationship. I think it's because Tally's afraid of liking someone too much, then getting burned. And Blake, well, he's a guy. Guys, in general, aren't big fans of the *relationship talk*.

8

"Let's get this over with," Tally says, picking up one of the rakes. She hands it to me and arms herself with the other. "After you," she says, nodding toward the door.

I start to take a deep breath in order to steel myself, but stop short when I'm hit by another wave of the awful smell. I step over the threshold, unsure of what to expect. The inside of the chicken coop is basically a huge box with a human-size door on one end and a chicken-size door on the other. One wall is lined entirely with nesting boxes, while the other sports long rods that I assume are perches. Tally and I begin working our way down the nests, pulling out the dirty hay. We set aside any eggs we find. It's straightforward enough. However, the hens seem determined to supervise, pecking at our boots and squawking orders.

"We'll be finished in no time," Tally says. I nod. We've only been working for about five minutes and we're already halfway down the wall. I'm pretty sure Tally jinxed us because just as she says that, she jerks her hand out of the nest she's cleaning. "Ouch," she says, holding her wrist. There's a slice in the rubber glove she's wearing. She ducks to peer into the dark box, then immediately jumps back with a yelp. "What is that?" she asks, pointing and backing up. A head with an enormous hooked beak and beady eyes emerges, and Tally and I both start inching toward the door as the rest of the bird exits the box. It's easily five times the size of any of the other chickens. A ragged comb flops to one side of the rooster's head. A giant rooster. And does he look mad.

"We should—" Tally says, dropping her rake and backing away from the monstrous rooster. I quickly back up and step over the threshold into the yard, followed closely by Tally. Neither of us seems to want to turn our backs on this behemoth, so we back our way to the gate. Tally keeps making these strange clicking noises and saying, "Good chicken," in a soothing voice. The rooster responds by stretching out his wings and giving an unearthly screech.

Tally screams, turns, and runs for the gate. I try to follow her, but my too-big borrowed rubber boots twist under my feet, sending me sprawling. The pain in the side of my face is immediate as my cheek hits one of the stepping-stones, but it's not enough to distract me from the fact that at any second I'm about to be attacked by the world's largest rooster. I throw my arms over my head.

"George!" It's Blake's voice. "Get over here." I peek out from under my arms and see Blake striding across the yard, his spiky hair bouncing with each step. George the rooster clucks at him. "Leave them alone," Blake says. I watch, horrified, as Blake reaches his hand toward George, certain he's going to pull back short one finger. But Blake just pats George's head, causing the rooster to make a satisfied noise deep in his gullet.

I sit up, holding my cheek. "Ouch," I say. It's only then that Blake notices that I'm hurt. His eyes get big and he's at my side instantly.

"Penny, are you okay?" I always love it when people ask

that when you are so clearly *not okay*. Tally hurries over, giving George a wide berth.

"Oh no," she says, her hands flying to her masked mouth. I look up at her, squinting in the bright sunlight. The movement brings tears to my eyes. I swipe at the wetness dripping down my cheek and my glove comes away with blood on it.

"Mom!" Blake yells, standing up. I try to stand as well, feeling dampness from the recent rain soaking into my jeans. "Don't move," Blake says, pushing me back. "Wait till my mom gets here. She'll know what to do. She used to be a nurse." He looks very pale.

"I'm fine," I say, eyeing George, who is edging toward me. "I just need to—"

"Blake?" I hear the latch on the gate, then quick footsteps. "Let me see," Blake's mom says, bending in front of me. She carefully lifts my goggles and slides them off. She removes the mask next. Then she gently touches my cheek, making me wince. "Sorry," she says. She tilts my chin and turns my head slightly. "I don't think anything's broken, but we should probably get a real medical opinion." She stands, reaches down for my hand, and helps me up. The world goes green for a moment and I wonder if I'm about to faint. "You okay to walk?" Ms. Wallace asks.

I nod, feeling like my head is full of jelly. Tally takes my arm and helps steer me through the gate and toward the truck. I hear Blake's mom talking on her phone behind me.

"Yes, we'll be right there," she says. Tally helps me shed my boots and gloves. Then she helps me into the truck and slides in beside me. Ms. Wallace climbs in behind the wheel. Blake stands watching. There's only room for three in the truck. "I called ahead to the clinic to make sure someone was there. Never know," she says. Blake lifts a hand as we pull away from their house. He still looks pale, and his hair is definitely a little wilted.

Ms. Wallace hands the phone to Tally. "Call Penny's mom. Tell her to meet us at Sandy's." I assume Sandy's is the clinic because Tally just nods. Blake's mom keeps looking at me out of the corner of her eye, checking on me without wanting it to seem like she's checking on me. Tally starts talking to my mom, telling her where to meet us. I hear my mom say something and then feel Tally looking at me.

"She's okay," she says, but she's not very convincing.

Sitting in the middle, I'm right in front of the rearview mirror. All it takes is a little shift to see myself. What I see is a girl with one eye nearly swollen shut and a stream of blood running from her eyebrow to her chin. Tally says goodbye to my mom and pokes the phone to end the call. She leans into me slightly.

"You doing okay?" Ms. Wallace asks, finally abandoning her quiet concern.

"Peaches and gravy," I say. Ms. Wallace shoots me a concerned look, but Tally actually laughs.

"She's okay," she says. Then under her breath, "Peaches and gravy. Awesome."

Chapter Two

If we were in Manhattan, Mom would have taken me to some fancy doctor wearing a white lab coat and an expensive watch. But this isn't Manhattan. This is Hog's Hollow. Dr. Sanford, aka Dr. Sandy, meets us wearing old jeans and a silver hoop in his ear. He takes one look at me and orders an MRI, so it's back in the truck and on the road to Lancaster. Tally calls my mom to give her the update. As soon as Gram and my mom arrive and fill out the paperwork, a nurse makes me lie down in a giant tube and tells me to hold still—"Don't even breathe."

When we're finished, the nurse sends me to the waiting room while she goes over the results with Dr. Sandy. My mom slides over on the couch, making room for me. Tally starts telling everyone what happened, embellishing only slightly when she describes George. "It was like *Attack of the Killer Tomatoes!*, but with a rooster, not a tomato." She has everyone laughing as she acts out the whole scene, playing herself, then me, then George. I smile in spite of the fact that I can feel my heartbeat in my face. Dr. Sandy comes in just as Tally is falling to the floor in imitation of me.

"The good news is that everything seems to be intact," he says. He pulls a sheet of paper from the folder he's carrying and hands it to my mom. "The not-as-good news is that I'm fairly certain Penny has a mild concussion."

"That's not so bad, right?" Tally asks, standing up. Dr. Sandy shakes his head. "Well, that's a relief," Tally says. Mom and Gram stand up to talk with Dr. Sandy. I try to listen in, but Tally slides over next to me. "Sorry about today," she says.

"It's not your fault," I say. "Just promise me that the next job won't involve chickens."

"Done," she says.

My mom comes over. "Come on, Penny. Let's get you home," she says. "Dr. Sandy says the best thing for you is rest."

Tally takes my arm as we walk to the car. I'm glad she does because I'm even dizzier than I was earlier. "I'll call Blake," Tally says. "Tell him we're not going to the movies." We stop beside Gram's car.

"No, Tally, you should go," I say. She frowns. "All I want to do is go home and lie down."

I slide into the backseat. "What about Saturn?" she asks.

My heart sinks when I realize I won't be seeing Marcus tonight. "I'll call Marcus when I get home," I say. That's not a phone call I want to make in front of a bunch of random people, even if some of those random people are my family.

"I'll call you tomorrow," Tally says. She shuts the door and steps back so Gram can pull the car out. She waves and heads toward where Blake's mom is standing and talking to Dr. Sandy. I lean my head back and close my eyes. Suddenly I'm really, really tired.

I must have fallen asleep on the way home because the next thing I know we're pulling into Gram's driveway.

"Look who's here," my mom says. I look up, feeling groggy, but as soon as I see who's sitting on our porch steps, I'm wide-awake. It's Marcus. I touch the side of my face. A bandage only partially covers my swollen eye. I glance down at my clothes. My Hello Kitty shirt has some suspicious brown stains and my jeans are nasty. I sigh. Whether it's debris from the bakery trash can or a coating of beach sand, I seem to have a habit of running into Marcus when I'm a mess. I climb out of the car, steadying myself on the door as I stand. Dr. Sandy warned me that I might be dizzy for a couple of days.

Mom takes my arm and walks with me toward where Marcus is standing. "Hi, Marcus," my mom says. "Guess you heard—" She doesn't finish her sentence, making me wonder exactly what he heard. *Penny, the klutz, finds yet another way to embarrass herself.*

"Blake called. He said Penny had an accident." He looks over at me. "You okay?" he asks. He seems genuinely concerned and not at all grossed out that I look like I've been dipped in some sort of sludge.

"I'm okay," I say. I look past him, searching for Sam, his golden retriever, but he's alone.

Marcus smiles when he realizes who I'm looking for. "I left him at home. I didn't think you'd want him jumping on you."

Mom hands me off to Marcus, actually transferring my hand from her arm to his. "Just a couple of minutes," she says. "Dr. Sandy said you need to rest." I nod, slightly amazed at how awesome my mom is being. Gram calls hello before disappearing into the house. Mom follows close behind, only pausing once to give me a concerned look. The door claps shut after them. It's quiet for a moment. I can hear the waves pull at the stones on the beach and the harbor bell in the distance. Then I hear a mournful cry from down the beach. Sam is obviously not that happy with his confinement.

"Poor Sam," I say.

Marcus shakes his head. "He's so dramatic. Last night we were out of his favorite chews, so I had to give him a dog treat instead. He acted like an orphan in a Dickens story."

I laugh, which I realize instantly is the wrong thing to do. Everything gets blurry and my knees get wobbly.

"Penny?" Marcus grabs my other arm to steady me.

"I'm sorry," I say. "I just . . ." He leads me up to the porch and lowers me onto the wooden bench.

"I'll go get your mom," he says, stepping toward the door.

"No," I say. "I just need to sit." I look down and start giggling. "I guess I am sitting." Marcus moves toward the door again. "Really," I say. "I'm okay." He looks at me uncertainly but comes and sits beside me. I'm very conscious of how good he smells and how horrible I smell. "I'm sorry," I say. "I'm sort of gross."

Marcus takes my hand in his, making whatever I started

to say disappear. "Last summer I worked at the boatyard. Just here and there when things got too quiet at home." I look at him, but he's looking at the water. I know he means after his mom died in a kayak accident out on the ocean. And how after her death, his dad pretty much just checked out. "I did what no one else wanted to do. Scraped barnacles. Fixed traps. Then one day Captain Steve says his sternman is sick. He tells me the job's mine if I think I can handle it." Marcus glances over at me. "You okay?" he asks. I must look as awful as I feel. I smile, careful of my face, which has, thankfully, gone numb. No matter how terrible I feel, I don't want to lose this moment. Marcus smiles back and squeezes my hand. And I feel a flutter in my stomach that has nothing to do with my concussion.

"I told Captain Steve that I could do it even though I had no idea what a sternman did. I found out pretty fast. I spent all morning dropping traps, hauling traps, and chumming traps while Captain Steve yelled at me." Marcus shakes his head.

"Chumming?" I ask. "Like fish parts?"

"More like rancid fish stew," he says. I make a face, making him laugh. "Finally we head back in and I'm standing on the dock waiting for him to get his wallet to pay me. And I hear boots on the deck behind me. Next thing I know, Captain Steve and his friends are dumping the remains of the chum barrel over me." Marcus makes a face. "Some sort of initiation." He looks over at me. The look on my face makes him laugh again. "So listen," Marcus says, leaning toward me. "I spent a week and a half last July smelling like rotten fish soup. You're not even close to breaking my record." He reaches up and lightly touches my cheek.

"I'm sorry I can't help with Saturn," I say softly.

"Me, too," Marcus says. He smiles and I swear if I weren't already dizzy from knocking my head on the ground, my head would be swimming. And suddenly a tiny part of me wonders if he's going to kiss me, but then there's a loud thump on the steps leading up from the beach. Followed by a flurry of movement out of the corner of my eye. Marcus turns just in time to stop Sam from launching himself at me. "How did you—" Marcus asks Sam. But Sam isn't listening. He's trying with everything he has to get to me.

"Hi, Sam," I say, reaching out to pet him. Sam stops straining immediately and focuses on trying to maneuver his ears under my fingers so I'll scratch them. I'm bummed at the interruption, but also sort of relieved. As much as I think I would want Marcus to kiss me, part of me isn't sure I'm ready. Because there's this tiny part of me that likes looking forward to it, kind of like when Gram bakes cookies and the smell makes me stand over the oven willing the timer to go faster. So as happy as I am when I bite into that first cookie, I sort of miss the looking forward to it. (Of course I do know that there's a big difference between a cookie and a kiss.)

Mom steps out onto the porch, making me even more grateful to Sam. Because even though I'm sorry he interrupted us, I'd have been mortified had it been my mom. "I hate to disturb you . . ." she says. Marcus's cheeks turn pink, making me sure he's thinking the same thing.

Marcus stands up, still holding on to Sam's collar. He reaches his free hand down to help me stand back up. I wobble slightly, making my mom hurry over to take my arm. "Let's get you inside," she says. Sam whines and pulls toward me.

"Bye, Sam," I say, reaching down to ruffle his ears one more time. I look up at Marcus, not wanting to say goodbye to him. "See you—" I pause, unsure of whether I'll see him before Monday at school or not.

"Let me know if—" Marcus begins, but a seagull chooses that exact moment to screech overhead, cutting him off. I start to ask him to repeat what he said, but suddenly I am so tired I can't even think straight to string just a few words together. It's all I can do to wave before Mom propels me inside and the door shuts behind us.

Chapter Three

By Monday afternoon, I'm starting to feel like a princess locked up in a high tower. Mom said no to school, so for two days, my life has pretty much been bed, couch, bed. The cool mom disappeared right after Marcus left, replaced by military nurse mom who seems determined to keep me horizontal and silent. Every time I ask if I can do anything other than sleep and stare at the ceiling, it's the same response: "Penny, you need to rest." All this resting is exhausting. I was so desperate that I actually begged her to let me go to school. Of course the answer was no. She let me talk to Tally, my dad, and Marcus on the phone for about two minutes, but other than that, it's been just me and Gram and the cats. Gram is slightly more sympathetic to my plight, actually letting Tally come over after school on Monday while Mom is still at the bakery.

Tally comes in bearing a box of Junior Mints. Well, half a box. "Sorry," she said. "I got hungry." She's wearing bright pink aviator glasses and a matching pink hat. She pulls off her hat, revealing that she's striped her hair pink, too. "What do you think?" she asks. "Too bright?"

"I like it," I say.

"We could do yours," she says.

"I like it *on you*," I amend. "So, how was the movie Saturday?"

I've only been couch-ridden for two days, but I feel like I've missed so much.

Tally makes a face. "Blake thought it was awesome. I thought it was gruesome. I totally don't get everyone's obsession with zombies. They're undead and gross and dumb. Got it." She flops down in the chair near the fireplace.

"How was school today?"

Tally shrugs. "Boring without you there." That makes me smile. "Oh man!" Tally says, sitting forward. "I have to tell you something."

"You kissed Blake," I guess.

Tally makes a face. "Ew. No." Then she blushes. "Okay, not ew. Just no. We're barely at the hand-holding stage." Then she frowns at me. "That was random."

"Sorry," I say. "My head—" I gesture vaguely toward my eye, hoping Tally will just assume that I'm still addled from my accident. The truth is, with nothing to do, I've been thinking about kissing/not kissing a lot. Tally isn't buying the whole *I hit my head and therefore cannot be responsible for whatever comes out of my mouth* excuse, but her news is obviously more important because she lets it slide.

Tally takes a deep breath. "Charity is moving to Paris."

"What?" I ask. I mean, I heard her. But it's like someone just told me I won the lottery or I just got picked to fly to the moon. "Really?"

"Okay," Tally says. "Charity *might* be moving to Paris."

She quickly outlines a conversation she overheard while helping her aunt install her new mobiles in the window at Parlin's Florist. "Poppy and Rhonda were talking about where to hang the dragon mobile when Mrs. Wharton bursts into the shop carrying a vase of flowers." I make a face. Charity's mom is not one of my favorite people. "She starts ranting about how she ordered French peonies and that what she got were clearly English." Tally stands up and starts acting out the scene. "So Rhonda calmly explains that she was lucky to find peonies of any kind at this time of year. But Mrs. Wharton isn't having it." Tally makes a face like she's been sucking on a lemon. "She tells Rhonda that if she couldn't get French peonies, she should have gotten irises. Because irises are widely recognized as the official flower of France."

"And everyone knows that," I say with as much sarcasm as I can muster.

"I know! Rhonda was totally calm. I would have chucked the flowers at Mrs. Wharton and told her to take her business elsewhere."

"What does this have to do with Charity moving?" I ask.

"I'm getting there," Tally says. "So in the middle of her rant, Charity calls. Mrs. Wharton puts her on speakerphone. Charity starts yapping about how there's some big storm in Paris and all of the flights have been grounded. And how she's done all this packing for nothing and now everything's ruined." Tally says it all in one breath, which I'm pretty sure is exactly how Charity said it. "So, Mrs. Wharton says, 'Don't worry. There's another flight in the morning.'" Tally says this last bit slowly for emphasis.

"Tally, I'm not sure—"

"There's more," Tally says. "So, Charity wasn't at school today. Charlotte said it was because she was at the airport!" Tally pauses. The fact that Charlotte is her source does lend some credibility to the claim. Until about three weeks ago, Charlotte was one of Charity's minions. But whether it was because she didn't like how Charity was bullying me or just got sick of letting Charity rule over her, she left the inner circle. Now she seems to want to be friends with Tally and me. Or at least she doesn't want to be enemies. It's hard to tell.

"So what do you think?" Tally asks.

"It seems too good to be true," I say.

Tally sighs and drops dramatically onto the other end of the couch. "I know," she says. "But wouldn't it be awesome?" I nod. A school without Charity always making fun of me, pranking me, and basically constantly trying to make my life miserable? *Awesome* doesn't begin to cover it.

"What does Poppy think?" I ask, thinking she might have a less biased opinion of what they heard at Parlin's.

Tally shrugs. "She told me not to count my eggs before they hatch."

"Your chickens?" I ask.

"Whatever," Tally says. I actually think Poppy's advice is good. Ever since Tally told me about her dad ditching her in a hotel room for three days while he was on tour and how Poppy dropped everything to go and get her, I've had even more respect for her. And that's on top of the fact that she's an amazing artist and one of the coolest people I've ever met.

Oscar, my orange cat, comes in and meows at Tally's feet. She picks him up and puts him on her lap. I roll my eyes at my fat cat. "He can jump," I say. "He's just lazy." I can hear him purring from where I'm lying on the other end of the couch.

"You're not lazy," Tally says, rubbing Oscar's ears. "You're just relaxed."

"Pfft," I say. "If he gets any more relaxed, he's going to be unconscious."

"Okay, girls," Gram says, walking in from the kitchen. She has Cupcake, her new kitten, in her arms. She's completely in love with him. He's super cute, but I like my cats big and sturdy like Oscar. "If Miss Penny is going to go to school tomorrow—"

"Really?" I ask. I've been begging my mom to let me go back. She kept saying, *We'll see*. That's usually just her nonconfrontational way of saying no.

"Dr. Sandy said you could go as long as you're up for it. And your mom said yes as long as you promise to call if you need to come home."

I start nodding a little too vigorously and have to hide the pain that shoots across my cheek.

Tally grins and jumps up, dumping Oscar onto the floor. "Yay!" I'm smiling both because I am apparently being released from confinement and because Tally is so enthusiastic.

Gram shakes her head. "Never thought I'd see two teenagers

so happy about school." She pretends to roll her eyes at us, but I know she's amused. She shoos Tally toward the door. Tally offers me a queenly wave before heading home. I give her a royal wave back from the couch. Just as Gram pushes the door shut behind her, the phone rings.

"I'll get it," I say, pushing myself up to sitting.

Gram shoots me a hard look. "Stay put." She walks into the kitchen and retrieves the phone from the counter. "Hello?" I ignore Oscar's meowing. He gives up after a few moments and leaps onto the couch. He winds his way up to my stomach and starts kneading me, trying to find a place to lie down. I close my eyes, waiting for him to get comfortable.

"Penny," Gram says. I open my eyes and see her walking toward me. "It's for you." My heart starts beating faster. Maybe it's Marcus, checking on me.

I take the phone from Gram, who doesn't let on who it is. "Hello?"

"Hey, Bean."

"Oh, hi, Dad." I'm a tiny bit disappointed.

"How are you feeling?" he asks.

"I'm better," I say. And it's true. The last time he called, I was so woozy, I could barely talk without slurring. "I get to go back to school tomorrow," I say.

"Good, good," he says, but he sounds distracted.

"Dad?" I ask.

"Sorry," he says. "There's a guy dressed in a silver jumpsuit serenading his pet goldfish. Listen." I hear a few guitar chords and a surprisingly deep voice comparing his fish, Loraine, to a sunset. "What do you think?" Dad asks.

"That is one lucky fish," I say, making my dad laugh. I can tell he's walking again as the sounds of traffic swallow up the music.

"You sure you're okay?" he asks.

"Dad, I'm fine. I mean, the leech bites still hurt, but—"

"Leeches?" My dad starts muttering about backwoods medicine.

I can't keep from laughing. "Dad," I say. "I'm joking. Dr. Sandford seemed totally legit. He had a white coat and everything." I don't tell him that it was pulled over a T-shirt with a dancing hula girl on the front. Some things are best left unmentioned.

"Ha-ha," my dad says, clearly less amused than I am. "I'd better go, funny girl," Dad says. "I have a big meeting uptown at Rain. You know. That fancy Vietnamese place you like?" I nod even though he can't see me. Of course I know. It was where the three of us had our last dinner together before my mom dropped the *we're moving* bomb. "If all goes well, I might have a big surprise for you." I hear voices and the sounds of cabs honking through the phone. "Be careful of those crazy chickens."

"Rooster," I say, but he's gone. Just as well. I'm not sure a rooster would be any less amusing. I scratch Oscar's ears, wondering if he's thinking the same thing I am. How did I go from a life of riding the subway uptown to eat Vietnamese food to a life of cupcakes and feral roosters?

Tally says she doesn't understand why they call it a black eye when it's obvious my eye is at least seven different colors.

"Eight," Blake says, after scrutinizing me for several moments. Tally raises one eyebrow at him. "No, really," he says. He manages to find indigo, navy, black (to which Tally says, "Duh"), olive, chartreuse, gray, ochre, and melon. He points to each one as he says it.

"Melon?" Tally asks. "That looks more like burnt sienna."

Blake shrugs. "Tomato tomato." He says it the same way both times, making me smile and Tally roll her eyes.

"How did you manage ochre and chartreuse?" I ask.

Blake shrugs. "I'm not unsmart," he says. His shirt has a photo of a swirled mound of what looks like rainbow-colored frosting with sparkling stars scattered all over it. The caption reads: UNICORN POOP.

He sees me reading his shirt and puts up his hand. "I already assured Tally that this is the only one with scatological humor."

"Yo, Wallace!" a guy calls from across the lawn. He twirls a soccer ball on his index finger. Blake nods, then looks back at us.

"Sorry, people," he says. "Gotta motor." He jogs over to where several other guys, who basically all look like clones, are standing. One of them punches Blake hard in the shoulder. Blake punches him back and they both start laughing.

"Boys are—" Tally begins.

"Unsmart?" I ask.

"Definitely," Tally says. The bell for first period rings, sending everyone running for the front doors. I have to hurry so I'm not late. I make it to my locker and quickly open it, pulling out the books I need for first period. Unlike at the beginning of the semester, my locker is devoid of dead fish, shaving cream, and a tsunami of pennies. Oh, life without Charity is going to be sweet.

In first period, Madame Framboise tries to get me to tell the class what happened to my eye. This would have been embarrassing, but not impossible. However, she wanted me to tell the story in French. *Ce n'est pas possible.* I finally end up pantomiming most of the story, which makes the class laugh. Charlotte smiles at me as I walk past to find my seat. That's way different from when she tried to trip me on the first day.

Despite the mountain of homework that every one of my teachers assigns, the thought of life without Charity has me floating down the hall as I make my way to fourth period.

Marcus stops me just before I walk into the art studio. "Hey," he says. He places his fingers under my chin and tilts my head. "Your eye looks better." My stomach flutters at his touch and I tell it to hush. "Want to have lunch together?" he asks. "I hear there's lime Jell-O."

"I was going to say no, but seeing as there's Jell-O . . ." I say.

"So I rank somewhere below lime Jell-O," Marcus says.

"But you're totally above blue raspberry or peach," I tease.

"It's good to know where I stand." He smiles at me and the corners of his eyes crinkle in a way that makes me feel all melty inside. "See you at lunch," he says, and heads toward the front office, where he works during fourth period. I float a few more feet off the ground. I drift into Miss Beans's class and to where Tally is sitting hunched over her sketch pad.

"Hi," I say. Charlotte smiles at me from the other side of the table. Looks like she's officially defected from Team Charity. I slide onto my stool, wondering if the day could possibly get any better.

"She's here," Tally hisses at me.

"Who's here?" Then I hear the too familiar laughter coming from the back table. Charity.

I feel like gravity just reasserted itself, but now it's about ten times stronger than it should be. "I thought she was in Paris."

Tally shakes her head.

"This stinks," I say. Charity chooses that moment to look over. She waves her fingers at me, which coming from anyone else in the whole world might seem friendly, but from her is positively terrifying.

"It gets worse," Tally says.

"How?" I ask. What could be worse than this? Just then Miss Beans's office door opens. She steps out, followed by a girl I've never seen before. Everyone stops talking and stares at her.

And not just because she's new, but because she is impossibly beautiful.

"That's how," Tally whispers. The girl follows Miss Beans to the front of the room.

"I'd like to introduce all of you to Esmeralda Fournier." The girl beams at us. I swear she actually gets prettier the longer I look at her. "She just arrived yesterday from Paris." Miss Beans looks at the girl, who just smiles. "She'll be spending the rest of the school year with us, so I hope you'll give her a warm welcome." Miss Beans nods toward the back table, where Charlotte's old stool sits empty. But Esmeralda isn't about to give up the floor.

"I am very excited to be here," she says. Her voice is soft and lovely. Her English is perfect, more than perfect with her exotic accent. "Charity has told me so much about all of you that I feel like I know you already."

Is it my imagination or did she just look at me? She walks to the back table and slides onto her stool. Even the way she moves seems striking, like she's a cross between a cat and a queen. Miss Beans begins talking about the next big project, something about public art, but I'm barely paying attention. Charity is leaning toward Esmeralda and saying something. Esmeralda looks up and this time I'm not imagining it. She's looking directly at me.

Chapter Four

The lunchroom is chaotic like always. There's the usual drama bomb at the cheerleader table. Several of the soccer players are having a belching contest, and two guys near the entrance are taking turns spraying Easy Cheese across the table into each other's mouths. Tally, Blake, and I sit at a table near the back as far away from the smelly trash cans as possible.

"I so did not see that coming," Tally says, nodding toward where Esmeralda is sitting with Charity and the rest of her minions. As we watch, Esmeralda laughs and tosses her hair, causing one of the passing soccer players to trip and almost drop his Frito pie. Tally looks slightly horrified.

"What?" I ask.

"The hair toss combined with the giggle is a very advanced move." She looks dejectedly at her peanut butter and cheese sandwich. (Totally gross, in spite of what she says.) "We're doomed," she says. I make a face at her. This is very un-Tally-like behavior. "She's like guy kryptonite."

"Who?" Blake asks around a mouthful of the second peanut butter and American cheese sandwich Tally brought for him. (He admits that it's gross, but says that if he eats it fast enough, he can mostly ignore the taste.) Tally nods toward Charity's table, where Charity is attempting the hair toss. She ends up with a mouthful of blonde curls for her effort. "Oh,

31

her. Yeah, she's in my PE class. She seems cool." Tally frowns at him. "What?"

"Nothing," she says. Blake shrugs and returns his attention to his sandwich. Tally turns to me. "Where'd she come from?" she asks.

"France," Blake says.

Tally rolls her eyes. "I mean why is she here now? I thought exchange students always started at the beginning of the semester."

"The word on the street is that her parents and the Whartons are old friends," Blake says. "So while her parents are in China on some business thing, they dumped her here."

Tally looks at him. "How do you know all this?"

Blake shrugs. "I have my sources," he says.

"Who?" Tally asks.

"They prefer to remain anonymous," Blake says.

"Hey," Marcus says, sliding onto the bench beside me. He bumps his shoulder against mine and smiles. Then he looks at Blake. "Mrs. Pittman told me she likes red velvet." Blake nods.

"Why would she say that?" Tally asks. Blake shrugs, but he looks shifty. "Wait." Tally narrows her eyes at him. "The school secretary is your source?"

"One of them," he says. "You'd be surprised how much intel a cupcake can buy you." Blake looks at me. "I'll need you to bring a red velvet cupcake to school tomorrow."

"Okay," I say, laughing. Tally just shakes her head, but when Blake steals one of her chips, she smiles at him. They might be only barely at the holding-hands stage, but you can tell they really like each other.

I glance over at Marcus, wondering if that could ever be us. Then I look at his tray. There's a vaguely gray piece of meat floating in a brownish sauce. "What is that?"

He cuts off a piece and chews it thoughtfully. "Hamburger," he says. "Or maybe chicken fried steak."

"Don't think, man," Blake says. "Just eat it."

"Good advice," Marcus says, taking another bite. "After school, I'm heading back up to Saturn. Want to come?" he asks me.

"I do," I say, "but I promised my mom I'd work the counter for her. I'm free tomorrow," I add, trying not to sound too eager.

"Cool," he says.

Tally kicks me hard under the table. She nods toward the front of the cafeteria. I look over and see both Esmeralda and Charity staring at me. I stare right back, refusing to be intimidated by them. But they don't look away. It's then that I realize they aren't looking at me at all, but at Marcus. Charity leans over and whispers something to Esmeralda, who smiles and nods. Marcus is too busy inhaling his mystery lunch to notice. But Charity sees me watching and grins. I glare at her, but it just makes her smile wider.

In the end I do look away first. I frown at my sandwich. (Peanut butter and honey.) I must make a frustrated noise aloud because Marcus glances over.

"You okay?" he asks.

"Absolutely," I say. I slide the tiniest bit closer to him until our shoulders are touching. He smiles at me and nods toward his coconut cream pie.

"Want some?" he asks.

"No Jell-O?" I ask.

Marcus shakes his head. "Turns out it was just a rumor. But there was pie." Even though I loathe all things coconut, I nod back. I take his fork and take a bite, reminding myself of Blake's advice. *Don't think. Just chew.*

"Yum," I say, earning a raised eyebrow from Tally. She is well aware of my aversion to coconut. I glance over at Charity again, who looks like she just took a bite of slimy coconut pie. I swallow, pleased to see that the bite of nastiness was worth it.

Gram is hanging a poster in the window of The Cupcake Queen when I arrive. I pause and read it before heading inside. "How many festivals does Hog's Hollow have?" I ask.

Gram tapes the last corner and turns toward me. "Hog Days, the Sugaring Festival, Spring Breakup, May Days, the Black Fly Jubilee, and, of course, Winter Fest," she finishes, gesturing toward the poster.

"That's a lot of festivals," I say.

"Mm-hmm," Gram says. She is distracted by something out on Main Street. She narrows her eyes at a truck idling behind a tractor towing a trailer full of pigs. "You have got to be kidding me," she mutters. She yanks the door open and stomps out onto the sidewalk. Mrs. Hancock, who owns the antique store next door, is sweeping the walk in front of her shop. "What's *he* doing here?" Gram asks. Mrs. Hancock turns to see what Gram is looking at. For some reason what she sees is completely hysterical because she lets out the loudest laugh I've ever heard. Gram glares at Mrs. Hancock, then marches out into the street where the old blue pickup truck is idling. I walk to the doorway and peer out. A guy with salt-and-pepper hair, wearing jeans and a flannel shirt, steps out of the truck and beams at Gram, who scowls back at him.

"This should be good," Mrs. Hancock says, smirking at me.

"You've got a lot of nerve showing your face around here," Gram says.

The older guy's smile widens. "Good to see you, too, Joy." Gram continues scowling at him. "I was in the neighborhood and thought I'd swing through."

"Since when is Hog's Hollow in the neighborhood of California?" Gram asks.

"Huh," the man says. "Thought you would have heard. You know, small town and all." I step out onto the sidewalk and let the door shut behind me. "I just bought the old Windham Farm." There's a fair amount of traffic backed up behind the man's truck, but most everyone is hanging out of their car windows enjoying the show. "Just came into town to pick up a few things and have a look around."

"Well, you've looked around," Gram says.

The man grins at her and then climbs back in his truck. He closes his door, but hooks his elbow out the window, still smiling at Gram. He tips his chin slightly and winks at her. "Guess we'll be seeing a lot of each other." *Holy cow,* I think. *He's actually flirting with her.* He pulls away, leaving Gram in the street watching him go.

"Hey," Marcus says, walking up. "Is that your grandmother?"

I nod. She's still standing in the middle of the road, forcing traffic to go around her. Nothing should surprise me in Hog's Hollow anymore, but seeing my usually unflappable grandmother completely unhinged is definitely bizarre. It's then that I notice Marcus isn't alone. *Esmeralda.*

"I don't believe we've met," she says, all sweetness and light.

"Sorry," Marcus says. "Esme, this is Penny."

"Hi," I say. *Esme.*

"*Enchantée,*" she says.

"Esme is in my bio class," Marcus says.

"Lab partners," she says, actually winking at me.

"She wanted to know if there was a good bakery in town," he says.

"I have a terrible sweet tooth," she chimes in.

I realize I haven't spoken in several seconds. "So, you brought her here," I say.

"Best bakery in town," Marcus says.

Esmeralda gestures at the sparkly gold lettering on the window. "So, all you do is cupcakes?" she asks. And I can't be sure whether her tone is one of genuine interest or smirky disdain.

"Yep," I say in what I hope is a nonconfrontational way. Suddenly Tally's comments about guy kryptonite and the way Esmeralda is standing so close to Marcus she's almost touching him make me feel *very* confrontational.

"Well, I can't wait to try one," Esmeralda says. I glance back over at Gram and note that she's still fuming, but at least she's making her way out of the road. Marcus holds the door open for both Esme and me.

"Thanks," I say.

"*Merci,*" Esmeralda purrs. She looks around. "What a cute shop."

Again, it's impossible to read whether she's serious or making fun. I walk around behind the counter and watch as she flips through the photo book full of pictures of the cupcakes I've designed. She oohs and aahs over them. I'm embarrassed at my jealousy. Esmeralda is new in town just like I was a few months back. If anyone should be nice to her, it should be me. I decide to give her the benefit of the doubt. It's not her fault that Charity is the Mean Queen. And I shouldn't judge Esmeralda based on her family association.

"So what can I get you?" I ask.

She holds up one delicate finger and moves away from Marcus, peering into the display case.

"Well, I'd like two mudslides," Marcus says. "One is for my dad," he adds. I tilt my head at him, which makes him laugh. "Probably," he admits. He leans on the counter, watching me while I pull out his cupcakes. "Sorry you can't come with me today."

"Me, too," I say, happy that he actually sounds bummed out. Unfortunately, it also makes me feel even more foolish for being jealous. Marcus was just being nice to Esmeralda. I'm the only one acting weird.

Gram is standing on the sidewalk out front talking to Mrs. Hancock, who is trying her best to match my grandmother's seriousness.

"Looks like the drama is over," I say.

"I don't think I've ever seen your grandmother that upset."

"Me neither," I say, folding a pink bakery box. "I wonder who the guy in the truck is," I say, mostly to myself.

"You should ask Blake," Marcus says.

"It will probably cost me another cupcake," I say.

Esmeralda walks back toward us. "I guess I'll have one of those blue ones," she says. Her enthusiasm is underwhelming.

"One blue velvet coming up," I say. I settle Esmeralda's round cupcake into a single cup and place Marcus's in a box. I tuck an extra one in his just in case.

Marcus fishes out a ten and hands it over. I pause, waiting for Esmeralda's money, but she's not moving. I make big eyes at Marcus, unsure of what to do, but he nods at the ten. Guess he's treating. Esmeralda waits until I hand him his change before saying anything.

"Marcus, you are so sweet to buy me a cupcake," she says, putting her hand on his arm. "Isn't he sweet?"

"Mm-hmm," I say, handing the cupcakes across the counter.

Esmeralda holds her cupcake up and examines it. Then she looks at me. "Which one is your favorite?"

"Either lemon or spice," I say.

"You must eat a lot of cupcakes," Esmeralda says. One of her eyebrows goes up the tiniest bit. I frown, unsure of how to take her comment. Then her hand flies to her mouth. "Oh my goodness," she says. "I am so sorry. I did not mean to suggest you are fat."

"It's fine," I say. But it's not really fine. Because even though I rarely if ever think about my weight, suddenly I am. And Esmeralda is. And Marcus, who is standing *right there*, is. And no one's saying anything.

"Well," Marcus says after what seems like a thousand years. "Guess I'd better go," he says. "See you tomorrow."

"Definitely," I say. Esmeralda makes a tiny wave of her fingers. I notice he holds the door for her again, making me wish he weren't quite so nice. They walk past the big window on the way down the sidewalk. I can't help noticing once again how perfect she is. It's like she's a different species from the rest of us. A more evolved, more beautiful, more charming, more exotic species.

I grab a towel and begin wiping the glass counter clean of fingerprints. Gram walks through the door, pausing to fix the wonky sleigh bells on the way in. "Was that Marcus I saw?" she asks.

"Yep," I say, scrubbing at a blob of icing.

"Who's the girl?" she asks.

"She's from France," I say as if that answers her question. I scrub harder. I'm trying to be fair to Esmeralda, but when it comes to Marcus, I don't always feel very rational.

Gram comes around the counter. I don't make eye contact with her. I know I'm acting nutty and so do not need her pointing that out to me. "You know," she says. "You were the new girl not too long ago." I don't answer her. "Just something to consider," she says.

"I know," I say.

"Careful," she says, pushing against the swinging door leading to the kitchen. "You'll wear a hole in that glass." The door swings shut behind her before I can reply. Gram's admonition has the opposite effect she intended. Now in addition to acting jealous and irrational, I'm embarrassed about being jealous and irrational.

"Stupid France," I say to myself. I glare at the blue velvet cupcakes. "Stupid cupcakes."

I hear Gram in the back talking to my mother. The words *the nerve of him showing up after all this time* and *over my dead body*, then *France*, float through the door. I put down the rag and start folding cupcake boxes. Mom pushes through the door.

"So," she says. "How's your head?" I reach up and touch where the bandage was. In all of the recent drama, I'd mostly forgotten about my head.

"Fine," I say.

"How was your day?"

"Fine," I repeat.

"How's the new girl?" she asks.

"Fine," I growl.

"Hmm," my mother says. She stands there watching me fold another box. "Everyone deserves a chance," she says.

"I know."

Mom smiles at me as if she's just fixed everything. "I could really use your creativity in the kitchen when you finish there," she says.

I nod, still folding. She heads back into the kitchen. I continue folding boxes for a few more minutes. There's a minor rush of customers, which manages to put me in a much better mood. By the time I meet my mom in the kitchen, I'm determined to stop acting so crazy. I stand with her at the counter, piping snowflakes onto a sheet of parchment. The whole time I try to talk myself out of my Esmeralda-induced paranoia. I mean, seriously, it's not like she really has superpowers. She's just a girl. A girl from France. A very pretty girl from France. A very pretty girl from France who seems to like my possibly almost boyfriend. I accidentally break one of the snowflakes I'm making, earning me a raised eyebrow from my mother. I give her an *everything's fine* smile. I start piping another snowflake. I mean, seriously. How much trouble can one girl cause?

Chapter Five

Gram refuses to say anything more about the strange encounter in the street and Mom says I'll just have to wait for her to tell me. I considered asking Mrs. Hancock at the antique shop, but every time I've been in town, she's been busy with customers. I finally decide to ask Blake. I tell him I'll give him two cupcakes. One for himself. One for his source. He says he'll see what he can do, but after three days, I still have no idea what the drama was all about.

Mom closes the shop early on Friday, insisting we head over to Dr. Sandford so he can check me out. I tell her I feel fine, but she won't budge. After almost a week, my eye is barely yellow and the cut on my eyebrow is completely healed. I sit on the edge of the exam table while he shines a tiny light in my eyes, checking first one eye, then the other.

"Any headaches?" he asks, turning my head slightly.

"No," I say.

"Double vision? Sensitivity to light? Trouble sleeping?" I shake my head. Definitely not the last one. Two afternoons of hauling iron rods, sheets of copper, and wooden scaffolding down a steep hill to load in Marcus's dad's truck, in addition to school and homework, have meant I pretty much drop unconscious about three seconds after my head hits the pillow.

"Well then, Miss Penny," Dr. Sandford says, taking off his

exam gloves and dropping them into the trash can. "I'd say you're all fixed up." He walks over to the door and pulls it open. I hop down from the table and follow him out to where my mom is waiting. She looks up from her phone when we approach. "She's all set," he says.

My mom dips into her purse for her wallet, but he waves it away. "Tell you what," he says. "Next time I'm in town, I'll let you buy me a cupcake." We both say thank you, which he also waves away. I decide that when I next talk to my dad, I'll tell him how nice Dr. Sandford is and what a good doctor he is. I won't mention the fact that he's wearing old Birkenstocks with wool socks and an ancient Grateful Dead tie-dye.

Mom and I head out to the parking lot. It's starting to get dark even though it's only six o'clock. "Brrr," she says, rubbing her arms. "It's getting cold." We climb into the car and she cranks up the heater. "Poppy called and asked if you wanted to come to dinner." We pull out of the parking lot and start heading back toward Hog's Hollow. "She said to tell you to wear blue. And just so you know, dinner at our house is probably soup and sandwiches." She frowns slightly. "Maybe just soup. I think we're out of bread." She looks at me apologetically, then back at the road. "It's been a crazy busy week. I just haven't had time to go to the store."

"Well, I do like soup," I say. It's true. I've even been known to eat soup for breakfast. "But if it's okay—"

"Of course," Mom says, turning onto another winding road lined with trees glowing orange and red in the setting sun.

"Gram's at some planning meeting. It'll just be me and the cats." Her voice seems a little sad, and I wonder if she's thinking about Dad. I'm not under any illusion that the divorce isn't happening, but it's hard. Fifteen years of marriage gone. That can't be easy for my mom. She reaches over and squeezes my hand as if to say, *It's okay.* I squeeze back as if to say, *If not yet, it will be.* The rest of the ride is quiet and I wonder what she's thinking. I glance in the side mirror and watch the leaves swirl behind us as we pass, but then I look forward again. I don't want to forget what used to be, but I definitely want to keep my focus on what's ahead.

I quickly change clothes when we get back to the house, pulling on a light blue T-shirt and jeans. Mom comes in carrying one of her vintage cardigans. It's navy with sequins and beading on the front. I'm skeptical, but I try it on. I stand in front of the mirror, trying to keep an open mind. "It looks good," I say.

"Don't be so surprised," Mom says. "I'm not totally hopeless." She offers to do my hair. I agree, letting her twist it into a knot at the nape of my neck. She pokes one of her beaded hair sticks into it when she's finished. She studies me for a moment. "A little lip gloss, I think," she says. I frown at her back as she walks toward her bathroom. She returns bearing not only rose-colored lip gloss but mascara.

"What's going on?" I ask.

"Nothing," she says. "I just thought you'd want to look nice." I let her apply the makeup and then turn to look in the mirror. I still look like me, but like fancy me. Mom beams at me over my shoulder, making me narrow my eyes at her. Suspicious. But she's shooing me, telling me to be back before ten. She hands me my blue fleece coat at the back door and ushers me out. I'm barely on the porch before the door clicks shut behind me.

It's a short walk down the beach to Tally's. It's even colder now, but so pretty. There in the darkness, the stars seem so close I could touch them. And the waves look silver in the moonlight. I glance at the Fishes' house on the way past, but the windows are dark. Even though I've seen Marcus every afternoon, it's all hauling and loading and unloading. By the time his dad tells us it's quitting time, we're both grimy and sweaty. It's not even remotely romantic.

Tally's house is bright, light spilling out of the windows onto the sand. I step onto the porch and raise my hand to knock. Tally opens the door before my knuckles even touch the wood. She yanks me into the house and closes the door behind me.

I pull off my coat and hang it on a peg by the door. Tally is watching me. "You look amazing," she says, demanding that I turn so she can look at my hair. Tally is wearing a turquoise-and-navy tunic embroidered with cream-colored flowers over navy leggings.

"I like your earrings," I say. Blue sea glass twisted with silver wire hangs from each ear. Tally smiles and shakes her head, making the earrings swing. She's changed the stripes in her hair again. Now they are turquoise instead of pink. And she's switched out her glasses for ones with blue rhinestones in the corners. The house is warm and smells amazing. Garlic and onions and underneath that something sugary.

Tally slides up next to me and puts her mouth near my ear. "Did I mention that my aunt is a little wack?"

"I heard that," Poppy says from where she's pulling something out of the oven.

"Good wack," Tally says more loudly. Poppy shakes her head, but she's smiling. Poppy is definitely not wack in my book. Tally beckons me to follow her. We round the corner and what I see makes me smile even more. The request to *wear* blue was only part of Poppy's plan. The whole dining room has been transformed into a blue-tinted fantasyland. Blue streamers. Blue balloons. Blue tablecloth. Blue dishes. And blue glasses in every shade from indigo to aqua.

"Is Blake coming?" I ask. Tally nods and grins. Luckily with them I never feel like a third wheel, but I am glad Poppy is here. It's a little less date-y and more family dinner-y.

The doorbell rings and Tally rushes to the front door. She returns with Blake in tow. He's wearing jeans, a blue velvet jacket over a white shirt, and a blue polka-dot bow tie. Seeing him makes me thankful my mom suggested I dress up a little. He's carrying a bundle of mail.

Poppy comes in, lights the blue tapers on the table, and dims the lights. She passes out blue fizzy drinks in turquoise wineglasses. Then she takes the mail from Blake. "Thank you," she says. Then she looks at Tally. "Are we almost ready?" she asks. Tally glances at the clock hung near the back door and nods. I take a sip of the drink, tasting ginger ale and something blueberry. Tally turns on polka music and we stand around feeling vaguely grown up and slightly awkward.

"So—" Blake says, looking at me. "How's the cupcake business?"

"Fine," I say.

"Good, good," Blake says, taking a sip of his drink. "Lovely weather we're having," he says. Tally rolls her eyes at him. There's a knock at the front door, saving me from any more of Blake's attempts at chitchat.

Tally flies out of the room, calling, "I'll get it!" I hear the door open and then her saying, "Come in. Come in." She returns grinning, followed by Marcus. He's wearing a denim shirt, dark jeans, and a navy suit vest. He smiles at me and my stomach flutters.

"Hey," he says, walking over. In the dimmed light, his brown eyes look more like dark chocolate than caramel. Seeing him makes my head swim.

"Hi," I say, suddenly so shy I can barely speak. *Get ahold of yourself, Penny*, I tell myself, but I'm not listening. I have this funny rushing sound in my ears and my heart is beating so fast, I wonder if everyone can hear it. I take a deep breath and let it out slowly.

"Oh, good," Poppy says, walking in. "We're all here. Dinner is just about ready. I just have to—" Whatever she just has to do is lost as she turns to walk back into the kitchen.

Marcus reaches up and touches the back of my neck. "You look amazing," he says softly.

"You, too," I say. I know I must be blushing like crazy. And I feel like I'm floating a couple of inches off the floor and only his hand is keeping me from floating all the way up to the ceiling. Tally is talking about some job she has lined up for us in the morning, but Marcus still has his fingers on the back of my neck and it's almost all I can focus on. Then I realize Tally is talking to me.

"So I told him no to repainting his barn," Tally says. "I mean, seriously. It's three stories tall." She looks at me, clearly waiting for a response. I put a serious look on my face and nod, which seems to be enough. "So he says we can just whitewash the fence. Whitewash. Who do I look like? Tom Sawyer?"

"You mean Huckleberry Finn," Blake says. "Tom Sawyer tricked him into painting the fence for him."

"An-y-way," Tally says, stretching it out so that it sounds like three separate words. "So do you think your mom can drop us off?" she asks me. "I'd ask Poppy, but her car is in the shop."

Poppy comes back in with her hands filled with blue dishes. "Yeah, poor Old Bessie," she says, referring to her vintage purple VW Bug. She moves past us and puts the steaming bowls on the dining room table.

"So do you think she can?" Tally asks me. Marcus drops his hand from the back of my neck to accept a glass of blueberry soda from Poppy. I realize Tally is waiting for my answer.

"Where?" I ask.

Tally rolls her eyes at me, but she's smiling. I'm pretty sure she knows exactly why I'm so distracted. "The Windham Farm," she says.

Something clicks in my brain. "Wait," I say. "Didn't someone just buy that?"

Tally actually slaps her hand against her forehead. "I swear I'm talking to myself half the time." Blake grins at me. "Yes!" Tally says. "His name's Dutch Ingamar or Ingamer or Inga-something."

"It's probably not Ingasomething," Blake says. Tally punches him lightly in the arm.

"So, Dutch I. moved here from California and bought the farm." She realizes what she just said. "I mean, literally bought the farm. He isn't dead."

I look at Blake. "So what did *you* find out?" I ask.

Blake shrugs. "Nothing really. Just that he and your grandmother used to know each other in high school."

"That's not really cupcake-worthy investigative work," I say.

"I'll keep digging," he says.

Poppy returns with two more dishes. "Okay, everyone," she says. "Dinner is served." We walk over to the table and spend a few awkward moments figuring out who is going to sit where. Poppy uncovers one of the dishes. "Blue mashed potatoes." She points to the various other dishes and plates on the table. "Blue corn rolls, bluefish, which isn't really blue, but just humor me. Purple asparagus. Also not blue."

"Sweet," Blake says. "Even the butter is blue."

"Eat up, everyone," Poppy says. She refuses to sit with us, claiming she has some work to do in the kitchen. "Call if you need me," she says. "Oh, and save some room for dessert."

"Blueberry pie?" Blake asks. Poppy nods. "Tally, your aunt rocks."

"Duh," Tally says. Poppy waves away the compliment as she heads toward the kitchen, but I can tell she's pleased.

In spite of its odd hue, dinner is amazing. Blake puts away enough food for three people, but still has room for two huge pieces of pie. The four of us tell Poppy we'll do the dishes. She disappears into her studio with the bundle of mail, a roll in her hand, and a serious expression on her face. Marcus and I wash, leaving Tally and Blake to dry and put away. With Marcus's arm touching mine every time he passes me a plate to rinse, it's a wonder everything's not broken. I check the clock once everything is put away. Quarter to ten. "I'd better go," I say.

"I'll walk you," Marcus says. We find Poppy in her studio. The roll, with only one bite out of it, is sitting on the end of the table. She's standing and reading a letter. One hand is in front of her mouth and there are tears in her eyes.

"Poppy?" She jumps at the sound of my voice. She quickly smiles and tries to blink back the tears. "Are you okay?" I ask.

"I'm fine," she says. She hurries to fold the letter and drops it onto her desk. Then she places her unfinished corn roll on top of it. "That was just a letter from—" She fusses at the scarf tying back her hair. "Just someone I used to know." She takes a deep breath and tries for another smile, but it's thin. She looks up at the clock over her workbench. Ten till ten. "Are you two heading out?" she asks.

"We are," I say. "We just wanted to thank you for dinner."

Marcus nods. "It was great," he says.

"It was nothing," Poppy says. "I'm just glad you enjoyed it."

I stand there for a moment longer, wishing I knew what to say. It's obvious that something in that letter really upset Poppy. Marcus touches my arm.

"Okay," I say. "Thanks again." Poppy gives us one more fleeting smile as we head back toward the kitchen. Before I pull the door shut I see her staring at the folded piece of paper sitting on her desk.

Tally and Blake wave goodbye from where they are setting up Scrabble. His mom is going to pick him up on the way back from her master gardener meeting, which Blake says is as dull as it sounds. Marcus and I pull on our coats and head out onto the porch. The last thing we hear before we shut the door is Tally talking her usual smack. "You're going down, Pineapple Head."

Then Blake's reply: "Bring it on."

Marcus takes my hand in his as soon as we step onto the sand. And I feel the same flutter, but I'm distracted by seeing Poppy so sad. "I hope Poppy's okay," I say. Marcus nods. We walk quietly for a few moments. I decide I'll try to talk to Tally about it later. For now, I want to enjoy my time with Marcus. Even though it's cold enough to see our breath, I feel warm inside. After the bright light and the noise, the beach seems soft and quiet. We walk down toward the water. The tide is low, exposing rocks and driftwood and shells. The wind is salty and cold, and makes me shiver. I can see lights on in the Fishes' house ahead of us. A blast of noise pours through the open back door.

"Uh, what was that?" I ask.

"Bagpipes," Marcus says. He grins and shakes his head. "When my dad said he wanted to learn to play an instrument, I thought it would be guitar or piano."

"It's an unusual choice," I say. "But building the whole solar system is a pretty hard act to follow."

"Good point," he says. Another wheezing note breaks across the sand. I have to bite my lip to keep from laughing. Marcus sees me and smiles. "The bad news is that there is no way to play the bagpipes quietly."

"What's the good news?" I ask.

"That he can't possibly get any worse," he says. A blast of chaotic notes hits us as we pass by the Fishes' porch, making both Marcus and me laugh. "I stand corrected," he says. We walk for several moments, smiling at his father's attempts at making music. A flash of light in the sky makes me look over.

"What was that?" I ask. I turn, following the splash of light as it streaks across the darkness. "Was that a falling star?" I ask, staring at the spot in the night sky where it seemed to disappear.

Marcus nods. "Probably. I saw something in the news about a meteor shower heading this way." He releases my hand and points almost straight above us. "There's another."

"That is so cool," I say. I back up, trying to see if I can spot another. The sand and rocks crunch under my shoes with each step. Crunch, crunch, squish. I barely register the change in the texture of the sand before my foot slides out from under me and I'm falling. Marcus tries to grab my arm to keep me upright, but it's no good. Suddenly I'm flat on my back on a wet mound of something that smells like last week's seafood special. I try to push myself up, but my hand slides away from me. There's a popping noise and something wet and cold hits my neck. "Ew!" I press my hands into the sand and try to rise, but there are more pops and more bursts of cold goo against my face.

"Penny," Marcus says. "Hold still." I feel his hands slide under my arms. And then he pulls me to my feet. The wet liquid sliding down into the collar of my coat makes me shiver.

I press my eyes closed and swipe at my face with my sleeve. "Let me guess," I say. "Alien slime?"

Marcus laughs. "Actually they're sea grapes." I open my eyes and look at the ground. Ropes of seaweed are decorated with clusters of giant mutant grapes.

"Huh," I say. "That's pretty much the most disgusting thing I've ever seen." Marcus smiles and brushes a wet strand of my hair from my cheek. Then he leans toward me. And I feel my heart beat faster.

"Penny?" he says.

"Yes?" I say softly.

"I think you"—he reaches over and pulls a strand of sea-weed out of my hair while I cringe—"have some seaweed in your hair." He pulls two more strands free and drops them to the beach. I sigh. Of course I do. I swipe impatiently at another rivulet of sea grape spew running down the side of my face. Marcus steps toward me and puts his arms around me. I let myself sink into him, feeling the warmth of his fleece coat against my cold cheek. And I feel like time just stops for a moment, like we could just stand there forever if we wanted to. But then I hear Gram yelling. Marcus and I both turn and see something being launched from our back porch and onto the beach.

I grab Marcus's hand and hurry toward Gram's house. We arrive at the base of the stairs, which lead up to our porch, just as projectile number two comes flying over our heads. A shower of tulips rains down on us. Around us all over the sand are a couple dozen more flowers, looking worse for the wear. We hear the back door open, then shut with a bang.

"Well, that happened," I say, at a loss. This is twice in a week that I've watched my usually levelheaded grandmother come unglued. "Guess I should—" I nod toward my house, unsure of exactly what I *should* do.

"Guess so," Marcus says. He seems disappointed, which makes me happy. "I had fun tonight," he says.

"Me, too," I say. Marcus starts to lean toward me. I lean in and close my eyes. *This is it. I'm about to have my very first kiss. On a beach, surrounded by flowers. Serenaded by music. Smelling of sea grapes.* I have to remind myself to breathe.

"Penny? Is that you, honey?" Gram asks.

My eyes fly open. I look up and see Gram squinting down at us from the porch. Thankfully she is standing in the light spilling out of the house and we are in the dark. I know she can't really see more than vague shapes.

"Yeah, it's me, Gram," I say. "Sorry," I mouth at Marcus, but he just shakes his head, smiling. "I better go," I say. Gram's next move is likely to flip on the floodlights. I'd like to avoid that if possible.

"I'll call you tomorrow," Marcus says. He tucks a strand of my hair behind my ear, and then lets his fingers trail across my cheek before turning to go. I watch him for a moment before turning to float up the stairs toward where Gram is waiting.

"Sorry," she says when I step onto the porch. "I wasn't thinking."

"It's okay," I say. And it is. I guess I'm a die-hard romantic. I want my first kiss to be magical. The kiss to which all other kisses are compared. I know it's ridiculous and completely unlikely, but at least that's the plan. "So what's with the flower bombs?" I ask, gesturing toward the sand below.

Gram's face goes hard. "If that man thinks that after all this time he can just waltz back in here and start courting me again like the last thirty-five years never happened"—she glares at the remaining tulip in her hand before chucking it over the railing—"well, he's got another think coming." She turns and heads back into the house, leaving me with a thousand questions. I hear bagpipes wheezing out the first few notes of what I think is "Mary Had a Little Lamb" and then a dog howling. I stand there listening to the first song die away and the opening stanzas of "Twinkle, Twinkle, Little Star" played badly and loudly accompanied by an extremely enthusiastic golden retriever until I'm shivering.

"Good night," I whisper. And it is.

Chapter Six

It rains all weekend, forcing us to put off painting the fence at the Windham Farm. It's just as well. Between homework and helping Mom pull together a giant catering order, I barely have time to get everything done. Tally drops by the bakery for a few minutes on Saturday and helps pack cupcakes into boxes, but with her own homework and helping at the ARK, she's slammed, too.

Marcus calls Sunday evening to tell me it's raining, which makes me laugh. Then he tells me to prepare myself. "My dad found someone to teach him how to play the bagpipes."

"That's a good thing, right?" I ask.

"In theory," he says. "But the guy's bringing his own pipes so they can play a duet."

"Ah," I say.

"I might go for a run during the lesson," he says.

"Good call," I say.

"See you tomorrow?" he asks.

"Definitely," I say. I hang up and grin at the phone for a minute before forcing myself to get back to work. My yet-to-do pile is still significantly bigger than my done pile. I sigh and reach for my French book. I'm still struggling in French, but Gram has been helping me memorize vocabulary words and practice simple phrases. She told me she's always wanted to visit France. I told her I'd think about coming along if she changed her plans and decided to visit another French-speaking country, such as Belgium or Switzerland. She just gave me one of her looks before going back to the book she was reading.

It's almost a relief when Monday finally rolls around.

The cafeteria is more chaotic than usual, which is saying a lot. I pause just inside the door to watch teachers herd students from their regular tables and force them to sit with people they barely even know. When a group of cheerleaders balk, Mrs. Hamm, the eleventh-grade English teacher, points to a poster hung on the wall. MAKE NEW FRIENDS!!! SAY NO TO CLIQUES! I spot Tally leaning against the back wall, nibbling on half of a sandwich. She's holding a piece of paper and is alternating between reading it and watching the chaos. I skirt around a cluster of scowling cheerleaders and weave in between dozens of people who are trying, like Tally, to eat their lunches standing up. Eventually I make it over to where Tally is standing.

"Hi," I say. Tally quickly folds the paper and stuffs it into her pocket. Her cheeks are flushed and she looks upset. "You okay?" I ask.

"Of course," she says. Then she gestures toward the commotion in front of us. "I just hate this." I nod. But I don't quite buy that the lunchroom reorganization is what's upsetting her. It's just more attempts to destroy the caste system. I sigh and lean against the wall beside her, wondering if the piece of paper she was holding is the same one Poppy was reading. I pull out my apple and take a bite, watching as Mr. Ellison, the vice principal, directs Charity and her minions toward a table near the trash cans. The minions comply. I suppose they are used to following orders, but Charity isn't about to give up her primo table without a fight. As soon as Mr. Ellison has moved on, Charity's right back to her old table. The minions are only seconds behind her.

"It might be a while before we get a table," I say. I slide down the wall and sit. Tally sits beside me. Madame Framboise leads a group of soccer players past and seats them with four guys playing Magic. The two groups barely acknowledge one another. I know the administration means well, but you can't force people to be friends.

We both watch as Esmeralda flits effortlessly between a table full of hardcore gamers and a cluster of cheerleaders before finally settling in at Charity's table. Slowly the tables in front of us begin filling up and the chaos dials down a couple of notches. Tally watches her for a moment before turning back to her lunch. While infinitely better than the lard sandwiches she was bringing a few weeks ago in an attempt to get back at Charity, salami and black raspberry jam is still pretty gross. I eat quietly, giving Tally a chance to talk if she wants to.

"I just don't get it," Tally says finally. She nods toward where Esmeralda has the whole table enthralled in something she's saying. "She's been here—what? A week? And she knows everyone." Talking about Esmeralda isn't exactly what I had in mind, but I go with it.

"Why does she bother you so much?" I ask.

Tally shrugs. "She just seems false, you know?"

"Maybe," I say.

"Like Charity 2.0."

"More like Charity 8.0," I say. Esmeralda is talking to the minions, who seem to be hanging on her every word. Charity is pretending not to care that she's not the center of attention, but it's obvious from the way she's attacking her carrot sticks that all isn't well at the popular table. Esmeralda finishes whatever she was saying and all of the minions burst into giggles. Charity snaps another carrot stick in between her teeth. "Maybe Esmeralda isn't that bad," I say. Although I'm not sure whether I actually believe that or just enjoy watching Charity get knocked down a peg or two. "I think we should keep an open mind," I say.

"Hm," Tally says. "You keep an open mind. I'll keep my eyes open."

The minions burst into another round of giggles. Charity rolls her eyes, picks up her lunch bag, and heads toward the trash cans. One of the Lindseys follows, but she keeps looking back at Esmeralda. After throwing away her trash, Charity watches Esmeralda holding court where she once ruled. She rolls her eyes again, spins on her heel, and heads toward the door. Unfortunately, her trajectory takes her right past where we're sitting.

"Just ignore her," Tally says. I try to, but the bite of sandwich I'm chewing turns to cement in my mouth, and my heart rate increases. I hate that I always react to her the way I do, but she's just so mean and random. Charity spots us sitting against the wall and smirks. She says something to Lindsey, who hiccups a laugh. My heart starts beating even faster and I feel sick to my stomach.

Charity pauses in front of us and shakes her head. "Look, Lindsey. It's Penny *Lame* and her lame little friend." She looks at me, waiting to see if I'll say anything. I try to think of something. Anything. But my brain just freezes. Then Tally starts laughing.

"Wow," Tally says. "You're almost as clever as you are pretty."

Charity is momentarily at a loss for words. Clearly she's trying to figure out if she's just been insulted or complimented. Then she gets it. She looks Tally over and shakes her head. "Nice skirt. Did you get that at the Salvation Army?" I glance over at Tally's denim skirt, which she made out of a pair of old jeans. Then Charity lowers her voice. "I hear they give discounts to orphans."

"Hey!" I say, finally finding my voice. "Lay off."

Charity moves away from us. The look on her face suggests that maybe she knows she overstepped a line. That was a low blow even for her. Tally calmly balls up her lunch sack and chucks it at the back of Charity's head. It strikes her ponytail and bounces off. Charity spins and glares at us. She mouths something. I actually have no idea what she said, which is probably a good thing. Then she stalks off toward the doors.

"I hate her," Tally says. "I wish she were—"

"Whoa," I say, putting my hand on her arm. "I know she's horrible, but you can't let her get to you. Just ignore her."

"Like you're one to talk," Tally snaps. She leans her head against the wall and closes her eyes. She takes a deep breath and lets it out. Then she looks at me. "Sorry," she says. "I don't know what's wrong with me."

"You do seem a little on edge," I say hesitantly.

"I think I'm just tired," she says. "I am sorry, though. Forgive me?"

"Of course," I say. We go back to eating our sandwiches, but it's obvious neither of us has much of an appetite anymore. I'm not buying that Tally is just tired. Something else is going on. But I decide not to push her. She'll tell me when she's ready.

Blake finds us sitting against the wall. He sits on the floor beside Tally and balances his tray on his legs. Blake takes a big bite of his pasta and smiles. He chews, swallows, and nods. "Say what you like about caf food, but this is the best spag bol I've ever had." I'm grateful for Blake's presence. Maybe he can shake Tally out of her funk.

"Spag bol?" I ask.

"Spaghetti Bolognese," Tally says. She leans forward so that she can see his T-shirt. "Save the Narwhals?"

"What? They're the unicorns of the sea," Blake says.

Tally looks at him for a long moment but obviously is at a loss for how to respond. She turns to me. "Are boys always this ridiculous?" she asks.

"I'm pretty sure," I say.

"I'm right here," Blake says. He takes another bite of spag bol and makes a happy sound. Clearly he's not that offended.

"Well, I have a history test that I'm only marginally prepared for," I say. "I'm headed to the library."

"See you after school?" Tally asks.

I shake my head. "Not unless you want to stack firewood. Gram's having three cords delivered today."

Tally makes a face. "Um—"

"I'm just kidding," I say. "I don't think it will take long anyway," I say. I collect my trash, gather my books, and stand. "I'll call you after," I say. I see Blake smirking as I walk away. I'm not sure but I think I hear him say, "City girl." Then Tally shushes him, but maybe I'm wrong.

I know it makes me crazy nerdy to admit it, but I like libraries. Actually I *love* libraries, and the HHHS library is really cool. And I can say that with some authority because the libraries in the City are pretty amazing. But what the library at HHHS is lacking in size compared to those, it totally rocks in style. And it's all because of Mrs. Zinnia. First of all there are plants everywhere. And she has rainbow catchers mounted in the upper windows, which, when the light hits them the right way, make the whole library light up. And she's constantly changing the artwork, asking artists from around the region to lend her new paintings and sculptures. Right now a guy who makes these crazy sculptures out of found objects has his pieces everywhere. I sit at the table under a giant octopus made out of a couple of pasta strainers, random silverware, and dozens of gears and springs and bits of glass. I spot Charlotte sitting at a table way in the back. She looks up and sees me. I wave. She gives me a smile but quickly looks back down at the book in front of her. Weird.

I spread out my history notes on the table in front of me and start running through them again. I can remember the names and the details, but never the dates, so when a shadow falls across my notebook, I'm mumbling numbers to myself in a way that might make me seem mental.

I look up. Marcus.

"Hey," he says. "I don't want to bother you. I just haven't seen you in a couple of days."

I smile. I do a little dance in my head. *Marcus missed me.* But then who should appear walking out of the rainbows? Esmeralda of course.

"Oh, hi," she says.

"Oh, hey," he says. And it's insane, but I try to figure out if her *hey* is the same as the *hey* I got.

Esmeralda looks at me. "Penny, right?" she asks. I nod in what I hope is a neutral way. I mean, seriously. It's not like we go to some megaschool with thousands of students. And besides, we have three classes together. And I sit right behind her in one of them. "Still studying for the history test?" I nod again. "Well, if you ever need help, let me know. My school in Paris was considerably more rigorous than the classes here."

"Thanks," I say, vaguely feeling like I was just insulted. The bell rings, signaling the end of lunch.

"I guess we'd better go. We wouldn't want to be late," she says. She tilts her head and smiles at Marcus.

"Yeah," he says. Esmeralda steps slightly away from us in a not so subtle *follow me* move. Marcus seems unsure whether he should go or wait for me to pack up all of my stuff.

"Go ahead," I say.

"Good luck on your test," he says.

"Thanks," I say, watching him walk across the library with Esmeralda. She pauses at the door, which he opens for her. Her *merci* followed by her musical laugh floats across the library. I sigh and close my notebook. As I walk to history, I tell myself he's just being nice to her because she's new. But what if that's why he's being nice to me, too? I shake my head and tell myself that's dumb. You don't go on walks on the beach with someone just because she's new. And you don't *almost* kiss someone just because you're nice. Do you?

Okay, three cords of wood is a lot. The pile of wood sitting in the middle of our front yard is huge. Gram informs me that when it's stacked, a cord is four feet high, four feet wide, and eight feet long. For the record, that's 128 cubic feet of wood per cord. Times three. Even with only the smallest break and both of us working, it's nearly dark before we finish hauling the last of it into the barn. Gram asks if I can finish up so she can start dinner. I'm just sweeping all of the bits and pieces of wood into a pile when Mom pulls into the driveway. She climbs out and regards me for a moment. I know I must be a sight.

Hair every which way and covered in sawdust and dirt and bits of bark.

"Looks like I'm right on time," she says.

"Ha-ha," I say. My mother is hysterical.

"Well, this should cheer you up," she says. She lifts a package from the front seat and hands it to me. It's from my dad. I take off my gloves and tear it open. I love getting mail. It's like mini Christmas six days a week. Inside is a blue blob of fabric and a long, flat box. I tuck the envelope under my arm and shake open the fabric. It's a T-shirt with what looks like Japanese printing on the front and a drawing of a cat with one paw raised. I hand the shirt to my mom and turn my attention to the box. It's wooden with a red lacquered top. I slide it open, revealing a pair of red chopsticks with a gold flowered pattern around the end.

"These are pretty," I say. Mom nods. "I guess he went to Chinatown?"

"I guess so," she says. It's out of character for him to send me anything at all, much less something so random. I check the envelope again and see a small sheet of paper. I pull it out. Printed across the top in bold type is PETER LANE ESQ.

> *Hey, Bean. I saw these and thought you might like them.*
> *Call me. We need to talk about Thanksgiving.*
> *Love, Dad.*
> *P.S. The mouse is for Oscar.*

Confused, I check the envelope again. Shoved way down in the corner is a tiny stuffed mouse with a long string tail. I pull it out and sniff it. Catnip. Oscar will be thrilled. "Guess I should call Dad," I say.

Mom nods. "Well, how about dinner first?" she asks. She smiles, but it's thin. And I wonder if she's thinking the same thing I am. Dad's *call me*s aren't generally good news.

"I just need to close up the barn," I say. She nods, but I can see the pain in her eyes. I know she's trying hard to be normal about my dad, but I also know just thinking about him is difficult for her. I hand her the empty envelope and the trio of gifts. "Be right in," I say. She heads toward the house as I turn toward the barn. I suddenly feel horribly sad. I know some of it is because I'm just tired, but some of it is because it strikes me that this will be the first Thanksgiving we won't spend as a family. I know I should have thought about it before, but I guess I was so wrapped up in starting school and Charity and just the whole divorce that it didn't really sink in. I turn off the lights in the barn, pull the heavy door across the opening, and hook the latch. I stand in the yard for a moment and look up. It's barely dark, the sky a deep navy shifting into black. And it feels too big and I feel too small. I realize that Thanksgiving is just the start. Then there's Christmas and New Year's and my birthday and then a whole new year of holidays.

And then, of course, there's the other thing. The thing that Mom and I have never really talked about. My dad's great at making plans, but he's not the best at the follow-through. In fact, he stinks at the follow-through. Mostly I just assume things aren't going to happen. That way if they do, it's a happy surprise. If they don't, well, then I'm not devastated.

"This stinks," I announce to the sky. I frown at the darkness. The sky doesn't seem to care one way or another. "Fine," I say, realizing how insane it is to be talking to the sky. Then I spot the first star, bright and shining. A tiny spot of light in the dark. And for some reason it actually makes me feel a little bit better. "Thanks," I say. Then I head toward the house to where I know it's warm and there's a shower and the smells of chili and homemade corn bread are wafting out into the yard. Just before I step inside, I look up one more time. Now instead of one, there are a hundred stars all twinkling for anyone who takes a moment to look. "Now you're just showing off," I say, but it makes me smile. And I head inside. Tired, but hopeful, and really, really hungry.

Chapter Seven

I leave messages for my dad on his work voice mail and his cell phone. I try texting him for the sixth or seventh time during breakfast on Friday.

"Still nothing?" Mom asks from where she's going over her calendar. I shake my head.

"He's probably just busy," I say. But this is classic Dad. He makes a gesture, which gets my hopes up, and then disappears. I take a look at the clock.

"I should go," I say.

"Is it that time already?" Mom sighs and pulls her hair back into a ponytail. She looks tired. I know the bakery has been busy and she still hasn't been able to find a full-time baker to help her. I hug her as I pass, something I need to do more often. Then I rush upstairs, brush my teeth, and try to wrestle my hair into something less chaotic than usual. I give up and just pull it back into a knot. I give myself one last look in the mirror. I'm wearing the shirt my dad sent for the first time. I grab my backpack and then go back for my new chopsticks on a whim. I quickly jam them into my twist of hair and head downstairs.

I grab my fleece and pull it on. Then I shoulder my pack. "Bye," I call as I head out the door. Mom waves from where she's still sitting, frowning over her calendar. I hurry to the bridge to meet Tally, but she's not there. I check my watch and realize I'm later than usual. Maybe she gave up and went ahead. By the time I get to school, I only have a few minutes to get to my locker and make it to class. I'm barely in my seat just as the bell rings.

School is mostly listen, write, answer questions about numbers or events or word choices. Repeat. And repeat. Art is a different story. Art makes me feel alive. It makes me feel like I fit. Not even the sight of Charity and her clones can make me stop smiling. I slide onto the stool beside Tally, who is frowning over a creased and stained letter.

"Hi," I say. She jumps at my voice and quickly slides the letter off of the table and onto her lap. "Tally," I say. "What is that?"

"Nothing," she says. She folds the letter and jams it into the front pocket of her backpack. When she sits back up, her cheeks are flushed.

"You sure you're okay?" I ask.

"Drop it," Tally says. Her voice is harsh and cold. Nothing like it usually is.

"Sorry," I say, feeling hurt.

Tally sighs and looks at me. "No, I'm sorry," she says. "I'm just being emo." She doesn't offer up a reason for *why* she's being emotional and I don't press it. "Any idea who that is?" Tally asks, nodding toward Miss Beans's office. Miss Beans is in there talking with some guy with long red hair pulled back into a ponytail and a tattoo of a fish on his forearm.

"No idea," I say. The door into the hall opens, spilling noise into the room. Then Esmeralda walks in. I notice once again how she doesn't even seem real. How can you get all the way to fourth period and still look like you just stepped out of a magazine? I glance around the room. Most everyone else looks rumpled or wrinkled or just tired. Even Charity's hair looks a little limp. But Esmeralda's hair falls in swirling waves across her shoulders. And her dress, which would look like a sack on anyone else, makes her look sophisticated in a way that should be totally impossible for someone only fourteen. As she passes, she leaves the faint smell of oranges in her wake.

I glance over at Charity, who is staring at me. "Nice chopsticks," she mouths. And I feel my cheeks go pink. What for four hours seemed cool and funky now seems stupid. I resist the urge to take them out. I don't want to give her the satisfaction. Instead I pull out my sketchbook. I told my mom if I had to make another snowflake cupcake, I might scream. She said I was welcome to come up with something new. I frown at the sketches I made during French class. A wonky penguin and a sad snowman. Not exactly my best work.

Charlotte comes in and slides onto the stool on the other side of me. "Hi," she says.

"Hi," I say. I still don't know how to act around Charlotte. I'm trying to be nice but cautious, but I have a feeling I'm mostly being awkward. It's just hard. Three weeks ago, she was laughing along with the other minions every time Charity pranked me or said something mean to me. And now she seems to want to be friends. I guess I'm just trying to keep an open mind *and* keep my eyes open.

"I like your hair," Charlotte says.

"Thanks," I say.

"What are you working on?" she asks.

"I'm trying to come up with a new winter cupcake design." I turn my sketchbook so she can see what I've done so far.

She looks at them thoughtfully. "A couple of years ago my family spent Christmas with my mother's family in Sweden. There everything was red and white. And everything was from nature. Birds and pinecones and reindeer." She smiles. "And gnomes. Lot and lots of gnomes." Her cheeks get pink. "Sorry," she says.

"Why?" I ask. "You just gave me a lot of great ideas."

She shrugs. "Charity always said—" She looks down at the sketch pad again. Whatever Charity always said to her must have been about as awesome as what she always says to me.

"Maybe Charity was wrong," I say. Charlotte looks sort of shocked, like I just suggested that maybe breathing air isn't good for you, but then she grins.

The door to Miss Beans's office opens. Miss Beans walks out, followed by the guy with the red hair. She lifts her hand to get everyone's attention. "I'd like to introduce Chad Stinson. Mr. Stinson is both a sculptor and painter. He's recently moved here from New York City." Miss Beans smiles at me. "I've invited him today to share with you all about the exciting new work he's doing." She steps back slightly, giving him the floor.

Chad Stinson holds up a handful of springs and a broken plate. "What would you call these?" he asks.

"Um, junk?" one of Charity's minions says.

Another says, "Trash."

There are the usual titters from the rest of the clones, but those are quickly silenced by one look from Miss Beans.

Chad Stinson isn't fazed; he just nods. "That's one way of looking at it. Anyone else?" I tilt my head, trying to see what he's seeing. He looks around the room from face to face. But then he looks at me. "What about you?" he asks.

"Um," I begin, drawing smirks all around from the back table. I ignore them and study what he's holding for a moment, trying to see what he sees, and then I say something before I really even think it through. "Possibility," I say.

Chad Stinson leans forward and really looks at me. "Nice," he says, nodding. "I was going to say inspiration, but I like your answer better." He puts the springs and the plate on the table and walks over to the corner of the room where a cart is covered with a drop cloth. He wheels it into the center of the room and then removes the cloth. Everyone leans forward to see what he's brought. Boxes and boxes of possibility. Broken clocks, mismatched silverware, a Mason jar full of corks. There are pipes and dials and a battered whisk. And a whole bowl full of doorknobs. Tally leans forward.

"Cool," she whispers.

Chad Stinson picks up an old broken windup clock. "Repurposing or upcycling is all about honoring what was with what could be." I see Tally nodding out of the corner of my eye and smile. She loves anything vintage or funky or just old. I love the idea of taking something that someone doesn't want anymore and turning it into something beautiful.

Miss Beans walks into her office and wheels out another cart. "Mr. Stinson and I are going to pass around some of his latest projects."

"Feel free to touch them, poke them, prod them," Chad Stinson says.

"But don't break them," Miss Beans says. She lifts the sheet from the cart she is pushing. At first it seems like another cart full of random objects, but then I see what looks like a birdhouse. It's not exactly like the one in the library. Instead of twigs, this one is made from colored pencil stubs, but it's obvious it's from the same artist. Miss Beans picks up one of the sculptures, a frog made from old clock parts and what looks like the gas tank of a motorcycle. She carefully delivers it to the closest table. She and Chad Stinson distribute different sculptures to each of the tables. We get a Ferris wheel made from a bicycle wheel and mismatched china teacups.

"Holy wow," Tally says.

"Holy wow?" I whisper. She just grins at me.

Miss Beans talks with Chad Stinson for a few minutes while we look at his work. I glance over at Charity, who is mostly rolling her eyes and looking bored. She glances over at me and sneers. Lovely.

"So, what do you think?" Miss Beans asks, walking over to us.

"Amazing," Tally says. Charlotte nods and smiles.

"What about you, Penny?" Miss Beans asks.

"Holy wow," I say. Tally just laughs and Miss Beans smiles. She walks back to the center of the room and raises her hand for everyone to be quiet again.

"As you might have guessed," she says. "This is your next project. Actually this is your final project for the semester, so I expect big things." She outlines the project, telling us how large our sculptures need to be (huge) and that they need to capture something about ourselves. "Glue, paint, and any kind of mounting materials are fine, but everything else has to either be repurposed objects or things you find out in nature."

We spend the rest of the class period poring over the boxes of materials and selecting things we want to use for our sculptures. By the end of class, I have a coil of wire, a copper finial from an ornate lamp, and a handful of wooden Tinkertoys. Tally has a box full of Christmas ornaments and an old film reel. Miss Beans tells us to put our finds into our cubbies. Then Chad Stinson spends the rest of the class demonstrating different techniques that he uses for his work.

After class Miss Beans asks for a volunteer to help put things away. I raise my hand, earning me an eye roll from Charity. She leans over to Esmeralda and whispers something, but Esmeralda is too busy talking with one of the clones to notice. Charity sits back up and frowns.

"Hey," Tally says. "Want me to wait for you?"

"No," I say. "Go ahead. I'll meet you in the lunchroom."

"You sure?" Tally asks, glancing over at Charity. I nod and wave her away. Charlotte, who is slowly stacking her books, cuts her eyes at Tally. The sight of her sitting in the library during lunch comes back to me. I realize I haven't seen her in the lunchroom after she stopped hanging out with Charity. And I wonder if she's been hiding out in the library ever since.

"Charlotte," I say. "Maybe you'd like to sit with us at lunch?" She looks from me to Tally and back.

"You sure?" she asks.

Tally nods. "Totally." Then she looks at me. "See you in there?"

"Yep," I say. Charlotte follows Tally out into the hall. Esmeralda is right behind them, trailed by the clones. Charity, who is still putting away her things, is left behind. I stand up and push in my stool, watching her. She looks sort of lost and sad, and for a moment, I feel sorry for her. Maybe everything isn't so awesome in mean girl land. But then she looks up. She narrows her eyes at me and I have the distinct feeling that she didn't want anyone, least of all me, to witness the fact that she was left behind. She picks up her things and walks toward me. She pauses, sniffs, and then makes a face.

"You might try to take a shower once in a while," she says. "Maybe then you wouldn't smell so horrible." Chad Stinson walks back into the room. Charity offers him her best pageant smile. "Later," she says to me before heading out into the hall. I cringe. With Charity even one word can unglue me.

I spend most of lunch helping box up the sculptures and then transporting them to Chad Stinson's truck. Miss Beans teases him about his truck's wonky paint job. It's mostly blaze orange, but the driver's-side door is fuchsia. He stands back and looks at it critically. "It's not horrible," he says. "Besides, it only cost me a little over seventeen dollars." He looks at me. "I did it myself," he says.

"He also did the body work himself," Miss Beans says, nodding toward the front bumper, which is held in place with blue duct tape and zip ties.

"Wait," he says. "You haven't even seen the best part." He opens the driver's-side door and steps back. The inside of the door, which at one time must have been leather or vinyl, has been replaced by green fun fur. "What do you think?" he asks. Miss Beans just smiles and shakes her head. He looks at me.

"I like it," I say. I wouldn't choose it, but I like that it's surprising and out of the ordinary and maybe just a little weird.

"I like it, too," Miss Beans says. Chad Stinson grins at us.

They thank me for my help and I head back inside, leaving them discussing whether he should repaint his truck lime green or grape. Apparently both colors are on clearance at Lancaster Hardware. And Chad Stinson says at three dollars a can, you can't really go wrong. Miss Beans isn't so sure and I have to agree. Sometimes you really do get what you pay for.

Chapter Eight

When my mom drops Tally and me off at the Windham Farm on Saturday, we're greeted by five huge buckets of white paint and plastic grocery bags containing a screwdriver, two rollers, and half a dozen paintbrushes. A thermos is perched on top of the pile. A note is wedged under one of the paint cans.

> *Felling dead wood on the back 40.*
> *Make yourselves at home.*
> *—Dutch*

Tally opens the thermos and takes a sniff, then an experimental sip. She makes a face. "Yuck," she says, extending the thermos toward me. "Black coffee. Taste it."

"Um, no," I say. Why do people always do that? Sniff something horrible, taste something disgusting. Touch something repulsive. And then after you witness their revulsion, they want you to do it, too. Tally screws the top back on the thermos and flips the note over. She reads aloud.

"Pineapple, sand castle, tulips, butterflies, polaroid, blue plate special." Tally looks at me with a question in her eyes. I shrug. "Either he's a genius or he's crazy," she says.

"Or both," I say. Tally pockets the note and we each grab a can of paint and a couple of brushes. We make our way around the back of the house, past overgrown lilac bushes, a garden full of rubbery rhubarb and spent irises, and a coop that's more a pile of debris than anything that might serve as a home to chickens. Tally disappears around the corner and I follow. She stops so quickly, I almost run into her back.

"What are you—" I look past her. "Whoa." It's the only thing I can think to say. Before us is the fence. I should say the FENCE, because it goes on forever, disappearing into a copse of pine trees only to reappear again hundreds of yards farther.

"Hello?" I turn at the voice and see Blake walking toward us, his four-wheeler helmet tucked under his arm. "Whoa," he says, stopping just short of where we're standing. "There has to be half a mile of fence. Maybe more."

"You act like you've never seen this before," Tally says. "You've lived in this town forever. Haven't you been past here about a million times?"

"Well, yeah," Blake says. "But who looks at fences?" His shirt has a giant white question mark on the front of it and the words YOUR DESIGN HERE below it. He walks to the nearest section of fence and begins stepping off the distance between posts. I hear him mumbling to himself. "Eight feet, two posts, four rails." He stands and studies the fence again. "What do you think? About thirty minutes per section?" Neither Tally nor I answer. Not having painted a fence before, I have no idea.

"Let's say thirty minutes," Blake says. "Give or take." He scans the fence line again and I can see his lips moving, counting. Then he's back to mumbling. "Half a mile of fence, 8-foot sections. 330 times 30 minutes." Then he stares at some passing clouds for a few seconds and announces that it's going to take Tally and me 82.5 hours to finish the job. "Plus breaks," he adds. Then he looks over at us, clearly pleased with his mathematical prowess.

I glance at Tally, who looks like she might start crying at any moment, and then back at Blake. "Not helping."

Then Blake does what every guy, including my dad, does when someone is about to cry. He freaks. He starts stammering that he was just guessing and that he is terrible with math and that he's sure it won't take us nearly that long seeing as how we're painting experts and all. Tally isn't buying it, but she does smile to make sure he knows she appreciates the pep talk. Even if it is all nonsense.

"It's a big job, but we'll get it done," Tally says.

"I'll help," Blake says.

Tally shakes her head. "No way," she says. "You have a paper and a lab report and that makeup test to do."

Blake makes a dismissive noise. "The paper's done. The lab report's cake. And the makeup test is for Mr. Nickel's bird class."

"Bird class?" I ask. I don't remember Blake taking ornithology.

Blake nods and makes his arms into wings. "Bird class," he says. "As in I'll fly right through."

Tally shakes her head at him, but she's smiling a little, so that's something. "Isn't there something else you're forgetting?" Tally prompts.

Blake looks at her blankly.

"Soccer practice?" she says.

Blake looks at his watch, then he makes a noise that sounds like a surprised chicken. When he looks up, there's panic in his eyes. "Sorry," he says. "I gotta go. Anyone who's late has to do pukinators until, well, until he pukes."

"Delightful," Tally says. "And that is why I'm not playing soccer." Blake pauses and frowns at her. "Oh, and the fact that I can't kick a ball to save my life."

"Later," Blake calls, jogging toward his four-wheeler. He pushes his helmet back on his head.

"When would you have to kick a ball to save your life?" I ask.

"Well, like an explosive ball," she says.

"Kicking an explosive ball is probably a bad idea," I say.

Blake climbs on his four-wheeler and starts it up. We watch as he steers down the driveway, sending up a rooster tail of dust in his wake.

"Guess we'd better get to it," Tally says, nodding toward the paint cans.

"Guess so," I say. My already low enthusiasm for the job plummeted even further after Blake's little mathematical assessment.

"Come on," Tally says, bumping me with her shoulder. "It'll be fun." I nod, remembering Gram's saying, "Once begun is half done." I know what she means. The hardest part sometimes is just getting started. And I totally get why that applies to scooping the cat box or cleaning my room, but this? The Great Fence of Hog's Hollow? I take a deep breath and follow Tally over to the nearest section of the fence.

From far away I couldn't really understand why Dutch wanted the fence painted, but up close it's obvious. If it was ever painted, any trace of it is long gone. Tally and I use the screwdriver to pry the lids off the buckets. Then we each take a bucket and a brush and start on a section. It's not hard work. It's just sort of fussy and messy, but soon we get into a rhythm. Tally tries to talk for a while, telling me about how she wants to sell the rest of the Rock Paper Scissors T-shirts at Winter Fest as a way to raise money for the ARK.

"What is Winter Fest exactly?" I ask.

"It's fun," she says. "A lot better than Hog's Hollow Days. For one, there's no Hog Queen. But there's also tons to do. There's a pancake feed and snowball fights and ice carving. And the Ice House." She pauses. "And then on the last night, they have fireworks." Her cheeks get pink.

"What?" I ask. She shakes her head and she blushes even more. "Tell me!" I say. She shrugs and turns away. Then she mumbles something. "Um, I didn't catch that."

She turns and looks at me again. "I said, 'That was when I first met Blake.'"

"During the fireworks?" I ask. She nods. "That's so romantic!"

"Don't tell him I told you," she says.

"I won't," I say. She smiles and we go back to painting. "Tally and Blake sitting in a tree . . ." I sing. She rolls her eyes at me, but I can tell she doesn't mind.

Every once in a while, I pause to rest my wrist and look around. Whatever we might think about the job itself, the location couldn't be better. The farm backs up against a thick forest. Red and orange leaves cling to the maple trees, while the pine and spruce are every color of green, from a deep viridian to a blue gray that reminds me of the ocean just before a storm. Tally seems better than she's been lately. Less stressed. And the mysterious piece of paper has yet to make an appearance. A flock of geese flying overhead starts honking like crazy. I look up and watch them until they disappear over the hills.

"Pretty, ain't it?" I jump at the voice behind me, sending a spattering of paint onto my already freckled shoes. There's a man standing a dozen or so feet behind us. Old jeans, a thick flannel shirt, and heavy hiking boots are all north woodsman, but the braided leather bracelet and longish shaggy gray hair would look more at home on someone riding a surfboard or rocketing down a ski slope. I recognize him from Gram's Main Street Meltdown. "Sorry," he says, blue eyes crinkling in the corners. "Didn't mean to scare you."

"Hi, Mr. Ingmar," Tally says. I can see her holding her breath, hoping she got his name right. I'm with Blake. It's probably not Ingmasomething.

"Hey there, Miss Tally." He narrows his eyes at her. "Although I'm pretty sure I told you to call me Dutch."

"Sorry, sir," Tally says. "I mean, Dutch."

"And you must be Penny," he says. He walks toward me with his hand extended. I put out my hand, but then think twice about it when I see how much paint is on it. "Pleased to meet you," he says, taking my hand. His hand is huge and warm and calloused. He squeezes mine briefly and steps back. He studies me for a moment, then nods. "You favor her," he says. "Your grandmother, I mean."

"Really?" I say. I don't look very much like my mother and only like my father in my hair color and around my mouth.

Dutch just smiles before turning toward the house. "Let's see if I can't rustle up some lunch for you two." Then he turns and narrows his eyes at us. "I'll bet you can knock out another section before I can whip something together." He turns away again, whistling off tune.

Tally grins at me. He's issued a challenge and Tally is about as competitive as they come. "Let's do two," she says. We get back to work, painting as fast as we can. "If I ever bump into Mark Twain," Tally says, "I'm going to have some words."

"If you ever bump into Mark Twain, run. Because it's a ghost. He's been dead for over a hundred years."

"Good point," she says. We are just finishing up the second section when a clanging from the front porch makes us both look over. "He has a dinner triangle," Tally says, laughing. "Awesome." We quickly cap the buckets of paint and wrap the brushes in the plastic bags from Lancaster Hardware. "Race you," she says, taking off running toward the house. I shake my head, but hurry after her. I easily catch up and begin to pull away. "No fair," she yells from behind me. But I'm not exactly sure what she's protesting. I place my hand on the side of the porch and turn and wait. It only takes a moment before she's standing in front of me. "Holy cow. You're fast."

Dutch appears in the doorway. "Well, get in here," he says. "Food's getting cold."

Tally and I look at each other. I shrug and we kick off our shoes at the door, adding them to the lineup of hiking boots, running shoes, and sandals with tire treads for soles and ropes for straps. I step inside first. Tally follows close behind. We both pause just inside the door and look around. The whole main floor of the farmhouse is one big room. A giant stone fireplace dominates most of the far wall, and a small kitchen huddles against the wall to our left.

"You can wash up over there," Dutch says, directing us toward the sink. Tally and I take turns at the faucet, pumping apple-scented soap into our hands and running them through the warm tap water. Dutch is standing beside one of the chairs, waiting for us. He nods toward the other chairs. It isn't until we're seated that he sits. A reminder of my father suddenly wells up inside of me without warning. He always waited to sit until my mom and I both were seated. He also always stood if we left the table. At the time, it seemed like unnecessary formality, but Dutch's easy courtesy makes me miss my father's quirky ways. Dutch bows his head briefly and I see his lips moving. I glance at Tally and see her wide-eyed, barely breathing. I wonder if something about this has triggered a memory for her, too. And it occurs to me how many of my friends have someone significant missing from their daily lives.

Dutch raises his head and looks at each of us for a moment, as if really trying to see us. Then he grins. "Well, dig in." He passes Tally a plate of only slightly mangled peanut butter and jelly sandwiches. "Sorry about those," he says. "I'm still hunting for the silverware." He nods toward the stacks of boxes at the far end of the room. "It's harder than you think to make PB&J's with a Swiss Army knife." Tally passes me the sandwiches and I add two halves to my plate before passing them back to Dutch.

"It's probably good that Switzerland is known for its neutrality," Tally says, studying her sandwich.

"And why's that?" Dutch asks.

"The Swiss Army knife isn't that imposing of a weapon. I mean, you're just as likely to flip open the scissors or a bottle opener as a blade."

Dutch nods as if seriously considering her observation. "Although the ruler-saw combo might give someone pause."

Tally looks around the sparsely furnished room. "You know what you need around here?" she asks.

"You mean other than a couch, a rug, and a couple of

bookcases?" He nods toward the boxes of books lined up in front of the fireplace.

"You need a pet," Tally says.

Dutch grins and looks over at me. "She's about to tell me about some poor, lonely dog who needs a good home."

"A good forever home," I say.

Dutch turns to Tally and leans back in his chair. "Okay, let's hear it," he says.

Tally is momentarily put off her game, but she rallies quickly. "Well, the way I see it, you have two options. First, there's Bear. He's a golden retriever. Not the smartest dog on the planet, but sweet and loyal. Or there's Lily. She's a herding dog. Crazy smart, but timid." Dutch nods, but Tally's not finished. "Or maybe you're more of a cat person. We've got dozens of them." She leans forward. "Literally."

"I'll tell you what, Miss Tally," Dutch says. "When you finish my fence, I'll swing by that ARK of yours." He takes a sip of his water and looks at her over the rim of his glass. "Although I will warn you. I tend to go in for the tough cases." He puts down his glass and smiles. "I like challenges." He glances out the big window that looks out over the pasture, then back at us. "Well, eat up. We've got us a bunch of fence to paint." We finish our lunch quickly and help Dutch carry the empty dishes over to the sink. He turns the water on and adds a good amount of soap.

"Mind if I use your bathroom?" Tally asks.

"Second door on the left at the top of the stairs," he says over his shoulder. Tally heads up the stairs, leaving me alone with Dutch. He glances back at me and nods toward a dish towel lying on the counter. "You can dry," he says.

I pick up the towel and wait while he scrubs and rinses the first plate. Dutch's directness reminds me a lot of Gram. I'm fairly certain I shouldn't mention that to her. In fact, she doesn't know Tally and I are here. I didn't exactly hide it from her, but I wasn't totally forthcoming with the details when she asked about our latest job. I told her we had some painting to do. She didn't ask any follow-up questions and I didn't offer any more information.

Dutch hands me the first washed plate, which I take carefully. As I rub it dry, a million questions flood my mind. Why did he move back to Hog's Hollow? Why did he leave in the first place? What's the deal between him and Gram? Why does the surfboard leaning in the corner of the living room look like it has a bite taken out of it? But every question I think to ask seems too personal, so I remain quiet. Dutch hands another plate to me and I carefully wipe it, like the task takes all of my mental energy so I can't actually speak.

"I'm looking forward to a proper snow," Dutch says, finally breaking the silence. "The stuff they have out West—" He shakes his head, like it's too depressing to even talk about. Then looks at me. "This will be your first winter here in Hog's Hollow." I nod. "You're in for a treat. Prettiest place in the world to be during the holidays." He hands me the last plate. "And I should know." The implication that he's spent holidays in a lot of different places hangs between us.

Finally I work up some courage. "Did you grow up here?" I ask. He nods. "What made you move back?" I ask.

"I've crisscrossed this country half a dozen times. Herding cattle in Montana, smokejumping in Oregon, roughnecking off the coast of Texas. I spent the last fifteen years running a surf shack down near La Jolla. But my heart's always been here." I hear the door open upstairs, then Tally's footsteps above us. "Hog's Hollow is home. Always has been," he says. Dutch looks at me. "I think I can finish up," he says.

I dry my hands and leave the towel on the counter. Tally hops down the steps and smiles at me. She nods toward Dutch, a question in her eyes. Did I get any details? I give her a tiny nod and then head up the stairs.

I step onto the landing and stop. The entire wall in front of me is covered in photographs. And not carefully framed, artfully arranged ones, but a giant mass. Just hung with push-pins, edge to edge. Some even overlap others. Big full-color ones and tiny black-and-whites barely bigger than a postage stamp. But they are all of the same things. Close-ups of faces. Old and wrinkled men with scars hang beside pink-cheeked toddlers with knit caps pulled low to keep out the cold. It's beautiful and slightly disconcerting. A hundred pairs of eyes peering at me, watching me. One woman has her hand in front of her mouth. Laughing, shining eyes. I lean in. I know that face. Gram. But young. Probably not a lot older than I am. I look into her eyes, so much like mine, as Dutch said. And I wonder what she was thinking. What made her laugh?

By the time I walk back downstairs, Tally and Dutch are already outside on the porch. I pull on my fleece jacket, push my feet into my shoes, and head out.

"I'm going to put blackberries there and plant some apple trees over there," Dutch says, pointing toward a spot to the right of the house.

"You do know it takes at least seven years before you have apples," Tally says.

Dutch shrugs. "I can wait." He glances over at Tally, who looks skeptical. "I'm old," he says, "but not that old."

"I know," Tally says. "Seven years is just so long." She looks at me for confirmation and I nod. Seven years is more than half my lifetime.

Dutch shakes his head. "You young 'uns. You want everything yesterday." He starts down the stairs and toward where we left off painting. "One day you'll figure out the best things are those you have to wait for." Tally makes a face and I nod again. Dutch smiles and shakes his head at us. "Come on," he says. "I'm not paying you to stand around." He steps off the porch and we follow. Dutch starts singing a song about planting watermelons on his grave. He insists we sing along, saying it's in our job description.

"I thought we were just here to paint," Tally says, picking up her brush.

"This is part of the *other duties as assigned*," Dutch says. "Now listen: You have to get the next part right or the song just doesn't make any sense."

We each take a section of fence while he teaches us the rest of the watermelon song. Within minutes, all three of us are singing about how chicken and biscuits are mighty fine, but they ain't nothing like a watermelon vine. Tally protests that when you're dead, you're not going to care about watermelons or chicken and biscuits, but Dutch just shakes his head and says she'll understand someday. Tally looks at me for support, but I can't stop laughing. And soon she's laughing with me. And hearing her laugh again after a long week of anger and sadness makes even the twenty miles of fence that still need paint bearable.

Chapter Nine

With Dutch helping, we are able to finish almost thirty sections by the time the sun is beginning to set over the trees. We help Dutch carry the buckets and brushes to his cellar door and then we walk back to retrieve our coats that we ditched during the warmth of the afternoon. Dutch looks at the fence, and then pulls out his wallet. He extracts two bills, folds them, and holds them out to Tally.

She tries to wave them away. "You pay when the job's done," she says.

"Consider it a down payment," Dutch says. Tally takes the bills and shoves them into the front pocket of her jeans.

"Thanks," she says. "We'll be back next weekend."

"And the weekend after that," I say, smiling.

Headlights dance across the lilac bushes as my mother's car pulls into the driveway. Dutch walks us around the side of the house and waves at my mother, who steps out of the car. She walks toward Dutch with her hand outstretched.

"Mr. Ingmar," she says. He takes her hand and gives it a squeeze before releasing it. "I've heard a lot about you."

"Some of it good, I hope," he says.

"Some," she concedes.

"Please call me Dutch," he says. "Everyone does." He looks

over at Tally and me. I cover a yawn with my hand, which makes Dutch smile.

"We should go," Mom says.

Dutch nods. "Of course."

The three of us pile into the car. Mom starts the engine and we head toward the street. As we pull out onto the road, I look back and see Dutch still standing there, watching us go. The look on his face reminds me of how I felt when I first moved to Hog's Hollow.

"He must get lonely out here all by himself," Tally says from the backseat.

"Yeah," I say. "Hog's Hollow is the best place to be when you feel like you belong."

"And the worst place to be when you feel like you don't," Tally finishes. Her comment makes me think of Esmeralda. And I wonder if she feels lonely, too. I can barely stand to be around Charity for a few hours during the school day. I'm not sure what I would do if I had to live with her. I decide that in spite of Tally's misgivings, I want to give Esmeralda a chance.

We drive past the Christmas tree farm and the Tide Mill Dairy, where the cows are making their trek up to the barn. We slow as the fog rolling off the ocean pours across the road. Then we make the last turn toward the beach and pull up in front of Tally's house.

Tally climbs out and I roll down my window. "Thank you so much for helping today."

"No problem," I say.

She ducks so she can see my mom. "And thanks for the ride," she says.

"Anytime," Mom says.

Poppy steps out onto the porch and waves. She has her reading glasses on and is holding a thick packet of papers. She steps into her clogs and walks over to us. "So how was it?" she asks me. The smile playing at the corner of her mouth hints that she's familiar with the fence at the Windham Farm.

"It was actually pretty fun," I say.

"I'm glad," she says.

"Dutch said next time he'll teach us how to juggle," Tally says.

"Excellent," Poppy says. She bends so she can see my mother. "Will you tell Joy that I'll drop the extension cords off in the morning? I thought I'd be able to dig them out today, but things got busy—" She gestures with the papers in her hand.

I glance at my mom, who is frowning. Tally stuffs her hands into her pockets and steps back from the car. Suddenly everyone is awkward and no one wants to make eye contact. It seems I'm the only one who has no idea what's going on.

Poppy is the first to recover. "I'll bet you're wondering what all of the extension cords are for," she says.

I nod, but what I'm really wondering about are those papers and why everyone's acting so squirrelly.

"Your grandmother likes putting up decorations for the

holidays," she says. Okay. A couple of wreaths. Some lights. I'm not sure why everyone is acting oddly.

Tally smiles. It's a little hesitant, but it's there. "It's awesome," Tally says. "Neon pink flamingos. Dancing polar bears. Lights that blink in time to the music." I try to picture what Tally's describing. It's hard for me to reconcile it with my down-to-earth grandmother.

I glance at my mother, who nods her agreement with what Tally's telling me. "It's true," she says. I've never seen Gram's house during the holidays. She always visited us in the City, claiming it was the one time of the year she preferred the press of humanity to the solitude of nature.

"Speaking of—" my mother begins. "We really should get home. When I left, the whole living room was covered in strings of lights and boxes full of flamingo parts."

"Ew," I say, making my mother laugh.

"Call me if you need anything," my mother says to Poppy.

"Thank you," Poppy says. She and Tally head to the porch, where they stand and wait while we pull out. I glance back and see them still standing there. Poppy has her arm around Tally and Tally is leaning into her.

"What was that all about?" I ask.

My mother turns onto the road and heads toward Gram's house. "What do you mean?"

"The papers and the awkwardness and the whole *call me if you need anything*," I say.

"Poppy's just dealing with some things," Mom says. We pull into Gram's driveway and up to the barn.

"Some things?" I ask. Mom shuts off the engine and looks at me. "You're not going to tell me anything, are you?"

She shakes her head. "I can't," she says. "I'm sorry." The barn door opens and Gram comes out with a giant flamingo tucked under one arm and an extension cord clutched in her hand. She smiles when she sees us and then heads over to a flock of flamingos leaning against the side of the house.

"We'd better go help," Mom says. She climbs out of the car and walks over to Gram, who points at the barn.

I make a face. And not because I don't want to help Gram. I'm happy to support any wacky scheme she has cooked up. I just hate being on the outside of things, particularly when those things seem to be about my best friend. I climb out of the car and join my mother as she hauls several more flamingos out of one of the storage closets at the back of the barn.

Once we have what Gram informs me is a *flamboyance* of flamingos positioned perfectly in the yard, we add top hats and tiaras (yes, half are wearing top hats, the other half, tiaras) and hundreds of twinkle lights. Then we stand back and watch as Gram plugs in the lights. The effect is overwhelming, both in a good and bad way.

"So, what do you think?" Gram asks.

"It's bright," I say.

"And—" Gram presses.

"Festive?"

"It's tacky," my mom says.

I turn and look at her, slightly shocked, but Gram just grins. "I was going for kitschy, but tacky's good, too," she says.

"Wait," I say. "You want it to look bad?"

Gram laughs. "Not bad. Memorable." She straightens one of the flamingos' top hats. She smiles again and it's positively gleeful. "People drive from miles around to see my little display. I wouldn't want them to be disappointed."

"Well, I'm sure they won't be," I say, gesturing at the brightly lit flock.

Gram just shakes her head. "Oh, Penny. This is just the beginning. We'll put the polar bears over there," she says, pointing toward the road. "And then there's the lights and the tree and, well, the roof."

"The roof?" I ask.

"Santa and his sleigh, of course," she says.

"Of course," I say, smiling.

"Unfortunately, something used Donner's torso for a nest this summer."

An image of a zombie reindeer prances through my head. "That's pretty gruesome," I say, making Gram laugh. The three of us walk toward the house for dinner and more talk about decorations.

Gram unplugs the lights on the way in, plunging the yard back into darkness. "We go live on the first of December."

"Ah," I say, because what else can you say when your mother has to step over a box of oversize ornaments just to reach the kitchen, and your living room looks like it was ransacked by Santa's elves?

"Who wants soup?" my mom asks from where she's pulling bowls down from the cabinet. My stomach growls in response. It's been a long time since PB&J's with Dutch. "I'll take that as a yes," Mom says.

"I'll get the bread," Gram says. She pulls a loaf of home-made sourdough from the oven, where it was keeping warm, and carries it to the table. I grab plates, spoons, and napkins and place them on the table at each of our spots. I add three glasses of water to the table and then help my mom carry over the bowls of soup. I have to nudge Oscar off my chair before I can sit. He hops down and proceeds to glare at me from the floor.

"So," Gram says after we say grace and start eating. "What have you been up to today?" she asks me. I glance at my mother, who cringes slightly.

"Tally and I were painting a fence," I say, keeping it vague. There's no telling how Gram will react if I tell her we spent the day with Dutch.

"No roosters?" Gram asks.

"Not that I saw," I say.

"Whose fence were you painting?" she asks, picking up the bread knife to slice a piece of bread.

I glance at my mother again, but she won't meet my eyes. I'm on my own. "We were at the Windham Farm," I say.

Gram slices the piece of bread calmly and places it on her plate. "That's nice," she says. Her tone indicates that she means just the opposite.

"So, you're not mad?" I ask.

Her laugh is only slightly disturbing. "Of course not. Why would I be mad?"

"You seem mad," I say. She puts down the knife with more force than necessary, waking Cupcake from where she was napping near the woodstove.

"What that man does is of no consequence to me."

I look at my mother. She's not buying it either. "Well, that's good," I say. "Because I was thinking maybe we could ask him to dinner." Mom's eyes get huge. "I mean, I remember what it was like to be new in town." My mom is fighting hard not to smile. Gram frowns. She's caught in her own trap and she knows it.

"Great," she says. Her voice is slightly shrill. "I'll look forward to it."

We finish dinner in silence. Me, relishing my tiny victory in the cold war between Gram and Dutch. Gram, simmering almost as much as the soup on the stovetop. And Mom, well, maybe it's sort of fun to see your own daughter outmaneuver your mother every once in a while. By the time we're finished eating, the sounds of bagpipes are starting to filter down the beach, accompanied by an off-pitch howl that rises and falls with the notes of "She'll Be Coming 'Round the Mountain."

"Well, that is just the icing on the cake," Gram says, picking up her bowl and taking it to the sink. "I'm going for a walk," she states. She has her coat on and is out the door before either my mom or I can say anything.

Mom smiles at me. "What do you say we clean up?"

I nod and start clearing the table while Mom fills the sink with soapy water. "I hope I didn't go too far," I say, standing beside my mom at the counter.

"No, you're fine," she says. "Dutch's arrival is probably the best thing that could happen to her even if she can't see it yet."

"I still don't know what happened between them," I say.

"He broke her heart," Mom says. It's simple, but the weight of what she said hangs in the air.

Chapter Ten

Gram is totally getting her revenge. She could have mentioned that Marcus was coming by in the morning to help hoist everything up onto the roof. She could have woken me up so I could at least brush my teeth. Instead, when I stumble downstairs, still blinking sleep out of my eyes and following the smell of freshly baked cinnamon rolls, it takes me a moment to realize that there are more people at the table than live at our house. In addition to Marcus and his dad, Tally, Blake, and Poppy are all standing, sitting, and leaning in various spots around my kitchen.

"Hey!" Tally says. "Your grandmother told us not to wake you." She smiles encouragingly at me. "Sorry," she mouths. Gram gives me her equivalent of the Cheshire cat's smile from where she's pouring juice into glasses.

"I think I'll just—" I start backing toward the stairs, where at the top I know there is a hairbrush and a change of clothes that don't look, well, slept in. I'm pretty sure there's also a toothbrush.

"Here," Marcus says, sliding over on the bench so there's room. I resist the impulse to look down at what I'm wearing. I know I've got on my comfiest sweatpants. Utilitarian gray and about two sizes too big. Topped with a cozy hoodie.

"Want a cinnamon roll?" Gram asks. I nod, trying not to open my mouth until I can eat or drink something. I have a feeling my breath isn't as fresh as it could be. I take the cinnamon roll Gram hands me and narrow my eyes at her. "Want another one, Marcus?" she asks, ignoring my look.

"No, thank you," he says, making Gram smile. She's all about manners and Marcus is all about being polite. I take a bite of my cinnamon roll and a little of my irritation fades away. I mean, how can you be grouchy when you're eating a cinnamon roll?

"How was painting yesterday?" Marcus asks.

I shrug. "Long," I say. "But Mr. Ingmar is really nice."

"I saw him at the hardware store yesterday buying an ax," Marcus says. He leans toward me and lowers his voice. "He was carrying a jar full of worms."

"Like fishing worms?" I ask.

Marcus shakes his head. "I don't think so. They looked—" He frowns. "Different."

"Different?" I ask, one eyebrow raised.

"Less wormy and more . . ."

"Different?" I suggest, smiling. He smiles back at me, and the clink of dishes and sounds of the coffeemaker popping and Oscar meowing under the table for a handout all fade. And it's just Marcus and me sitting together in the warm kitchen filled with the smells of cinnamon and sugar. And—

"Hey!" Blake says, slapping Marcus on the back. "You ready?" I look up and see everyone putting their coats on and heading toward the door. Tally is grinning at me and I feel my cheeks flush.

"Yep," Marcus says, picking up his plate to carry it to the sink.

Gram waves him away, telling him she'll clean up later. "It's the least I can do to repay you for all the hard work."

"I'll take payment in cinnamon rolls any day," Blake says. Gram grins and follows him out of the house.

"You coming, Penny?" Marcus asks.

I nod. "Be right there," I say. Tally hangs back while Blake and Marcus follow Gram outside.

"Sorry," she says. "I tried to get your grandmother to let me go up and wake you. You know, *warn* you, but she said to let you sleep."

"Don't worry about it," I say.

"Well, from what I could see, Marcus doesn't care about all that stuff anyway."

"What stuff?" I ask. "You mean, brushed hair and fresh breath?" Tally laughs and tells me she'll see me outside. I hurry upstairs and throw on some jeans and quickly brush my teeth. Whatever Tally says, I'd still rather not look like a complete mess every time Marcus sees me.

I dash back downstairs again before Gram even makes it back inside. I grab my fleece and head outside, where the wind has picked up and is blowing the pom-poms on the snowmen's hats and making their bells jingle.

"Hey, Penny!" I step into the yard and look up to where Mr.

Fish is standing anchoring a giant tree into place beside the chimney. "Does it look straight?"

"A little to the right," I yell. He moves it slightly and I give him a thumbs-up. He lashes the tree to the brick while Marcus holds it steady.

"Can you help me?" Poppy asks, walking toward me. Her arms are filled with bundles of Christmas lights. I rush over and take the staple gun hanging from her fingers and the box of staples she has pinned between her chin and her shoulder. I help her pile the lights on the back deck. Then the real work begins. Poppy tells me Gram not only wants a lot of lights, but they have to be artistically interesting. And considering my grandmother is a photographer and Poppy is a glassblower, this is a significant request. I note that these are no ordinary lights. There are at least five shades of blue, a couple of orange, and a trio of green.

"Whatever happened to traditional red and green?" I ask.

Poppy shakes her head and smiles. "Your grandmother got these special delivered from Poland last spring. These and about seven hundred painted wooden eggs."

"Eggs?" I repeat, wondering if eggs at Christmas is some unique Hog's Hollow tradition.

Poppy smiles. "For her Easter tree."

"Wow," I say. "Seems like Hog's Hollow goes all out for every major holiday."

"And some minor ones," Poppy says, starting to sort the lights into piles. "Like National Food on a Stick Day."

"Really?" I ask.

Poppy smiles at me. "You'll see." I begin sorting the blue lights into indigo, aquamarine, periwinkle, cobalt, and navy. Poppy begins sorting the greens. "Tally says you'll be in New York for Thanksgiving," she says.

I shrug. "Maybe," I say like it doesn't matter one way or the other. "I'm not sure."

Poppy glances over at me, but she doesn't comment. I look over at Tally, who is wearing Frosty's top hat and trying to put a Santa hat on Blake, but he keeps dodging away. "I wish Tally's dad would—" I'm not sure how to finish. Tally's dad chose his music career over his daughter months ago. I'm not sure even if he did decide to see her over the holidays, it would make any difference.

"Me, too," Poppy says, reading my mind. Then she sits back on her heels and looks at the piles of lights. "So, any ideas?" she asks.

I tilt my head and look at the different shades of blue. "What if we did an ombré pattern? You know, like navy along the bottom, then indigo, then cobalt—"

Poppy starts nodding. "We could finish up at the top with white lights."

"It's a lot of lights," I say.

Poppy nods. "That's why we started today. Last year it took more than a week to put everything up."

"Wow," I say.

Poppy nods. "It was pretty wow. I have photos somewhere,

but they really don't do it justice. It's definitely a you-have-to-have-been-there thing."

I look over at where Blake and Tally are still trying to inflate the snow globe. "I'm glad I'm here now," I say.

"Me, too," Poppy says.

We spend the next three hours positioning lights and using the staple gun to tack them into place. Poppy had the idea to add swirls and loops to my color design, so by the time we have a couple of feet in place, it's starting to look like the waves breaking just off the shore. I'm feeding lights to Poppy as she perches on top of the stepladder to reach around one of the windows.

"Wow," Blake says, staring at our work. "That looks amazing."

"Thanks," I say.

Mom pulls into the driveway and climbs out of her car, a stack of pizza boxes in her hands.

"That also looks amazing," Blake says.

"Who wants pizza?" Mom calls. Blake is already at her side, helping her carry the pizza to the deck. The sun has warmed us up and Blake has taken his jacket off. His shirt has a giant octopus flying through space with the words CELESTIAL CEPHALOPOD. Weird.

We all finish whatever we're working on and make our way to the deck, where Mom has the pizza boxes and Gram has glasses of lemonade. "You grab the pizza and I'll get us some lemonade," Marcus says from just behind my shoulder. I take one of the pizza boxes and carry it over to a bench along one side of the porch. Marcus joins me with two glasses of lemonade in hand and Blake in tow. Tally is close behind.

Blake snags a slice of pizza and takes a big bite. "Best day ever," he says.

"You always say that," Tally says, taking her own slice.

"Warm sun. Cool breeze. Gooey pizza. Pink flamingos. What could be better than this?"

I look out at the water and a sky that is almost too blue to be real. Blake's right. It might not be the best day *ever*. But at least top ten. I turn back and see Marcus looking at me. He smiles and I immediately amend my opinion. Blake's right. Best day ever.

After pizza, Gram tells everyone to go home. "I can't thank you enough," she says.

Before Marcus leaves, he asks if I want to walk Sam later and, of course, I say yes.

Later, I'm trying to outline a paper on the global ramifications of World War I when Mom comes in and sits on the edge of my bed.

She takes a deep breath, which gets my attention. "I just got off the phone with your dad." One look at her face and I know what she's about to say.

"He didn't want to talk to me?" I ask.

She shakes her head. "He was about to get on a plane. He said he'd call you once he landed."

"Let me guess. No Thanksgiving?"

She sighs and nods. "He said he has some big meeting he has to attend. Something about a new acquisition. He's flying to Japan tonight." Well, at least that explains the gifts. "I'm sorry," she says.

"It's fine," I say, but from my voice, it's clear. It's not fine.

"No," Mom says. "It stinks."

I shrug. "It does, but—" I shrug again and lean back against the wall. The truth is even before the divorce, I didn't see my dad very much. He was always traveling or working late. Part of me was sort of glad when we moved because as much as I missed him, at least he had a really good excuse for not being around. Finding new excuses for his absences was a lot harder when he lived in the same house as us. I guess deep down I thought things might be different once we moved away. Like "absence makes the heart grow fonder" and all of that. But it's obvious that things aren't working out as I'd hoped.

"I was thinking," Mom says. "Maybe we could invite Tally and Poppy and Blake and his mom and—"

I sit up and look at her. "Dutch?" I ask.

She nods. "It might be easier if there were other people around."

"She is less likely to freak out."

"I know Marcus and his dad are gone," I say. Over pizza, Marcus told us about the Fish Family Traditional Last-of-the-Year Camping Trip. Marcus told me the last time they did it was before his mom died. Apparently they got rained out and the three of them spent the night in a motel eating junk food from the vending machine and watching old black-and-white monster movies. He confessed he wouldn't be totally bummed if it rained again this year.

"Are you going to tell Gram? About, you know," I ask.

"I think maybe it can be a surprise," Mom says.

"Good thinking," I say.

Mom pats my leg through the quilt I have pulled across my lap. "I'm really sorry about your dad," she says.

"Yeah, but at least he sort of tries," I say. Although I'm not sure I believe even that. "Tally's dad just bailed." Tally hasn't heard from her dad in months. My dad's still around. But sometimes I wonder, is barely trying better than not trying at all?

We sit in silence for a couple of moments until Oscar meows. Mom bends and puts Oscar on the bed. He immediately walks to my math book and lies down on it, making finishing my homework even more challenging. Mom stands up and walks to the door, but then pauses before heading out into the hall. "Keep in mind that just because someone else's life is different doesn't mean it's harder."

I start to disagree, but then I stop and just nod. She turns and walks toward the stairs. I sigh and scratch Oscar behind the ears, making him drool on my book.

"Gross," I say, even though I don't really mean it. Oscar just looks at me and rubs his face even harder into my hand. I think about what my mom said. Maybe she's right. Maybe Tally's life isn't harder or easier. It's just different. Sometimes nothing is better than something. If the something keeps hurting you over and over.

Chapter Eleven

Marcus calls me after dinner to see if I still want to go on a walk. "Sure. When?" I twirl around the kitchen, making Oscar look up from his nap.

"How about now?" he asks.

"Sure," I repeat. I already have one arm in my coat before we hang up. "I'm going for a walk," I say loudly so that Mom and Gram will hear me from where they are sitting in the living room. Mom is researching new cupcake recipes and Gram is stitching up the holes in some giant red stockings that didn't summer over very well.

"Wear a hat," Mom says.

"Okay," I say, because we've had this argument a million times and I've lost a million times. Even though I've presented solid empirical evidence supporting my position that an uncovered head does not equal pneumonia, Mom's not buying it. I rummage in the bin by the door and pull out a hat I bought at a funky shop in SoHo. It's gold and green with a big purple velvet flower stitched on one side. I tuck my hair behind my ears and pull it on. I gently push Cupcake out of the way so she can't make a break for it. She's under the illusion that she'd survive more than one day without canned tuna and a warm fire. I mean, seriously. Her name's Cupcake.

I step out onto the deck and pull the door shut behind me. It's gotten a lot colder since the sun went down. And even though I wouldn't admit it in a million years, I'm glad to have a hat. I walk down the steps to the sand and head down the beach toward Marcus's house. The wind sends the thready gray clouds scuttling across the sky. I spot Sam an instant before he sees me. He covers the distance between us in a matter of moments, chuffing and sneezing all around me as I bend to pet him. Even though he's gotten a lot better about not jumping up on people, I still make sure to keep my hands where he can reach them so he has no reason to try.

"Cool hat," Marcus says, jogging up to where Sam and I are standing.

"Thanks," I say, now doubly glad to have it. "Where to?" I ask.

Marcus nods past me toward where the beach narrows and eventually turns into a trail, which threads through the trees and to the next beach over.

We walk side by side, laughing as Sam sprints ahead, churning up sprays of sand in his wake. And as much as I love the moments when I can barely breathe because Marcus is holding my hand or touching my face, I also love it like this. Laughing and happy. When Sam realizes we aren't right behind him, he runs back to us, urging us forward. But he quickly grows tired of our pace and sprints away again. The third time he returns dragging a piece of driftwood more than three times his length. He drops the ginormous branch in front of us, then sits, wagging his tail hopefully.

"Sorry, buddy," Marcus says. "That one's a little too big for fetch." Sam tilts his head at him, making me laugh. Then as if understanding him, runs off again in search of a better size stick. "Are you going to see your dad over break?" Marcus asks.

I stuff my hands deeper into my pockets. "No," I say.

"Oh," Marcus says. He's quiet, waiting for me to explain or not. I love that about Marcus. He respects space when people need it. Maybe it takes going through something painful to make you into a good friend. Like maybe you need to hurt so that you can see past your own life and your own problems. We walk across piles of rocks. They crunch under our feet, reminding me of the icy snow in Central Park.

"My dad's going to be in Japan," I say, seeing if I can convince myself it's okay if I just say it out loud.

"I'm sorry," Marcus says. Because what else can you say when someone says her dad is more interested in closing some big business deal halfway across the world than spending Thanksgiving with his daughter, who he hasn't seen in almost six months?

We walk in silence for several moments. And I wonder what he's thinking. And I wonder if I asked him, would I get a real answer? And not what I usually say when someone asks me: "Nothing." Which is a lie. Because I'm never thinking about nothing. Marcus takes my hand; for once it doesn't send me flying up into the sky. It just feels comforting and takes some of the sting out of my dad bailing on me. Marcus leads me toward where the trees touch the beach. We step onto a winding trail that leads us deeper into the woods. The trees press close against us, forcing us to walk single file. I have to step carefully to keep from tripping on the exposed tree roots. Because I'm watching the ground, I nearly run straight into Marcus, who is stopped in the middle of the trail.

"Look," Marcus says, pointing out through a gap in the trees. I step around him, but he catches the back of my coat. "Careful," he says. "It's a long way down." The trail has led us upward as well as in. We're standing on the edge of a ledge of rock, looking down on the sand and water below. The two lighthouses, one on each edge of the bay, are lit up. Their lights dance across the fog.

"It's beautiful," I say. "And kind of spooky."

Marcus starts to say something, but there's a crashing in the woods behind us, which makes both of us turn. Images of headless horsemen and yetis and evil wood elves come to mind. Then Sam bursts out of the trees, panting and chuffing. He jogs directly up to me and drops a stick at my feet. He sits and looks at me expectantly. I pick it up, trying to ignore the fact that it's all gooey with dog saliva. I try to hold it with just two fingers, and then I toss it back down the trail from where we came. And Sam tears after it.

"We should probably head back," Marcus says. "I still have to finish studying for my French test."

"Ouch," I say, smirking. "And you with no tutor to help." Like I'm one to talk. Even with all of the extra studying and

Gram's help, I'm still just staying afloat. Marcus smiles at my teasing.

"Actually," he says. "I wanted to talk to you about that." Something in his voice makes me brace myself. Charity was tutoring Marcus in French, but he stopped working with her when he found out how awful she was being to me. Marcus starts toward home and I follow, saying a little prayer. *Please not Charity. Please not Charity.* "Esme offered to help me if I needed it."

I'm thankful that I'm walking behind him and he can't see my face. It's not Charity, but in some ways Esmeralda is worse. Like Tally said, she's boy kryptonite. I'm not certain I want Marcus spending a lot of time with her. And then it occurs to me that maybe Esmeralda doesn't even know about me and Marcus. Not that there is a me and Marcus—at least not yet. And I wonder if he even thought to say anything to her about me.

We break free from the trees and Marcus turns and looks at me. "Madame Framboise was the one who suggested it. Esme said she wasn't sure she should because she didn't want to make you jealous, but I told her you're not like that."

I nod, realizing I'm caught. If I say no, then I'm just admitting that I am, in fact, jealous and even more that Esmeralda was right. "You should totally work with her," I say, trying to sound more confident than I feel.

We walk back toward my house. Marcus takes my hand as soon as we can walk side by side. I start to pull back because of the dog drool still clinging to my fingers, but Marcus just laughs and squeezes my hand tighter. Sam sprints down toward the water, then leaps away with a yip when the waves swell toward him. I still feel off about Marcus working with Esme, but I tell myself I'm being ridiculous. It's just tutoring. He wasn't drawn in by Charity; why would Esmeralda be any different? But a tiny voice says, *But she is different. Isn't she?* I tell the tiny voice to hush.

"So what *are* you going to do for Thanksgiving?" Marcus asks.

I'm grateful for something to think about other than Esmeralda. I tell him about my mom's big scheme for getting Gram and Dutch in the same room. "Things could get ugly," I say. He grins. He was present for both the Main Street Showdown and the Tulip Bomb, so he knows exactly what I mean.

We're at my house sooner than I would like. Time with Marcus always seems to go faster than regular time, like a minute is a second and an hour a handful of minutes. We stop just short of Gram's house and I think tonight has to be it. Marcus is definitely going to kiss me. No tulips. No interrupting dogs.

That's when I see the mountain of sand. I tell myself not to pay attention to it. It's nothing. But then Marcus sees it, too.

"What's that?" he asks. We walk toward the mound of sand. Boot prints spiral all around it and there's a shovel and several buckets and a box full of seashells. A figure is crouching down at the edge of the water, filling a pail with more wet sand.

Marcus lets go of my hand and steps slightly in front of me. I squint into the darkness. I can't tell who it is until he stands up.

"Dutch?" I say. He whips around and I can see his face in the dim light. He looks an awful lot like a deer caught in someone's headlights. He walks toward us. Sam thunders down the beach straight at him. His hackles are raised and he plants himself on the sand between Dutch and us. I've never seen him look so fierce. Dutch stops, clearly nervous.

"Sam," Marcus says. "It's okay." Sam hesitates, unconvinced, but he comes over to sit in front of me. The message is clear: *I've got my eye on you.*

"Hey there, Penny," Dutch says, walking toward us. He's still nervous. And not just about my furry protector. He nods at Marcus, who nods back.

"This is Marcus," I say.

"Nice to meet you, sir," Marcus says.

"Likewise," Dutch says. They shake hands like we're just meeting on the street in the middle of the day and not in the dark on an empty beach. Sam seems mollified by the exchange and proceeds to leap into the pile, leaving a dog-shaped impression in the sand.

"What are you doing?" I ask Dutch. I keep my voice low because it's obvious whatever he's up to, he doesn't want anyone to know.

"Well, you see—" He looks from the pile of sand to our house, then back to the sand.

"Never mind," I say, letting him off the hook. It's apparent it's something for Gram. And it's equally apparent that it's a surprise. What little I know of Dutch is that it's sure to be an interesting one.

"You won't rat me out, will you?" Dutch asks. I shake my head. The relief on his face is immediate.

Sam keeps leaping into the pile, scattering sand everywhere. "We'd better go," Marcus says. "Before all of your work is destroyed." He smiles at me and maybe I imagine it, but it seems like he, too, wishes there was more time. "See you tomorrow, Penny?"

I nod. "See you." Marcus starts away from us, waving for Sam to follow. Sam pauses, looking at me. He wants to make sure I'm safe before he leaves. "Go ahead," I say. He chuffs and hurries after Marcus. The darkness swallows them up after only a few yards. I glance over at Dutch, who is smiling after them. He looks at me and his eyes twinkle.

"What?" I ask.

He just grins and shakes his head.

I frown. "Well, I'll leave you to it," I say. "Whatever *it* is."

"Night, Penny," Dutch says. "And thanks."

"Don't mention it," I say. And I mean it. If Gram thinks I'm conspiring with *the enemy*—well, let's just say I'd rather stay neutral in this war. I start toward the stairs.

When I walk in, Gram asks me how the walk was and I tell her it was good. She studies me over the rims of her glasses and I swear I see the same wistfulness in her eyes that

I saw in Dutch's. Then it's gone, replaced by her usual no-nonsense look.

"I hear you're staying here for Thanksgiving," she says.

"Yes," I say.

"Well, good," she says. She stands up and walks over to me. "I'm glad you'll be around," she says. "With just your mom and me, well, that didn't really seem like enough for a proper Thanksgiving." She touches my cheek for a moment and I know there's more that she'd like to say about my dad canceling, but she doesn't. And I appreciate both. The acknowledgment that what he did was wrong, but also that she doesn't say it out loud. "Your mom already went to bed," she said, "but she asked if you'd peek in and say good night." She starts toward the back door. "I'll just lock up," she says.

"No!" I say a little too loudly. She turns and looks at me. "I'll do it." I know my voice sounds a bit shrill.

"Okay," she says, looking at me like I've lost my marbles. "Then I'll just say good night." She gives me the eyeball as she walks past, but, thankfully, she doesn't press the point. Hopefully she'll just decide I'm being an emo teenager or something and not think twice about it. Once she's in her room with the door shut, I walk around turning off lights and making sure all of the doors are locked. I peek in on my mom. The lights are off and her eyes are closed, but she's still awake. She waves me over. She reaches up to hug me. She pulls me down so that my ear is close to her mouth. "So, what's Dutch doing down on the beach?" she whispers.

"I don't know," I whisper back.

"A mystery," she says. She squeezes me one more time and then lets go. "I love you," she says.

"I love you, too," I say back. Oscar meows at the doorway. Clearly he's ready for bed. "See you in the morning," I say, pulling the door shut behind me. I climb the stairs to my room. Oscar runs up past me, hoping to get the prime spot on the pillow.

By the time I climb into bed, I realize how tired I am. But it takes me a while to fall asleep. Both because my cat keeps stealing the covers, but also because even though it's not for me, I can't wait to see what will be on the beach when we wake up. And even more, what Gram's reaction will be.

Chapter Twelve

Whatin the world?" Gram's voice spills in through my open window. I blink my eyes open and look at my clock. 5:30 a.m. I start to roll back over, but then I remember about Dutch and the pile of sand. "Well, I never," Gram says. I throw off the covers and hurry down the stairs. The back door is open and I can see Gram standing on the deck. Her mug of tea sends up a spiral of steam into the frigid air. I hurry outside and join her at the railing. The wood deck is cold on my bare feet and for a second I wish I had taken a moment to pull on some sneakers. But then I see what's on the sand in front of our house and all thoughts of cold and shoes fly away.

"Wow," I say. And it hardly captures what I'm seeing. Dutch has built a sand castle. But not like any sand castle I've ever seen before. This one is enormous. Four tall turrets with actual stones set in the walls surround a giant courtyard filled with gardens of seaweed and tufts of sea heather mounted on sticks for trees. The moat is carved deep into the sand surrounding the castle. A piece of driftwood serves as the drawbridge. Bits of blue and green sea glass wink in the stained-glass windows of the keep.

"Come on," I say to Gram, pulling at the sleeve of her robe. She resists at first, but her curiosity gets the best of her and she follows me down the steps to the beach. The sand castle is even more impressive close up. It's at least five feet across and four or five feet tall. But it's the level of detail that's so amazing. Huge arches curve over doorways, and actual windows that let light pour through are cut into the sandy towers.

"He must have been out here all night," I blurt out. Gram narrows her eyes at me. "I mean, I assume it was Mr. Ingmar," I say, because I don't want Gram thinking I'm on a first-name basis with the enemy.

I glance up at the porch, where Mom is standing, smiling. I smile back at her but am careful to fix my face before Gram spots it. Gram doesn't say anything else, but she stays on the beach looking at it long after I tell her I'm going in because I'm afraid my toes are going to freeze and fall off.

"It's amazing," I say when I climb up to where my mom is standing. "Did you know that he could do that?" I ask.

Mom shakes her head. "I'm afraid I don't know much of anything about Dutch," she says. "Your grandmother never would talk about him. And I was too young to remember him when he lived here before."

"You think this might change her mind about him?" I ask.

Gram turns and heads up the steps toward us. "Who wants toast?" she asks. She's inside and the door is shut before either of us can say anything.

"Maybe," Mom says, frowning. We stand and look down at the castle for several more minutes before we're both too cold. I follow Mom inside, brushing my feet off before I step into the house. Gram is standing at the counter, a faraway look in her eyes. Burned toast sits on a plate to her right. I smile at this. Dutch has my unflappable grandmother rattled again. But this time she doesn't seem mad, just thoughtful.

I think about sand castles all the way to school and wonder if Dutch just thought it would be cool to make one or if it means something to him and Gram. I spot Tally leaning against her locker, looking at that piece of paper again. She stuffs it into her pocket when she sees me. I decide to just ask. "What is that?"

"What?" Tally asks.

I raise my eyebrow. She raises hers in response.

I sigh and shake my head. "Forget it," I say. We stand there awkwardly for several moments, looking everywhere but at each other. I finally break the silence and tell her about the sand castle.

She pretends to swoon. "That is the most romantic thing I've ever heard," she says.

"What is?" Blake asks, walking over. I retell the story to Blake, who has a very different take on it. "He could have just bought her a card." Both of us glare at him. He puts up his hands and starts backing away, mumbling something about having to see someone about something. Tally just smiles and rolls her eyes. Both of us know Blake got it. He pretended not to just to mess with us. He's a lot less obtuse than he pretends to be.

*　　*　　*

By the time third period is over, I've heard Charity make the same announcement at least four times. She's telling anyone who will listen (and at a volume that those of us trying not to listen can't help but hear) that she and her parents and Esmeralda are going skiing for break. First off, who cares? And second, the thought of either Mr. or Mrs. Wharton skiing is so ridiculous that it seriously detracts from the impact of her story.

"I just feel bad for her," I say after we are subjected to the fifth retelling of the ski trip to end all ski trips. Tally is leaning against the locker next to mine and watching the show while I change out my math books for my sketch pad.

"Why?" she asks, glancing down the hall to where Charity is holding court. "She's exactly where she wants to be: the center of attention."

"Not her," I say. "Esmeralda."

Tally makes a face. "Why?"

Esmeralda walks past us, barely looking our way.

"I wouldn't wish living with Charity on my worst enemy. Would you?" I say, looking at her.

She sighs. "Okay, no," she says. "But I still don't trust her."

"Maybe we just need to give her a chance," I say.

"What? To stab us in the backs?" Tally shakes her head.

"I just remember what it was like to be new here," I say.

"Well, me, too," Tally says. "But—" She sighs again. "Fine," she says. "I'll be nice, but that's it."

Esmeralda heads into the art room, glancing back only once to where we are. She looks lost and sad.

"See?" I say. "Come on." Tally and I head toward the art room, threading our way through the clusters of people spilling out of the classrooms. A soccer ball whizzes by, nearly clipping Tally on the side of the head. She ducks just in time and the ball bounces against the row of lockers behind us.

Jacob, one of Blake's less cerebral friends, jogs by. He grins at Tally. "Good reflexes, dude."

Tally rolls her eyes at me. We head into the sanctuary of the art room only to find Esmeralda crying at the back table. She looks up, with tears streaming down her face. She quickly ducks behind her waterfall of hair, but it's too late.

"See?" I repeat. I grab a box of tissues from the bookshelf and walk over to Esmeralda. Tally follows a few steps behind. "Here," I say, placing the box of tissues on the table. Esmeralda looks up and gives me a watery smile. I sit on the stool that Charity usually occupies. Tally stands just behind me.

Esmeralda takes a tissue and blots at her eyes. Either she's wearing waterproof mascara or her eyelashes really are eight feet long. I feel like a total jerk just thinking it. She's clearly hurting and all I can think of is my own vanity.

"Thanks," Esmeralda finally says. "I guess I'm just homesick." Tears course down her cheeks again. She hiccups a laugh. "Of course there's no one at home. My parents are in China." For a moment I can't tell whether she's sad or angry. Maybe both.

"It's too bad you couldn't have gone with them," I say. "Not that we're not glad you're here," I add quickly. I glance over at Tally, but she's just watching us. "I'm sure they miss you, too," I say.

"I'm sure," Esmeralda says. I can't tell whether she's being sarcastic or not. Esmeralda gives her eyes one last blot and takes a deep breath. "I just feel so alone. They wouldn't even let me keep Marcel. They took him with them."

"Marcel?" I ask.

"My dog," she says.

"Oh," I say. Because what do you say to that? They took her dog with them, but not her? And I feel sick to my stomach. I've been judging Esmeralda for what she looks like. Somehow I got it into my head that beautiful people have perfect lives or something. But underneath all of that, she's just like us. Just like me.

"Well, listen," I say. "You aren't alone." I glance back at Tally, but she's just standing there frozen, like she can't decide what to do with everything she's heard. I look back at Esmeralda. "There's an animal shelter here in town called the ARK. Tally volunteers there and so does Marcus. If you ever need a dog to hang out with, you just call me and we'll go over there together." I feel Tally poke me in the back, but I ignore her.

"Thanks," Esmeralda says. She looks at the tissue in her hand and then at me. "I'm sorry," she says. "I'm embarrassed."

"It's fine," I say. "We've both been there." I glance back at Tally again and, thankfully, she's nodding. Well, that's something.

"I just don't want Charity to know that I was—" She nods at the tissue. "You know."

"Don't worry," I say. "Your secret is safe with us." I stand and pick up the box of tissues. "So when you get back from skiing?" I ask.

Esmeralda smiles. Tally takes the box of tissues from me and walks to the bookcase to put them back. I linger for a moment, to see if Esmeralda wants to say anything else. But then the door opens and in walks Charity, followed by her clones. I back up to let them pass.

"You lost?" Charity asks, smirking at me. "I believe the loser table is over there." She points to where Tally is sitting at our table with her sketch pad open in front of her. I walk to our table and slide onto my stool.

"See?" I whisper. Tally nods. I pull out my sketchbook. I glance over at Esmeralda, who already seems fine. Other than slightly pink cheeks, which make her positively glow, she still looks amazing. When I cry, I look like the Thing from the Black Lagoon for about an hour afterward. "You said you'd give her a chance," I remind her.

"One," Tally says. "But that's it."

I frown at my sketchbook. It's not like Tally to be so cold. But if I were ditched by both of my parents, I'll bet I'd be a lot more closed off than she is. Tally just needs time. She'll come around.

Miss Beans comes out of her office, carrying two black cases. She places them on the center table and opens first one and then the other. They are filled with professional-quality semipermanent art markers. "To make good art, it helps to have good materials. I've brought my markers to share with you. All that I ask is that you take care of them and return them to the cases at the end of the class." I glance around the room. No one else seems that impressed. One of my art teachers in the City let me use her markers once. She had seventeen different shades of blue and more than a dozen of green. When I got home I asked my mom if we could get some. She told me each one of them cost over five dollars. So that was a no.

When Miss Beans tells us we should get to work, I'm the first one up and walking to the markers. Charity is right behind me. I quickly select an orange the color of sherbet and a pink the color of Oscar's tongue. Charity takes the cap off of a purple marker and examines the brush tip. She spins to ask one of the minions something and the marker whips toward me. I pull back, but not before the brush tip slides across my cheek.

Charity turns back. Her eyes are huge. "Oh no. I am so sorry," she says.

"I'm sure," I say.

Miss Beans glances over from where she's grading sketchbooks. "Everything okay?" she asks. She's looking at me. Unfortunately, so is everyone else.

I nod and retreat back to my table. Tally glares at me. "Say something," she says. I shake my head. "Then I will."

"Leave it," I say. I know how this one goes. I say something. Charity denies it. Miss Beans says something to Charity.

Charity gives me a false apology. I still have a purple stripe on my cheek. Tally goes back to working on her sketchbook, but she's pressing her pencil so hard into the page that it tears.

"Tally," I say. "It's okay."

"Stop saying that," she says. "You always say it's okay, but it's not." She shoves her sketchbook to the floor, stands, and rushes from the room. Everyone looks from where Tally disappeared out the door to me. I start to go after her, but Miss Beans is already up and headed toward the door.

"Keep working, everyone," she says. She walks out into the hall and to the right, following Tally's path. Everyone stares at me for a couple of moments before going back to their projects.

"Good going, Penny *Lame*," Charity hisses.

"Leave me alone," I say. My voice cracks, hinting at the tears I'm only just holding back. Charity finds this hysterical.

"Leave her alone," Esmeralda says.

Charity rolls her eyes at her, but it works. She leaves me alone. I try to focus on my sketchbook and ignore the giggles from the back table, but it's hard.

Miss Beans comes back after several minutes. She comes over to me and sits on Tally's stool, turning so that her back is to everyone.

"Tally's going to go home," she says. "She asked if you could gather up her things."

I nod, wishing I could do more than just stack books for Tally. Miss Beans frowns at my cheek.

"Please don't say anything," I plead.

Miss Beans looks at me for a long moment. "I won't," she finally says. "This time." She gets up and walks toward the back table, where they are still whispering and giggling. "Get to work," she says. Charity glances up at her with big eyes. "Yes," Miss Beans says. "I mean you, Miss Wharton."

Charity's cheeks flush, but she goes back to drawing. Miss Beans walks toward the other side of the room, inspecting everyone's work. I try to draw, but it's a mess. I glance over at Charity to see her staring at me. She doesn't say anything. She just stares. And somehow that's far more terrifying than if she actually said a word.

I'm in the library later looking for books to read over break, seeing as how I'm not going anywhere. I'm checking out the new arrivals shelf when I hear Esmeralda's musical laugh. I know people always use that phrase to describe someone who has a pretty laugh, but I never quite knew what it meant until I heard Esmeralda. Her laugh literally sounds like the beginning of a song. Mine tends to run more toward the sound of a chicken clucking. I try to ignore her giggling and focus on the books in front of me. But I realize I've flipped through half of them without even reading the titles because I'm wondering if she's here with Marcus. I pick up the next book and stare at it. *Okay. I'll just look. That's it.*

I peek around the bookcase and see Esmeralda sitting beside Marcus. And I think about saying hello, but then I don't want Marcus to think I'm checking up on him. I'm trying not to be *that way*. I try to disappear back around the corner.

"Oh, hi," Esmeralda says. I freeze. Marcus looks up at me and I have no choice but to walk over. "You were looking for us?" Esmeralda asks.

"No," I say. "I was actually just looking for a book." I hold up the book in my hand as evidence.

Esmeralda reads the title aloud. "*Preparing for Zomb-ocalypse: A Survivalist's Guide.*" I glance down at the book and sigh. Of course. Out of the two dozen new books on the shelf, this is the one in my hand when they catch me spying.

"Well," I say. "It's good to be prepared." I throw in a laugh for effect, but I clearly don't have Esmeralda's gift. Rather than melodic, I sound like a chicken in pain. Marcus smiles at me. Well, that's something. At least he finds me amusing. "I don't want to bother you," I say, backing toward the exit. Unfortunately, in my haste to get out, I back right into Mrs. Zinnia's giant antique globe. I spin to catch it, but the zombie apocalypse guide and my general klutziness get in the way. The stand falls with a loud thud, spilling the globe out onto the floor. It proceeds to roll toward the magazine rack at an alarming speed. It hits the base with a resounding boom, toppling the whole thing backward and sending periodicals flying in every direction. The globe ricochets toward the fish tank.

I drop the zombie guide and hurry after it. The globe strikes the fish tank stand, sending a tsunami of water up and over the side. Only a miracle keeps the tank upright and all of the fish inside. Only I didn't take into account the splash back from the tidal wave. I succeed in stopping the globe's destruction, but end up drenched in fishy-smelling water in the process. Marcus is the first to reach me, followed by Esmeralda. He looks worried. She looks, well, not covered in fish tank water. Mrs. Zinnia bursts out of her office to see me standing, dripping, clutching the giant globe to my chest.

"Oh my goodness," she says, hurrying over. "Penny, are you okay?" I nod, wishing I weren't. Like maybe I could be unconscious or something. But no, I am fully and horribly conscious. Mrs. Zinnia looks around at the path of destruction. "What happened?" she asks. I try to come up with a lucid explanation, but I can't find one in the midst of my embarrassment. "Well, never mind," she says. "Let's just get you cleaned up."

She takes the globe from me and gestures toward her office. I follow her, my feet squishing in my now wet sneakers. I know I shouldn't look back, but I do. Marcus looks concerned. Esmeralda looks, well, lovely as usual. Mrs. Zinnia shuts the door behind us so that I can get cleaned up in private. I am able to dry off well enough, but the fishy smell stays with me. I walk back out into the library just as the bell rings. I help Mrs. Zinnia clean up the mess, drying the globe and resettling it into its stand. Then we reorganize the magazines and check on the fish. The last item I pick up is the cursed zomb-ocalypse guide. I tell myself it's fine. Marcus has seen me in a lot worse condition. It's just that this time Esmeralda was there smelling like oranges and not fish. And I know it's not her fault. I put the book away and head toward the library door, wondering if maybe Cinderella's stepsisters always felt like this. Like maybe they weren't ugly after all. They just weren't as pretty as Cinderella. Well, if that's the case, I have to hope that Marcus prefers the interesting stepsister type.

Chapter Thirteen

Mom drops me off at the ARK on her way to Lancaster. She's delivering a last-minute Thanksgiving order. Mom asked me to be creative and they came out awesome. I made four different kinds. Some have a turkey leg made from a mound of frosting, graham cracker crumbs, and a white chocolate "bone." Others I made to look like a dish of peas and carrots. I made the carrots out of orange Starbursts and the peas are chewy SweeTarts. The mashed potatoes came out the best with a yellow Starburst for the butter and a pool of caramel sauce for the gravy. The last kind just has mini pecan pies on top with a tiny scoop of vanilla frosting for the ice cream.

Mom tells me she'll be back in a little over an hour to pick me up. She's not about to chance Gram being there alone in case Dutch arrives early. I walk down the long driveway and around the side of the house to where the shelter is. I'm actually pretty nervous about seeing Tally. I haven't spoken to her since the meltdown in art class. I thought she'd call me, but she never did. I almost didn't come this morning, but I thought bailing might make everything worse.

I don't see Tally, so I head toward the building housing the exotic pets. The ARK is really just a bunch of buildings nestled among the trees between Monica's house and Six Mile Lake (which for the record isn't six miles long. It's six miles from town). It's obvious from looking at it that Monica just added buildings as she needed to. Nothing matches. The dog building is blue. The cat building is pink. And the exotics building is half-and-half. I head straight for this last building, which overlooks the lake. Most of the animals in the exotic building aren't really exotic at all. They are just common lizards and parakeets, but there are a few really odd residents. In addition to Snowball, the wingless albino vulture, there's Poe, a raven with a permanently broken wing and a limp. And the newest resident: Winston Churchill, a blind snowy owl. He's my favorite.

I pull open the door and head inside. The heat lamps over the lizards' cages give everything a rosy glow and warm the whole space. I walk back to Churchill's cage and give him the peanut butter and sunflower seed cookie I made for him. I know he'd prefer some kind of rodent, but I'll leave that for Monica. I brought extra cookies for both Poe and Snowball because they'd raise a stink if they saw me feeding Churchill and they didn't get anything. The door opens just as I'm giving the last of the cookie to Poe.

"I thought I saw your mom pulling out of the driveway," Tally says. She's carrying bowls of cut-up apples and lettuce leaves for the lizards and a takeout container of crickets for the snakes. I pass out the fruits and veggies while Tally handles the live dinner. I know the snakes need to eat and I know they're just crickets, but I still can't quite bring myself to do it. Tally's more pragmatic. *Everyone has to eat.*

The heat lamps flicker when Tally accidentally bumps one with her elbow. She cringes, but they stay on. She frowns at a spot on the ceiling in the corner where water is starting to seep in. Then she looks at me. "I'm sorry I was such a jerk," she says. "Are you still mad?"

I shake my head. "I just don't understand what's going on," I say.

"I can't talk about it."

"Can't or won't?" I ask. I'm trying hard not to be offended, but it's not easy. Clearly something is really wrong. I don't understand why she won't talk to me.

"Can we talk about this later?" she asks. She turns and walks toward the door. She pulls it open and is out in the yard before I have a chance to respond.

"I guess we'll have to," I say to myself.

I help Tally pass out treats to the dogs. It takes a while because each of them wants to play. I'm throwing a tennis ball for a bulldog named Henry when Tally finally breaks the silence. "I saw Esmeralda and Marcus sitting together in the library."

"She's tutoring him," I say.

"I'll bet," she says.

"What's that supposed to mean?" I ask. I throw the tennis ball a little harder than I intend. Henry looks at me, a little accusatory. He's not terribly athletic, but he goes after the ball anyway.

"Penny, you're not stupid."

"Thanks for that," I say.

"Obviously she has her sights on Marcus," she says.

"She's not Charity," I say.

"No," Tally says. "She's not. She's worse."

I shake my head. "When did you become so cynical?" I ask.

"Hmm. Let's see," Tally says. "Maybe when my dad dumped me with Poppy? Or maybe when my letter to him got returned with a big stamp on it saying he refused to accept it? Or maybe when he—" Tally shakes her head. There are tears in her eyes.

"When he what?" I ask.

"Nothing," she says. "You wouldn't understand."

"Try me," I say. There's the sound of car tires on the ARK's gravel driveway. I turn and see my mom pulling in.

"You should go," she says.

"I can ask her to wait for a minute," I say.

Tally swipes at her eyes impatiently, like her tears are irritating. "Just go," she says. Her voice is raw with anger.

"Why are you mad at me?" I ask.

"I'm not," she says. She closes her eyes. "Please just go." She turns and walks back toward the exotic building without saying goodbye. The back door of Monica's house squeaks open. I turn and see Monica stepping outside.

"Penny?" she calls.

"Be right there," I say. I look back at Tally, who is still walking away from me. Then I head toward the car, where Monica and my mom are standing and talking.

"Thank you anyway," Monica says to my mom. "But my

son and his family are driving down from Maine. They'll be here soon."

Mom smiles at me. "I was just asking if Monica wanted to join us for dinner," she explains.

"Thank you for your help, Penny," Monica says.

"Anytime," I say. Then I remember my conversation with Esmeralda. "Do you think it would be okay if I brought someone from school here next week to see the animals?"

"Of course," Monica says. "There's always cat boxes to scoop and dogs to walk."

I smile at the thought of Esmeralda scooping a cat box. Undoubtedly she'd find a way to do it that would make it seem exotic and stylish.

"Well," she says, "I need to get my pies out of the oven and help Tally finish up so I can get her home. I'm not sure what I would do without her around here."

Mom and I climb into the car and pull out. "Did you have a good time?" Mom asks.

"Mixed," I say.

Mom looks at me for a long moment to see if I'm going to elaborate, but when it's clear I'm not going to give up any more details, she just pats my hand. It's a pretty lame gesture, but then I guess I'm being pretty lame, too. I pat her hand back. Mom pulls the car out onto the road and we start home.

I'm finishing setting the table when Tally and Poppy arrive for Thanksgiving dinner. Poppy hugs everyone, but Tally just gives us each a tiny smile. (Everyone but me, that is.) I'm hopeful that when Blake and his mom arrive, it will ease some of the tension, but it doesn't. It's obvious to everyone that something's really off.

Gram puts everyone to work. She directs Tally and Blake and me to set out the fruit and cheese for everyone to nibble on while we wait. Tally and I are both quiet, looking everywhere but at each other. Blake tries to fill the silence, telling us about his mom's new chocolate avocado raw foods pie that she made. He leans toward us. "Even I wouldn't eat it," he says loud enough for his mother to hear.

She smiles from where she's standing at the counter spooning cranberry sauce into a dish. "It was pretty gross," she says.

"Pretty gross?" Blake asks. "It was green."

"Greenish," his mother says.

Mom keeps checking the clock and looking out the front window while pretending not to look out the front window. Thankfully Gram is too immersed in mashing potatoes and making sure the gravy doesn't have lumps to notice.

Gram asks me to go out and fill the wood basket so that we can stoke the woodstove before we eat. I grab the wicker basket, glad to do something away from the kitchen and the awkwardness. I walk out onto the front porch and pull the door shut behind me. I step onto the driveway just as Dutch is pulling in. I wait while he parks, then head over to his truck.

"Hey there," Dutch says, climbing out of his truck. "Need some help?" He gestures toward the basket I'm carrying.

"I've got it," I say.

"Let me rephrase that," Dutch says. "Can I help?"

"Sure," I say. I pull the barn door open and flick on the lights. He follows me inside and together we fill the basket. It's not really a two-person job, so we're finished in only a couple of minutes. Dutch brushes his hands together to get the sawdust off of them. Then he picks up the basket.

"I'll get this if you'll grab what's on the front seat." We walk back outside and I shut off the light and pull the door closed. Dutch looks up at the low-hanging clouds. "Looks like it might snow," he says. I open the passenger's-side door of his truck and pull out a foil-covered plate. Then I push the truck door shut with my hip. I start toward the house but realize Dutch isn't behind me. I turn and see him still standing in the same place, looking at the sky. I walk back over to him and wait.

"You nervous?" I ask.

Dutch looks at me. "That obvious, huh?"

"Sort of," I say, hedging a bit. "But listen. Gram might be mad. But she'll work it out. She always does." Dutch nods, but I can tell he's not convinced.

The front door opens, making both of us jump, but it's not Gram. It's Tally, propelled outside by Blake. He gives her one last push and then shuts the door behind her. Tally turns as if to go back in, but we hear the lock click into place. She rolls her eyes and makes a menacing face at the door. I know Blake's likely watching her through the peephole and probably laughing. Then Tally turns toward us.

"Hi," she says as if nothing unusual just happened.

"Hi," I say.

"Tally," Dutch says, dipping his head a little.

Tally walks right over to me and hugs me hard, almost making me drop the plate. "I'm sorry," she says.

"Me, too," I say, feeling tears spring to my eyes.

"I was a jerk," she says. I start to say something, but she shakes her head. "Don't deny it. I was."

"A little," I say.

"Forgive me?" she asks. "Again?"

"Of course," I say. I glance over at Dutch, who seems vaguely amused.

Tally nods her head at the plate. "What is it?" she asks.

"You'll see," Dutch says. He takes a deep breath and then lets it out slowly. "I guess we better get this over with."

"Um, it's dinner. Not an execution," Tally says.

"She might poison his food," I say.

"True," Tally says, heading toward the house. "Or pour gravy on his head."

"Or drop a pie in his lap," I say, following her.

"This isn't helping," Dutch says. We make it to the front door, which is still shut.

"Let us in," Tally says.

"Have you two made up yet?" Blake calls from inside.

"Yes," we say in unison. The lock clicks open and the door pulls inward.

"Well, good," Blake says. "I'm sorry I had to get tough with you two, but there's only just so much emo chick stuff a guy can take." He looks past us to where Dutch is standing holding the firewood. "Oh, hey, Dutch," he says. He backs up to let the three of us pass.

"Blake," Dutch says, nodding his head.

Gram comes around the corner, stopping any further conversation. She narrows her eyes at Dutch and then at the three of us, standing with him. Blake scoots around her on one side while Tally and I move around her on the other. All three of us are eager to get out of the line of fire.

"Hello, Dutch," she says.

"Afternoon, Joy," Dutch says.

"You can put the wood over there," she says, pointing toward the fireplace. She narrows her eyes at the plate I'm carrying. "What did you bring?" she asks.

Dutch puts down the wood basket so that he can take the plate from me. Then he steps toward her as he lifts the foil. "Pineapple upside-down cake," he says. Gram peers at the cake. "I remember you like it."

"I do," she says. She doesn't even crack a smile. She's not going to give him an inch. She takes the plate from him and turns toward the kitchen. "I imagine you'll want to wash up before we eat." It's a statement. Not a question. "Penny will show you where." We all stand around staring at each other. I think we all had braced ourselves for a giant meltdown. The complete lack of drama has left us all stunned. Gram comes back out of the kitchen and looks at each one of us. "I'm sorry to disappoint you all," she says. "I know you came for a show, but all you get is a meal." She says it with a smile, which makes everyone relax. Even Dutch smiles. Then Gram points the whisk she's holding at him. "You'd better watch yourself, Mr. Ingmar. I'm still as riled up as I was. I just don't want to ruin dinner."

"Yes, ma'am," Dutch says. But then just before Gram retreats back into the kitchen. A tiny smile. Meant only for him. I just happened to be standing where I could see it. Dutch picks up the wood basket and carries it over to the fireplace. And I wonder if he saw it, too.

At first I'm not that thrilled about Tally and Blake and me having to sit at the kids' table. But the truth is Gram's table is so small that we'd be knocking into one another every two minutes if we all tried to cram around it. Plus, Tally says she has something to talk to us about. Gram lets the three of us serve ourselves first from the dishes lined up on the kitchen counter. Then we retreat into the living room and sit on the floor around the coffee table.

"I've been thinking," Tally says. She takes a bite of turkey and waits.

I glance at Blake, who is shoveling mashed potatoes into his mouth. "Well, tell us," I say.

Tally grins at me. "The odd jobs aren't bringing in enough money for the ARK. Monica has a long list of all of the things that need fixing or replacing. Even if we paint ten miles of fence, it's not going to be enough." I nod and take another bite

143

of potato. "So, Poppy and I were listening to NPR while we were driving to Lancaster."

Blake and I cut our eyes at each other. NPR is the inspiration for most of her wild ideas. Tally sees us look at each other and frowns.

"Easy, Tal," Blake says. This doesn't help. "Look, you know we're in," he says. "Whatever it is." He looks at me for confirmation. I nod. Absolutely. "I was all for the Rock Paper Scissors Society; the Fruitcake Initiative; and the Waste Not, Want Not Drive. I also dressed up as a giant acorn for Arbor Day last year." I can't help staring at him. Other than the RPS Society, I have no idea what he's talking about. "I think I've earned the right to ask a few questions."

Tally frowns at him, but then she nods. "Agreed," she says.

Blake takes a big bite of mashed potatoes, then asks Tally if she likes seafood. He opens his mouth to show her the potatoes inside.

"Anyway," she says, ignoring him. "These odd jobs are earning us a good amount of money. But what we need is something big that will draw money as well as media attention."

"Like what?" Blake asks.

Tally looks from him to me and back again, creating dramatic tension. "*Avantouinti*," she says.

"Bless you," Blake says.

Tally sighs. "It's Finnish for 'winter swimming.'" She smiles.

"So you want to do a polar plunge?" Blake asks.

"Not exactly," she says. "I mean, polar plunges are awesome, but there are literally hundreds of them. Maybe thousands. I want to do something different."

"Like what?" I ask.

"Pudding," she says. I look at Blake, who shrugs. "I want to put on a pudding plunge."

"You want us to jump in pudding?" Blake asks.

"Yep," Tally says. She grins from me to Blake and back.

"So people pay money to jump in pudding," Blake says, making sure he understands.

"Not just that," Tally says. "We get people to pay money to see *other* people jump in pudding. You know, like Sheriff Abrams or maybe Charlotte's dad?"

I smile. Charlotte's father is president of the bank. I've never seen him without a tie on, much less covered in pudding.

"And just think of the merchandising opportunities!" Tally grins at us. "So what do you think?"

"We're going to need a lot of pudding," I say. "And something to hold it in."

"And a place to have it," Blake says. "And permits and lifeguards. Not to mention towels and a shower station."

Tally frowns. It's clear she hadn't thought about all of that.

"We can do this," I say.

Blake looks at me. "We can?"

"Of course," I say. I sound more certain than I am, but it has the desired effect. Tally is smiling again. "Let's see if we can hold the Pudding Plunge at Winter Fest," I say. "I'll bet the dairy has a big enough vat to hold the pudding. And we can find pudding. There has to be a bulk pudding supplier somewhere."

"We still have a big problem," Blake says.

"What's that?" I ask.

"What flavor pudding?"

"Chocolate," Tally and I say at the same time.

Blake nods. "It's a classic."

Gram pokes her head out of the kitchen and asks if anyone has room for pie. Blake's up and heading toward the kitchen before she even finishes her question.

Blake comes back with three plates and a whole pie. He cuts pieces of pie for Tally and me. Then he cuts the biggest wedge of pie for himself. He starts to transfer it to his plate. There's no way the plate is going to be big enough.

"Why don't you just eat out of the pie pan?" Tally asks. She's joking, but Blake's eyes get big and he leans forward.

"Is that cool?" he whispers.

I shrug. I'm not sure whether it's cool or not, but we are at the kids' table. And it's not like anyone is under any illusion that Blake is actually going to return to the kitchen with leftover pie.

"Go ahead," I say.

"Seriously?" he asks. I nod. He takes a huge bite of pie, closing his eyes as he chews. "I'd *avantouinti* all day long for pie."

"You'd sell your soul for pie," Tally says.

"Not my soul," Blake says. "But maybe my appendix or part

of my liver." He looks at us. "Did you know that your liver is the only organ that can regenerate?"

"Can we not talk about your liver?" I ask.

"Why? Are you losing your appetite?" Blake asks, looking longingly at my piece of pie. He starts singing a song about his liver. Something about donating just a sliver because he's a giver. I pass the rest of my pie to him. Blake looks at Tally to see if she's going to give up her piece.

"Dream on," she says, taking a big bite. "I am immune to your superpowers."

"His superpower is being gross?" I ask.

Tally laughs. "That's every guy's superpower," she says.

"I only use my power for good," he says.

"And pie," I say.

"And pie," he says. Blake polishes off the rest of the pie and stands up. He offers to take our dishes to the kitchen, which seems suspicious. But from where we're sitting, we watch Gram pressing the leftover pie from the grown-ups' table on him. He feigns being full for about two seconds, but then caves. Dutch slides over on the bench to make room for him to sit down. So, while Tally and I are still relegated to the kids' table, Blake has somehow managed to wrangle a spot at the adults' table and get more pie to boot.

Dutch says something to him that makes him laugh. And I see my mom smiling, too. It's weird. Even with everything over the past few months, she seems happier than I've ever seen her.

And definitely more relaxed. Hog's Hollow seems to suit her. It seems to suit all of us. I glance over at Tally to see if she's thinking the same thing. There are tears in her eyes. She tries to blink them away.

"Thanks for agreeing to help," Tally says. She looks past me and out of the window. "I just want to do as much as I can while I'm here." She smiles at me, but her smile doesn't make it all the way to her eyes. Tally stands up and heads toward the adults' table, leaving me sitting alone at the kids' table, wondering what she meant by *while I'm here*. She slides onto the bench beside Poppy, who puts her arm around her. I shake my head. Something is going on, but no one wants to tell me anything.

Chapter Fourteen

It rains for three whole days following Thanksgiving. The first day, Tally and I play board games and make popcorn and help Poppy box up dozens of her new mobiles. Then we help my mom at the bakery, baking dozens of blue velvet cupcakes for a baby shower. The second day, we spend at the ARK, mopping up water leaks and trying to keep the dogs from going stir crazy by taking them out for wet walks in small groups. I try several times to get Tally to talk about what was making her so sad on Thanksgiving, but each time, she starts talking about something else or pretends not to hear me or leaves the room. She finally just tells me to drop it and so I do.

By day three we're so bored that by early afternoon, we are literally lying in the middle of Tally's living room floor and staring at the ceiling.

"I am so bored," Tally whispers.

"Me, too," I whisper back. We quickly learned not to say it too loud. The last time we said it, Poppy overheard us and made us go sweep out the garage. Mr. Blick, one of Tally's cats, comes over and sits on my chest. Pumpkin, her giant orange cat, climbs onto Tally. We lie like that for several minutes just staring at the ceiling fan twirling above us.

Poppy peeks in and asks if we want to go to the movies in Lancaster. We're up, spilling cats onto the floor before she even finishes her invitation. "Don't you want to know what's play-ing?" she asks.

"It doesn't matter," Tally says, making Poppy laugh. She spins and looks at me. "Call Marcus." I shake my head. She turns to Poppy. "I mean, if that's okay."

She shrugs. "Why not?" I can think of a million reasons why not, starting with *he might say no*. Poppy goes to change out of her studio clothes.

Tally turns to me. "I'll call Blake." She nudges me. "Come on," she says. "What's the worst that could happen? He says no?" I nod. "He's not going to say no."

She picks the phone up off the kitchen counter, dials, and hands it to me. I back away, waving my hands. Tally rolls her eyes and puts the phone to her ear. "Oh, hey, Marcus," she says. "This is Tally. Penny wanted to talk to you." She hands the phone to me. I glare at her, but take it. What else can I do?

"Hi," I say. "How was fishing?"

Tally rolls her eyes.

Marcus says it was good. "Good," I say back. I take a deep breath. "Poppy offered to take Tally and me to the movies. Blake's going to come, too. Probably. I called to see if you wanted to come."

"Oh," Marcus says. Then there's a long pause. I bite my lip. "I can't." I wait, but he doesn't say why.

"Well, maybe another time," I say.

"Yeah," he says.

"Okay, then," I say. "I guess I'll talk to you later."

"Bye, Penny," he says. Then there's a click.

I look up at Tally. "He can't," I say.

"Well, he probably has a good reason," she says.

I nod, but if he did, wouldn't he have said so? I feel sick to my stomach. Why did I have to call? Now it's awkward and horrible.

"Well, forget boys, then," she says. "We'll just make it a girls' night."

Poppy comes out of the back, pulling a sweater over her head. "So, is Marcus going to walk over or should we pick him up?" Tally shakes her head. Poppy glances at me. "Well, I'm sure he was just busy."

I nod. But it wasn't just that he didn't want to come to the movies. It was his voice. He sounded weird and distant.

"Come on," Tally says. "I'll buy you your own box of Junior Mints. And I won't eat any of them." I follow Tally and Poppy out to the garage.

The movie turns out to be a double feature. *Casablanca* and *An Affair to Remember*. Tally and I've never seen either of them. Poppy, it turns out, has seen them about a dozen times. She cries during both of them. When the lights finally come on at the end of the second movie, she's still blotting her eyes.

"So romantic," Poppy says.

I glance over at Tally, who is completely dry-eyed. "So unrealistic," she says. "In movies everything leads up to this one perfect moment," she says. "Life isn't like that." She looks at me, waiting for me to agree.

"I guess," I say. I frown. But maybe I want that. One perfect moment.

Poppy smiles. "Well, whatever you say, I think it's romantic." Tally sighs and rolls her eyes, making Poppy laugh.

We filter out with the rest of the crowd. Thankfully it's finally stopped raining, but the fog is so thick, it reminds me of the airstrip in *Casablanca*. We climb into Poppy's car and start back toward Hog's Hollow. We have to drive through downtown Lancaster, which compared to Hog's Hollow is huge. We stop at a traffic light. Tally is talking about how movie stars just aren't as glamorous as they used to be. Poppy is fiddling with the defroster, which doesn't seem to be working. I use the sleeve of my coat to clear a tiny circle in the foggy window. I look out of the window at Pat's Pizza. The sidewalk out front is packed with people waiting for a table. There's a girl outside with hair just like Charity's. When she turns, I realize it is Charity. Awesome. But then I see who she's talking to. Marcus. She says something and he nods. Then she leans in and gives him a hug, and I feel my stomach drop. Then the light turns green and we're pulling forward. Well, I guess I know now why he couldn't come to the movies with us.

I look away from the window and close my eyes, willing myself not to cry. I try something I read once about listing things in your head to keep yourself from crying. I start listing the first thing I think of: cupcake flavors. Lemon, vanilla, carrot, pumpkin spice, mudslide. Mudslide. Marcus's favorite. Tears prickle at the corners of my eyes. I'm grateful it's dark, but still I lean forward a bit to let my hair cover my face. The worst thing would be for Tally to see. She'll want to know what's wrong and then she'll want to talk about it. And the last thing I want is to talk about it. I feel sad and humiliated and a small pinprick of anger. I swipe at my cheeks and tell myself to keep it together at least until I'm alone. Strawberry, white chocolate walnut, blue velvet . . .

Poppy drops me off at my house on their way home. I end up helping Gram organize the rest of the twinkle lights for the house. But it's not distracting enough. I keep seeing Charity hugging Marcus again and again. Like it's on a loop. Gram, my mom, and I have a late dinner of leftover turkey and pineapple cake. I pick at my dinner. When my mom comments, I tell her I just ate too much popcorn at the movies.

I help with the dishes, but then I tell them I'm going to go upstairs and read. My mom looks up from where she's filling the kettle. "You okay?" she asks.

"I'm good," I say. She frowns. I'm the world's worst liar.

"Do you want to talk about it?" I shake my head. "If you change your mind, I'm here." I walk over and hug her. She puts down the kettle and hugs me back. "I love you," she says.

"I love you, too," I say.

Upstairs I lie in bed and try to read, but I give up after reading the same page three times. I put the book down and shut off my light. Then I lie in the dark feeling sorry for myself. Even

Oscar pushing under the covers, followed five minutes later by Cupcake, aren't enough to cheer me up. I lie on my side staring out the window at the water, playing the Marcus and Charity movie over and over in my mind until I finally fall asleep.

On Monday, Miss Beans tells us we'll have every art class for the rest of the semester to work on our sculptures. Charity walks in just as the bell rings. She glides past our table and smirks at me. Just seeing her makes my stomach hurt. After a whole night of replaying her hugging Marcus over and over, the sight of her makes me feel like throwing up.

I pull the bundle of twigs I collected on the way to school out of my backpack. I move to an empty table and start laying them out to make the framework for the dirigible I'm building. The only thing I can do at this point is distract myself. Unfortunately, Charity doesn't make it easy. Her voice cuts across the hum of the pencil sharpener and the low drone of everyone talking as they work. Tally leaves the dog she's constructing out of table legs and tin cans to help me tie the framework together.

Charity is loudly describing her ski trip in detail. Apparently she was a natural. "Gregory said my form was flawless," she says. Her minions are listening, barely. Every time Charity pauses, one of the Lindseys breaks in and asks Esmeralda if she had fun or what she was wearing or what Gregory said about her form. Esmeralda just smiles and offers mostly one-word answers. Charity's response is to talk louder and pepper her stories with digs about Esmeralda's lack of ability on the slopes. She's clever about it, though, saying everything with a smile.

"Do you want this to stick out here?" Tally asks, pointing to the twig I just attached.

"Of course not," I snap. "Why would I want that?"

Tally looks at me with big eyes. "O-kay," she says.

"Sorry," I say. "I'm just tired."

Tally nods. She continues attaching twigs to the frame. "Have you talked to Marcus yet?" I shake my head. "Don't worry," she says. "I'm sure he was just busy."

I nod. I can't bring myself to tell Tally what I saw in front of Pat's Pizza. I feel bad enough just thinking about it. I don't want to talk about it.

"You should just talk to him about it," she says.

"I don't think so," I say.

Tally shrugs, but I can tell I've disappointed her. "Whatever," she says. "It's what I would do if I were you."

I look at her like she's lost her mind. "Like how you're talking to me about what's been bothering you?" I ask.

"That's different," she says.

"I'm sure," I say.

Tally pinches her lips together. She's mad, but she knows I'm right, so I'm not backing down.

"Maybe we should talk about something else," she says.

"Fine," I say.

"Fine," Tally says. She takes a deep breath and flips a page open in her sketchbook. *Pudding Plunge* is written across the top. Below it are dozens of numbered items. "First we need to—"

"Tally," I say, putting my hand on the page. "I can't."

"Look, I know it's a lot, but—"

"No," I say.

"So what?" Tally says. "We're not doing it?"

I sigh. I know how much this means to Tally, but with school and Marcus and the bakery and my dad and Charity, suddenly it just feels like too much. I could say I'm busy with the bakery or homework or even stacking firewood, but none of those things is the reason I can't take this on. It's more that I'm tired from the inside. Tired of my dad bailing. Tired of Marcus lying to me. And if I have to be really honest, the drama with Tally is exhausting me as much as anything. So, it's not the busyness, although that's there. It's all of the sadness and anger and confusion that's weighing me down—draining my energy.

"Maybe we just need to get someone to help us," I say.

"Who?" Tally asks.

I frown. My mother and Poppy are both out. They're swamped with work. Then it hits me. "What about Gram?" I ask. "This is a pretty dead time for her. Holiday portraits are all finished. And there's only a few weddings at this time of year."

"Oh my goodness," Tally says. "You know who else we should ask? Dutch!" I make a face. "It's perfect!" I shrug. It could go either way.

"Excuse me," Charity says loudly. "Can you two keep it down? Some of us are trying to work." The minions all smirk at us. It's then that I notice what they're wearing. Two of the Lindseys have butterfly clips that are identical to Esmeralda's in their hair. The third Lindsey has a blue-and-pink polka-dot scarf knotted around her neck that looks suspiciously like the one Esmeralda wore on her first day of school. Esmeralda gives me a tiny smile. I smile back. Charity sees our exchange and narrows her eyes at me. My stomach flips over, but I don't look away. I smile at Esmeralda again before going back to my project. The nice part of me wants to be nice to Esmeralda. The not-so-nice part of me wants to get back at Charity. I have a feeling befriending Esmeralda would really get to her.

By the time the bell rings, Tally and I have figured out a strategy for trying to get Gram and Dutch together and get them to pull together the Pudding Plunge with only minimal help from us. "Hurry up," Tally says. "I'm starving."

"You go ahead," I say.

"You sure?" she asks.

"I need to finish this," I say.

Charity walks past and gives me a little wave. That can't be good. Tally's back is to her, so she doesn't see.

"Do you want me to stay?" Tally asks.

I spot Blake waiting outside in the hall. "No, go ahead. I'll catch up."

In moments, everyone is packed up and gone. Miss Beans tells me to close the door when I leave and heads to the teachers' lounge. I work through lunch, framing out the whole balloon of the dirigible. The bell signaling the end of lunch rings just as I'm tying the last joint. I pack everything away and then I carefully pick up my sculpture and carry it back to the cubbies. It's too big for the space, so I have to leave it on top of the shelving unit. I push it way back, where there is no chance for it to be knocked over. Then I grab my bag and head out, pulling the door shut behind me.

The hall is packed. I merge into the press of people all trying to get to their lockers, trade gossip, and generally goof off. I step around two guys loudly debating whether a lightsaber or a plasma gun would win in a duel. I slide free of the mash of people and stop at my locker. There's a funny smell, like nachos, but I decide it must be from the cafeteria. It must be taco day or something. I spin the dial and lift the latch. I'm so unprepared for what's inside that it takes me a moment to get it. There's something neon orange coating the entire inside of my locker. The smell hits me hard and I flinch back. It's cheese. My jacket was draped over my books, so the cheese didn't get on them. But my coat is covered. I look around for Charity. I thought she was through with stuffing gross things in my locker. I guess I was wrong. I fold my jacket in on itself to contain the cheese and push it to one side. The door is nasty, but that's going to take longer than I have to clean up. I glance around to see if anyone has noticed me and my cheese-covered locker, but no one is looking at me. Even though it's not my fault. Even though I've done nothing wrong, I feel ashamed.

Because even if I don't think I've done anything to deserve this, maybe other people do. No one normal gets cheese poured all over her stuff. Do they?

"Oh, Penny!" I turn and see Esmeralda walking toward me. Great. Of all the people, it has to be her. Perfect, beautiful, smart, and completely cheese-free. Esmeralda walks over next to me and peers into my locker. Her eyes widen.

"What happened?" she asks.

"Nothing," I say. Even if my locker smells like a fiesta, I don't want her help.

"*Qu'est-ce que c'est?*" she asks, pointing at the goo clinging to my locker door.

"Cheese," I say.

She makes a face. Clearly *le fromage français* is not neon orange. "I'm so sorry, Penny," she says.

"Thanks," I say. Then the bell. And Esmeralda says she's sorry again and that she'll see me in class. Then she walks away. Right past Charity, who is standing not twenty feet from me, watching me and smirking. She offers me a little wave and then she also walks away. I want to follow her. I want to tell her off, but I'm too angry. And when I'm too angry, I usually start crying. And the very last thing in the world I want to do is make Charity think she can make me cry. I slam my locker shut and then instantly wish I hadn't. Because I hear the distinctive sound of cheese product being flung from one surface to another.

Don't look, I tell myself. *Just walk away.* So I do.

Chapter Fifteen

The bakery is dead. I've been here two hours and I've rearranged the cupcakes three times and cleaned the windows twice and still no one has come in for cupcakes. The only person to walk through the door is the UPS guy with an envelope for my mom that I have to sign for. I stare at it, wondering what it is. Last time something like this arrived, it was the papers my mom had to sign for their divorce. I put the envelope on the back counter and go back to working on my algebra.

I try calling Tally, but no one answers. And maybe that's just as well. I want to talk to her, but everything is just so weird between us. One minute we're fine and laughing over something and the next we're barely speaking to each other. I had to stay late to clean out the cheese, so I didn't get to see her after school. The janitor kept glaring at me every time he'd make another pass with his mop. Like this was my fault. What exactly does he think I did? Cheese bomb? Thankfully he gave me a pair of gloves so I was saved from actually touching it, but I still had to smell it and see it. As far as I can tell, Charity must have just poured it into my locker through the vents. I guess I should be thankful. She could have opened my locker and dumped it right on my books. Yes, thankful she only poured it through the vents. Funny how a little nacho cheese can really change your perspective.

The janitor finally took pity on me and told me he'd finish up. I gathered my books together and picked up the plastic bag with my coat stuffed inside and made my way to the front of the school. I tried to ignore the fact that I smelled like old nachos as I made my way down the sidewalk to the bakery.

I'm almost all the way through my homework by the time Mom gets back from her delivery. I hear her in the kitchen, talking to someone on her phone.

"I'll have them notarized, and I'll put them back in the mail right away," she says. Then she's quiet. I peek through the crack in the door. She's leaning against the island and listening. "Just take it one step at a time," she says. Then she says goodbye and hangs up. She takes a deep breath and sighs. I push into the kitchen.

"What was that about?" I ask.

"What?" Mom asks.

"The phone call," I prompt. I was on the outside of everything as my parents were splitting up. I'm not about to let that happen again.

The front door jingles and my mom smiles. "Sounds like we have a customer," she says. She is past me and through the door before I can say anything. Then I hear her talking with someone about Tahitian versus Madagascar vanilla. I head out to the front, figuring once this customer leaves, I can try to talk to her again. I wait for a woman to finish her order for three dozen Snickers cupcakes. She wants them with gingerbread men on top.

"I want them to be festive," she says.

"Of course," Mom says. She's amazing. I've never ever seen her get impatient with a customer. Even when they ask the dumb questions like do the banana walnut muffins have nuts in them? Or are our maple bacon cupcakes vegan? I pretend to straighten the cupcakes while Mom finishes writing out the order and the woman leaves with a handful of samples.

"Anyway," I say. Mom looks at me and for a moment I think she's going to tell me something, but then she spots the envelope.

"When did that come?" she asks.

"About an hour ago," I say.

She checks her watch. "I need to run over to the bank," she says. She grabs the envelope and heads for the front door. "I'll be back in a bit." The bells on the door jingle as she walks out. I watch her make her way across the street and down to the bank.

"Seriously?" I say out loud.

I'm back to homework when I spot her walking back. But she doesn't come into the bakery. She just keeps going to the other end of the street. I step onto the sidewalk, braving the cold, and watch her head into the post office. "Seriously?" I say out loud again. Mrs. Hancock, the owner of the antique store next door, gives me a funny look. I smile at her, but she just mumbles something about teenagers and heads back into her shop.

By the time Mom returns, Gram is back from taking holiday photos of some family who insisted that their nine-foot banana ball python be in every photo. I try a couple more times to ask Mom about the phone call and the envelope, which clearly are connected, but she isn't talking, except to tell me that she'll tell me everything at some point. Unless, of course, she can't. Yeah, that's super helpful.

Tally isn't waiting for me before school again, so the first time I see her is in art class. She's looking at the sheet of paper again.

"Hey," I say, sliding onto the stool beside her. "Where were you?" I ask.

"When?" she asks. She refolds the piece of paper she was looking at and stuffs it into the front pocket of her backpack.

"This morning," I say.

"I overslept," she says. She pulls out her sketchbook and starts doodling, drawing dots and crosses and curlicues and stars.

"You okay?" I ask.

"Yep," she says. She keeps doodling, refusing to look at me.

"Tally—" I say.

She shakes her head, silencing me.

Charity and her clones come in. Charity barely glances in our direction on her way to her seat. I lean over to tell Tally about the cheese in my locker, but Charlotte walks in. I don't really want to talk about everything in front of her. She starts heading toward us, but someone at the back table clears her throat. Well, fake-clears it. It actually sounds like ahem-hem. I glance over and see Charity is looking at her. Big surprise.

Charlotte pauses in the middle of the room. She looks from Charity to me and back again. Then she frowns and walks over to Charity's table. She sits on the stool next to Charity and stares at the desk in front of her.

"Wow," I say. I actually thought Charlotte was done with Charity. She's eaten lunch with us a few times and even talked about volunteering at the ARK. Tally looks up and then over to where Charlotte is sitting. Charlotte glances over at us, but then quickly away. Tally just goes back to doodling as if nothing happened.

Miss Beans comes out of her office. She makes a couple announcements about when our sketchbooks are due as well as a request to stop leaving the caps off the glue. Then she tells us to get to work. "You can talk," she says. "Just work *while* you talk." Unlike some of my teachers, she seems to get that we sometimes have a lot to talk about and that the ten minutes in between classes isn't enough time to say all we have to say.

For once, though, Tally and I don't seem to have much to say to each other. We work quietly for most of the class period. By the time class is almost over, Tally is all but finished with her sculpture, while mine still looks like a big white blobby thing that vaguely resembles a whale with a pointy nose.

I sigh. "Maybe I should do something else."

"It'll work," Tally says.

"I just hope it doesn't implode," I say. Although not as deadly and catastrophic, my dirigible is about as flight-worthy as the *Hindenburg*.

"It would be historically accurate to have it self-destruct," she says. "But it would be in really bad taste." Tally offers me a tiny smile, which I take as a good sign. Then she helps me smooth the last of the paper over the framework.

When the bell rings, I tell Tally to go ahead to the cafeteria and that I'll meet her there.

Once everyone is gone, I stand back and look at the dirigible, trying to see it for the first time. It's not terrible. There are places where the papier-mâché is uneven, but once it's painted and hung, I'm not sure anyone will notice.

I'm carrying the dirigible toward the cubbies when the door to the classroom opens and Chad Stinson walks in. "Oh," he says. Not hi. *Oh*. Weird.

Miss Beans pokes her head out of her door. She sees me and says the same thing. *Oh*. Then, to Chad, "Be right there."

"Take your time," Chad Stinson says. He puts the paper grocery bag he's carrying on the nearest table and comes over.

"Hi," he says. "Penny, right?"

"Right," I say.

"Wow," he says, peering at my sculpture. "May I?" He nods toward the dirigible.

"Sure," I say.

He reaches out and taps it gently. "Nice job. Getting papier-mâché this thin without sacrificing the integrity of the structure is really difficult."

I want to say *tell me about it*, but I just say, "Thank you."

Miss Beans comes out of her office. I look at her and raise

an eyebrow. Her hair, normally pulled back in a no-nonsense ponytail or held in a bun on top of her head with pencils or the ends of paintbrushes, is down around her shoulders. And I'm pretty sure she has on fresh lip gloss.

"Wow," I say, looking at the clock. "I just realized I'm starving." I quickly put away my project and then grab my books and my bag. There's a folded piece of paper sitting on the floor right where Tally's backpack was. I pick it up and examine it, realizing it's not just *a* piece of paper, but *the* piece of paper.

"We have plenty—" Chad Stinson says.

"What?" I ask, turning to look at him.

"Food," he says, nodding toward the paper sack.

"Oh no," I say. "It's Frito pie day in the caf." Like that explains why I'm running out of the room like my head is on fire. "Bye." I glance back at Miss Beans, who is smiling and shaking her head.

I step out into the hall and pull the door shut behind me. I look at the piece of paper I'm holding, trying to decide whether to read it or not. If I read it, I'll know what's going on, but I'll also be betraying Tally big-time. I slide the paper inside my sketchbook without opening it. Tally's friendship is too important to risk over one piece of paper.

I head toward my locker to drop off my books. I have to pass the library on the way to my locker. I try not to look. I actually tell myself out loud. *Don't look.* But, of course, I do. And, of course, I see them. Marcus and Esmeralda sitting across from each other. He's reading something from the book and she's twirling a piece of her hair and looking lovely. He says something and she laughs and leans toward him. She points to something in the book in front of him and he leans closer to read what she's pointing at. Their heads are only inches apart. And for a crazy moment, I think they're going to kiss. Right there in the library. But then Esmeralda looks up and sees me. She smiles and nods toward where I'm standing and spying. I try to hurry away before Marcus can see me, but somehow I manage to trip over my feet and almost, but not quite, run into a post. I duck my head and quickly walk away. Why am I always such a spaz? Will there ever be a day when I can just be normal?

I head to my locker to retrieve my lunch. I spin the dial and open the door. A paper drops to the ground at my feet. I pick it up and unfold it. It's pink with a border of tiny hearts along one edge. The initial C is embossed into the top in curlicue script.

Be careful. Things are not as they seem.

C. No big mystery there. Charity. I frown at the note, then crumple it up and chuck it into the nearest trash can. I don't know what game she's playing at, but I don't want any part of it. I grab my lunch and head toward the cafeteria, where the smell of Frito pie is blending nicely with the smell of grungy soccer uniforms and sweaty feet.

Chapter Sixteen

Okay, for people who have never worked in the food industry, the words *grease trap* would be somewhat disgusting. But for anyone who has worked in any kind of restaurant or other purveyor of food, the words *grease trap* have the ability to induce nausea, a deep-seated fear, and possible complete cerebral shutdown. Until about ten minutes ago, I was in the first category, blissfully unaware of the horrible secret lurking just under my feet.

When I arrive Mom announces that it's time to clean the grease trap. Apparently that's the big job she needs help with. I say, "Sure." Because first of all she's paying me. And second, it's my mom. And third? Well, I'm still ignorant. She tells me to get a bucket and rubber gloves. Then she hands me a giant spatula I've never seen before and tells me to follow her.

We head out the back door and around to the side of the building where there's a door to the cellar. *Cellar* is actually a pretty nice way of describing the space beneath the bakery. More like scary room with rusty drains lit only by bulbs hanging from extension wires. Mom flips the switch and leads me past the hot water heater and the oil furnace and to the far side of the room. Sitting in the corner, connected to a bunch of pipes, is a metal box. It's about four times the size of a shoe box.

Mom reaches into her pocket and pulls out two of those paper masks that dentists always wear when they're cleaning your teeth. She hands one to me and puts the other on. This is when I start thinking maybe this grease-trap thing isn't going to be the cakewalk I thought it was going to be. She tells me to put on the rubber gloves. Then she kneels in front of the box and pries up the top. She lifts the cover and places it to one side.

"What is that?" The question is out of my mouth before I even realize it. Mom laughs. She's kneeling in front of what can only be described as the most disgusting substance on the planet, and she actually laughs. She puts on her gloves and takes the spatula from me.

"Just hold the bucket for me," she says. I kneel beside her. For the record, I have never smelled anything as horrible in my life. And I've had up-close-and-personal experience with many species of poop. Chicken, cat, dog, cow. And I attend school daily with a bunch of guys who somehow believe that enough cologne will cover the fact that what they really need is a shower and some deodorant. Mom starts scooping the brownish yellow sludge into the bucket one disgusting spatula full at a time. Once it's empty, she takes the bucket from me. She retreats upstairs and returns with another bucket full of hot, soapy water. I help her wash the inside of the trap and the lid and put the whole thing back together. Finally we're finished.

"Well, that was gross," I say. Clearly I have a knack for

stating the obvious. We head back upstairs, where Mom tells me to just throw away my mask and gloves. She washes her hands, then heads out front to see if Gram needs any help. I wash my hands at least half a dozen times, but the smell of the grease seems to cling to me. Finally I give up, deciding I'm not going to get clean until I can get home and get a proper shower. Preferably a long, hot one. I console myself with the fact that as long as I stay in the kitchen, I won't see anyone I know. Then the back door opens.

"Hey, Penny," Mr. Fish says.

"Hi," I say. *There goes the hiding-out-in-the-kitchen plan.* Well, at least it's only Mr. Fish. He props the door open and heads back outside to his delivery truck parked behind the shop. I walk over to the door to see if he needs a hand. Mr. Fish is loading crates of milk and boxes of butter onto a dolly. He balances one last crate of cream cheese on top, tips the cart, and starts pushing it toward me. He pauses and turns back.

"I forgot the sour cream. Can you grab it?"

"Got it," a voice from inside the truck calls. Marcus. Well, so much for remaining unseen. I glance down at my apron. Gross. I look at my shoes. Double gross. I don't even bother with my hair. After crawling around in the basement, there's no telling what it looks like. Then I remember him hugging Charity on the street in Lancaster and him laughing with Esmeralda in the library and I tell myself I don't care.

Marcus jumps down from the back of the truck, holding

two big tubs of sour cream. "Oh, hey," he says, spotting me standing there. "I was hoping you'd be here."

I frown. This isn't exactly how I thought this would go. I thought Marcus would be awkward or distant or something. "Hi," I say hesitantly.

"Where do you want me to put this butter?" Mr. Fish calls from inside the bakery. I'm grateful for the interruption. More than ever I don't know how to be around Marcus. I head back inside and direct Mr. Fish to just leave the butter on the counter. We're baking all afternoon anyway, so it won't matter if it sits out. My mother comes into the back to help put everything else away and sign Mr. Fish's clipboard.

"Thank you for fitting us into your schedule," she says. "The orders just keep stacking up. And with Winter Fest right around the corner—" She takes a deep breath. "Anyway," she says. "We would have been up a creek without this."

"It's no problem," Mr. Fish says. Then he turns to me. "I'm looking forward to seeing the new holiday cupcakes."

I laugh. "Yeah, me, too." The decorations are pretty lame right now. Snowflakes, gingerbread men, Santa hats. Not exactly original. "I'm open to suggestions," I say.

"What about bagpipes?" Mr. Fish asks.

"Christmas bagpipes?"

"Or Hanukkah," Mr. Fish says. "Either way."

"Nothing says Merry Christmas like bagpipes," Marcus teases.

I see Marcus out of the corner of my eye smiling at me. I don't look at him. I don't want him being nice to me right now.

Mr. Fish shakes his head. "You just wait. Bagpipes are making a comeback." He accepts his clipboard back from my mother and grabs his cart. He rolls it toward the door.

"See you later," Marcus says, following him to the door.

"Bye," I say softly.

He pulls the door shut behind him and I stand there for a moment, wondering what *later* means in guy-speak. In my limited experience, it can mean anything from an hour from now to next week. I wish they would be more specific.

"Penny," my mother says from the stove. I turn and look at her, thinking she'll tell me how it's obvious how much Marcus likes me or how it was so nice of him to come by to see me. Something supportive. "Does this buttercream seem grainy to you?" she asks, holding up a spatula full. Or maybe not.

I help my mother crank out some big orders. Mostly holiday parties. Just before closing, Gram pokes her head into the kitchen and asks if I can help her. I walk out front, where there's a line. Gram is taking care of the first order, so I look to who is next. It's Mrs. Whippet, the mayor's assistant. Gram says if you want something done in this town, she's the one you need to go to. She's on her phone. She pulls it away from her mouth just long enough to announce she wants to place an order. Then she's back to talking with whoever is on the phone about something somebody said to someone that was *unbelievable*.

I grab the order pad and wait while Mrs. Whippet walks down the counter, looking at all of the cupcakes. Mrs. Whippet finally orders. I write it all out. She makes me read it back to her to make sure I've got it right. She holds out her hand for the order pad and pen. She's so intimidating that I just give them to her almost without question. She writes *NO NUTS!!!* and underlines it four times, pressing hard enough to emboss the sheets underneath. Then she hands it back to me.

"I'll pick them up on Friday at five twenty." I nod and write that on the order. "P.M.," she says. I nod again and she waits.

"Oh," I say. I write that on the order, too, although I'm not sure why. I look up again, but she's already back on her phone and heading out of the shop. *Yikes.* By the time I'm finished, Gram has cleared out the rest of the customers.

"How was Mrs. Whippet?" Gram asks.

"Intense," I say. I pass her the order pad.

She looks at it and laughs. "Yep," she says. "That's Mrs. Whippet for you."

"Call me if you need any more help," I say. I head back into the kitchen, where my mom is working, hoping for a little less intensity. My mom is at the sink scrubbing cupcake pans. Mrs. Whippet's intensity should be sort of familiar. In the not too distant past, my mom was like that. But in the last few weeks, she's been way more relaxed, so I guess I've forgotten what it's like. I ask my mom if she needs any help.

She narrows her eyes at me. "What are you up to?"

"Nothing," I say. "Can't I just offer to help my mom?"

"Of course," she says, handing me a scrub brush. I understand her incredulity. I've probably announced a hundred times how much I hate cleaning the cake pans. It's my least favorite job. Oh, wait, it's my second-least favorite. Cleaning the grease trap is my new number one.

We work in silence for several minutes. The bell on the front door rings occasionally, announcing new customers. Gram will call if she needs us. But I'm hoping she doesn't call because I have some questions for my mother.

"So," I say. Mom cuts her eyes at me. Suspicious. I press on in spite of the look she's giving me. "The phone call and the envelope," I say.

"What about them?" she asks.

"Well, the last time someone delivered an envelope I had to sign for—" I don't finish. I still can't really talk about my parents' divorce without feeling like I'm going to cry.

Mom looks at me for a moment. Then her face softens and she puts her brush down. "Oh, Penny," she says. "I'm sorry. Of course you'd think—" She sighs. "Well, I'm sure you didn't know what to think." She turns and looks at me. "The envelope and the phone call aren't about you. Or about your dad and me."

"Then what is it about?" I ask.

She frowns. "I can't tell you."

"Is it bad?" I ask.

She shakes her head. "No," she says. "Well, if it works, it won't be. If it doesn't . . ." She glances down at the soapy water. Then she looks back at me. "But things look good."

"Are you ever going to tell me what's going on?" I ask.

"At some point," she says.

"I guess that will have to be enough," I say. I put down my brush. "So, I'll just—" I start to back away from the sink. I mean no sense in me washing pans anymore, right?

"Oh no," Mom says, picking up my brush and handing it back to me. "You're in this now."

"Fine," I say. I plunge my hands back into the water and start scrubbing again.

Mom starts singing a goofy song about cupcakes and cabbages and crabgrass and kumquats and other things that start with the letter *c*. I point out that *kumquat* starts with a *k*, which she says is precisely why it's so tragic. My mother is so weird.

On Friday it's finally dry enough for us to finish decorating Gram's house. Everyone except Tally and me and Gram are working or have soccer practice or have unknown things keeping them busy, which Tally says is perfect. We still need to convince Gram to help with the Pudding Plunge. We know Dutch will be on board, but getting my grandmother to agree is going to be difficult.

I'm tacking the last of the lights to the side of the house, and Tally is tying new bows for the reindeer. I think about the folded piece of paper I have stuffed into the pocket of my jeans. I keep trying to find a moment to give it back to Tally, but it never seems right. She's going to think I looked at it even though I haven't. I can't very well give it back in front of Gram, so I guess I'll just wait.

"Tell me again why Dutch can't help us?" I ask my grandmother. I glance over at Tally, who smiles at me. It's the third time I've asked. The first time Gram didn't actually answer at all. She just left the room. The second time she made a vague statement about him—and this is an exact quote—*He's busy with that thing.*

"Penelope Lane," Gram says. She's exasperated, which means Tally's and my plan to get her to call Dutch is moving along nicely. "Will you please drop it?"

"Absolutely," I say. "But—"

Gram sighs. "But what?" she asks.

"I'm just not sure the three of us are going to be able to get the reindeer up on the roof by ourselves. And it's going to be dark soon." I nod at the sun slowly sinking toward the hills. Gram looks over at the herd of wooden reindeer leaning against the side of the house.

"*And* the weather is supposed to get really sketchy later in the week," Tally says.

I cut my eyes at Tally. I really have no idea what the weather forecast is. And I'm willing to bet that Tally doesn't either, but I just go with it, hoping Gram is as ignorant of the weather as we are.

"Really sketchy," I say. Gram sighs again. I know I almost have her. "I'm just thinking of all of those disappointed children who are expecting to find your house all lit up for Christmas."

Gram looks at me. "I'm sure," she says. She looks over at Tally, who is trying to look like she's thinking about the poor children, too. Gram throws up her hands and heads toward the house. "Fine! I'll call him." Tally leans over and gives me a fist bump. "I saw that!" Gram says.

Tally and I finish the lights that Poppy and I were working on while Gram is making her phone call. We start wrapping the porch railings with lights, striping them red and white like candy canes. I'm still trying to find the courage to give Tally the paper when she stops and stares at something over my shoulder.

"Wow," Tally says. I turn to see what she's looking at. Gram is stepping out of the back door. She has traded her stained barn coat for the bright green one I bought her for her birthday. And if I didn't know better, I'd think she put on some makeup.

She walks over to us and looks at us. "Not one word," she warns. There's the sound of someone pulling into our driveway. Then we see Dutch's pickup through the trees.

"Whoa," I say. "He sure didn't waste any time getting here."

"Hush," Gram says. But when she thinks we're not looking, I see her smile.

"Hello?" Dutch calls.

"Back here," Gram says. He comes around to the back of the house and climbs the steps up to the porch. He's holding something square and black in his hand.

"Joy," Dutch says, smiling at Gram. "Ladies," he says, nodding at me and Tally. "Thought you two might have fun with this," he says, handing me what he's holding. I take it from him and turn it around. It's an old Polaroid camera. The kind that spits out the photo as soon as you take it.

"Cool," Tally says. "A vintage camera."

Dutch looks at Gram and they both laugh. "I guess vintage is better than old," Dutch says.

We spend the next hour mounting all nine reindeer on the roof along with Santa and his sleigh. We also use up three packages of film taking photos of one another. We finish just as the sun finally disappears behind the hills. Finally Gram calls it *Christmas* and we go inside for tea and homemade blueberry muffins.

"If Blake were here, I know what he'd say," Tally says.

"Best day ever?" I ask. I look at the photos spread on the table between us and pick up one of Tally and me. Our heads are scrunched side by side so that we can both fit into the photo. I grab a Sharpie out of the jar on the bookshelf behind me and write in the white space below the photo. *Best Day Ever.* Then Tally and I proceed to write the same thing on all of the photos. Even the one she accidentally took of her foot. Dutch picks up one of Gram looking out at the ocean. Her eyes match the green of her coat and the green of the water. He reads our caption and nods. *Best Day Ever.*

"Speaking of best days," Tally says. She nudges me with her foot under the table. We agreed I should approach them about the Pudding Plunge. By *agreed* I mean I lost at Rock, Paper, Scissors. (Three out of five.)

"Tally and I were thinking of putting together an event for Winter Fest," I say. Gram nods and sips at her tea. "You know, as a fund-raiser for the ARK." I take a deep breath. "And we were hoping that you two would help us with the organization. We're just so busy with school and the bakery and painting—"

"Really busy," Tally says. "Tests and art projects and papers. Not to mention the science fair."

I frown at her. The science fair is in April.

"What are you planning for the fund-raiser?" Gram asks. That's a good sign. At least she's asking for more details. Tally quickly outlines her idea for the Pudding Plunge.

"What flavor?" Dutch asks. It's his only question.

"Chocolate," Tally says. She grins. "Obviously."

"What do you say, Joy?" Dutch asks. "It is for the animals."

Gram takes another sip of her tea and then puts her cup on the table. "I'll do it," she says. "For the animals."

Tally grins at me and I smile back. I glance over at Gram, who is shaking her head slightly. She knows what we're up to, obviously, but she's not mad, which is a very good sign.

We sit and pass photos back and forth in between bites of muffins. Gram and Dutch start making a list of things that they need to do for the Pudding Plunge. Dutch leaves first, saying he has to stop by the feed store. (Which is weird since he doesn't have any animals.) Tally leaves right after, saying she's on dinner duty since Poppy's slammed with last-minute

Christmas orders. I still have the piece of paper in my pocket when she leaves. I wimped out.

Gram says she needs some Penny Time. Maybe for some people, hanging out with their grandmothers would be boring, but Gram isn't like most grandmothers. First she shows me how to make a projector using her cell phone, a shoe box, a magnifying glass, and some odds and ends from the junk drawer. Then we move the furniture, stretch a white bedsheet across the wall, and set it up. I make popcorn while Gram gets the movie going. She picks an old Alfred Hitchcock movie, which she swears is scary. I'm skeptical. I mean, how scary can an old black-and-white movie be? But when the wind slams the back door open, I jump about a foot and spill half of my popcorn on Oscar, who was sound asleep on my lap. Gram just gives me a self-satisfied smile. I figure after Tally and I snookered her into working with Dutch, I probably deserved it.

The phone rings just as I'm getting into bed. I hear Gram answer and then hear her coming upstairs. "Penny?" she says. "It's for you. It's your dad."

"Oh," I say. I sit up on the edge of the bed and Gram hands me the phone. I sigh and put it up to my ear. "Hi," I say.

"Hey there, Bean," my dad says. He's doing that thing he always does where he's overly enthusiastic. It might have worked when I was five, but not so much now. I just let the silence grow. "So, how was your Thanksgiving?" he asks.

"Fine," I say.

"Good," he says. "Mine was good, too," he says. "I had sushi." He pauses, waiting for me to respond, but I don't. "Listen," he says. "Sorry about having to cancel on you."

I start to say it's fine like I always do, but it's a lie like it always is. "It's not okay," I say.

"What?" he asks.

"It's not okay," I repeat. My stomach churns. I hate confrontations. But I also realize that I hate getting walked over constantly. I take a deep breath. "Dad, you do this all the time. You bail on me and then apologize like that's going to make it all right." I close my eyes. "But it doesn't," I say softly. The silence stretches out between us. "Well, say something," I say finally.

"I'm not sure what to say," he says.

I shake my head in frustration. All he has to say is that he messed up. That he was wrong. And that he won't do it again— and actually not do it again.

"I should go," I say. "It's late."

"Oh," he says. "Of course." Then there's a pause. "I love you," he says.

"I love you, too," I say. I say goodbye and hang up. I sit and stare at the phone in my hand for a long time before I get up and carry it back downstairs. Gram looks up from her book. I can feel her gaze on me, but I don't look over. She stands up, walks over to me, and puts her arms around me. Then she just hugs me.

Chapter Seventeen

On the way to school on Monday, I tell Tally about hanging out with my grandmother. She makes me describe the projector in detail. "Your grandmother is so cool," she says.

"I was thinking we could have a movie night on the beach next summer. We could hang a sheet up near the dunes and have s'mores and a fire. I mean, the picture quality wouldn't be awesome, but it would still be pretty good," I say.

"Yeah," Tally says. She's a lot less enthusiastic than I thought she'd be.

"Or not," I say.

She puts her hand on my arm. "It's a great idea," she says. "I was just thinking about last summer before I met you. And how I'm really happy we're friends."

"Me, too," I say. I glance over at her. She definitely doesn't seem happy. More like wistful and a little sad.

Then she shakes herself. Literally. "Sorry," she says. Then she grabs the sleeve of my jacket and pulls me to go faster. By the time we make it to school, we're nearly running. She pulls the door open and heads inside. And I follow, wondering what that was all about.

Charlotte walks past, well, scurries past. It's so bizarre that Tally, Blake, and I are all watching her.

"What's her deal?" Blake asks. "I thought you guys were friends now."

Tally just shrugs like it doesn't matter to her, which is weird. Charity is waiting for Charlotte near the front doors. Charity's body language makes it clear she doesn't like to be kept waiting.

"Well, I'm out," Blake says. He walks away without saying goodbye.

Tally is still staring at Charity and her minions. With the addition of Charlotte, the count is up to five. Tally would say six because she sees Esmeralda as one of the minions. Esmeralda smiles over at us. Tally just makes a face and turns away.

"Tally," I say, "what's with you?"

"What do you mean?" she asks.

"I don't know," I say. "One minute you're fine. And the next—"

"Sorry," she says. "I'm just . . ." I wait, thinking here it is. She's going to tell me what's been bugging her, but then the bell rings. "See you in art?" she asks.

"Okay," I say. She heads toward her locker and I head toward mine, which still smells vaguely of cheese.

I finally have my dirigible looking, well, dirigible-ish. And I have Esmeralda to thank for a lot of it. She actually came over and asked if I wanted some help. Charity looked furious, but Esmeralda didn't seem to care. Esmeralda is the one who suggested I paint it to match the sky. "Like *le camouflage.*" (Which is apparently a French word.) She's also the one who helped me figure out how to attach the gondola to the balloon. (Also a French word.) Tally is completely silent the entire time.

"Are we still on for this afternoon?" I ask Tally when Esmeralda heads over to the supply cabinet for more glue.

"For what?" she asks. She's back to doodling in her sketchbook. Hundreds of stars crowd together, taking up two full pages.

"Puppy-cups?" I say. Tally asked my mom if we could make some dog-friendly cupcakes to sell at the bakery to help raise money for the ARK.

She shrugs. "I guess."

Miss Beans walks to the center of the room and asks for our attention. "I have an exciting announcement to make. The Winter Fest committee has agreed to allow any of you who wish to donate your pieces to the silent auction held during the festival. As you know, proceeds from the auction go to support various groups in the community. This year, they have selected the ARK as the recipient."

Tally grins.

I lean over to her. "Did you know about this?"

She nods. "Monica and I talked about it, but I didn't want to tell you until it was for sure."

Miss Beans looks around. Maybe everyone's blood sugar is a little low because it's almost lunchtime, but no one seems that into it.

"I'm in," Tally says.

"Big surprise," Charity says.

"I'll just pass around a sign-up sheet," Miss Beans says. "Now back to work."

I go back to tying on the gondola and Tally returns to her stars.

Esmeralda just sits quietly on the other side of me, sketching. I glance at what she's drawing. It's startlingly good. I guess I shouldn't be surprised; she seems to be awesome at everything. It's a simple line drawing of a dog, but it's so realistic that it almost looks like a black-and-white photograph.

"That's really good," I say to Esmeralda. She smiles at me. Tally frowns at what Esmeralda is drawing and then stands up and walks toward Miss Beans's office. I watch her walk away and sigh. Then I turn my attention back to Esmeralda.

"Is it Marcel?" I ask.

She looks at me and smiles. "You remembered his name." Then she looks back at her drawing. "I just miss him."

"You can still come to the ARK sometime with us. There's some pretty cute dogs there. I mean, they're not Marcel, but . . ."

Esmeralda shakes her head. "I don't think so," she says. She nods toward where Tally is talking to Miss Beans.

"She'll be fine," I say, but, in truth, I'm not totally sure. She's been acting so erratic lately. Esmeralda isn't convinced either. "Well, I don't have a dog, but I have a giant cat who thinks he's a dog. If you want, you could—" I pause. Did I just invite Esmeralda to my house?

"I'd like that," she says. Tally is heading back to our table.

"Great," I say. Tally sits back on her stool and starts drawing stars again. Esmeralda gets up and drifts back to her table. Then Tally looks at my sketchbook. The edge of a piece of paper is poking out of the top. Her eyes narrow.

"Is that mine?" she asks. She yanks it out of my sketchbook. Tally glares at me. "You stole this?"

"No," I say. "I found it on the floor. I was just looking for the right time to give it back to you."

She shakes her head. "Well, then I guess you know."

I shake my head. "I didn't—"

"You want to hear my favorite part?" Tally asks. She unfolds the paper on the table in front of her.

"Tally, I didn't—"

"'The petitioner requests that any legal obligation between himself and the aforementioned minor be severed,'" Tally reads. She looks at me. "It almost makes my dad giving me up sound okay." Tears form in her eyes. She swipes at them impatiently. "Turns out it's totally legal to cut ties with your daughter."

"Tally," I say softly. "I didn't read it." She looks at me for a long moment and then closes her eyes. "I'm so sorry."

She shakes her head. Tears slide out from under her eyelashes and down her cheeks. "Just leave me alone," she whispers.

The bell rings and she's the first out the door. And I'm left sitting alone staring at a stained and crumpled sheet of paper that is far worse than I ever imagined.

*   *   *

I don't see Tally before the end of the day, but I head to the bakery right after school. I have all kinds of ideas for decorating the puppy-cups. Making cupcakes might be the last thing Tally would want to do, but I'm hoping she shows up. I start laying out the ingredients in between helping customers. Peanut butter and oats and pumpkin and blueberries. It sounds gross, but they were a hit with the dogs at the ARK.

Mrs. Whippet arrives to pick up the order for her daughter's birthday. The order was for three dozen gingerbread cupcakes with brown butter frosting topped with a tiny gingerbread cookie. I do what I always do. I find the ticket, search through the cooler for the order, open the box to show it to Mrs. Whippet (who nods), tape the box shut, and take her money.

I head back to the kitchen and start mixing together the puppy-cup batter, figuring the fun part is really the decorating anyway. I tell myself that Tally's just running late. I'm pulling the last batch out of the oven when Mrs. Armitage arrives for her order. Snickers with a gingerbread man on top. (Because she wanted them to be festive.) She's excited to see how they look and peeks in the box when I am ringing her up. Not only does she look in, but she sniffs. Several times.

"Is everything okay?" I ask.

"Actually—" she begins. I turned toward her, tape in one hand and her change in the other. "These smell an awful lot like gingerbread."

"Oh," I say. "You're probably just smelling the ginger-bread cookies." I nod toward the tiny gingerbread decorations.

"Yes," Mrs. Armitage said. "You're probably right." And so I tape the box up and send her on her way.

I mix up the frosting for the puppy-cups and fill the pastry bags. I make up a couple of sample puppy-cup designs. A dish with a bone in it. A fire hydrant. A doghouse. Mom comes back to pick up the cupcakes for her last delivery.

"Hey," she says. "Those are cute."

"Yeah," I say.

"I thought Tally was coming by," she says.

"Me, too," I say. I want to tell her about the letter. I'm almost certain it's part of the phone calls and notarized papers, but what if it isn't? I don't want to betray Tally. She's angry enough already.

"She's probably on her way," Mom says.

"Probably," I say, even though I know it's a lie. When Tally told me to leave her alone, I did. But maybe I should have run after her.

"Do you think you two can lock up tonight?" she asks. "I thought I'd head home after this last delivery and make a proper dinner. You know, something other than soup."

"I don't mind soup," I say.

She kisses the top of my head. "I know, but something else might be nice for a change." I help her carry the boxes to her car. "Just don't forget to turn off the ovens," she says.

"I won't," I say. She climbs into her car. She waves as she pulls away. I walk into the kitchen and get back to work on the puppy-cups.

By six, I've given up on Tally showing. I wrap up everything for the puppy-cups and put it away. I'm just about to lock the door when the phone rings. It's Mrs. Armitage. She starts by apologizing for bothering me. And then she tells me a long story about how she has a terrible sweet tooth and how much she *loves* our Snickers cupcakes. And how she decided that the guests at her holiday party the next day wouldn't notice if she snuck just one. Right? I make a hurry-up gesture with my hand, wondering why Mrs. Armitage's secret snacking is any of my concern.

"So, imagine my surprise when I bit into the cupcake and found out that it was gingerbread," she says. Okay, maybe I'm distracted by seeing Marcus driving past on his four-wheeler. But it takes me several long seconds for everything to sink in. And while I do agree that it is terrible that I gave Mrs. Armitage gingerbread instead of Snickers, I am more concerned with the fact that at this very moment a dozen or more little girls are arriving at the Whippet house to celebrate Daisy turning seven years old. Daisy, who has such a terrible peanut allergy that she's been hospitalized several times.

"Mrs. Armitage," I say, interrupting her second apology for bothering me. "Can I call you right back?" I hang up before she can answer. I find the order receipt and call Mrs. Whippet's cell phone number. But it clicks over to voice mail. I try their home number, but that, too, just asks me to leave a message. I try my mom's phone, and then Gram's and then the house phone, but no one answers. I stare at the receipt, unsure of what to do.

"Marcus," I say aloud. I so do not want to ask for his help, but I can't think of anyone else. I run to the door and look up and down Main Street. There's his four-wheeler at Ed's Minimart. I sprint down the street, not bothering to even take off my apron. He's just coming back out, carrying a carton of eggs. He looks up and sees me.

"Hey," he says. "I was just going to stop in and—"

"I need your help," I blurt out.

"Okay," he says. I quickly explain my dilemma and how I *need* to get to the Whippet house on the other side of Tide Mill Farms. And can he please drive me over there? "Sure," he says. "Grab your coat."

"No time," I say. He takes off his coat and gives it to me. And if I weren't so freaked out, I probably would have melted right there in the middle of the parking lot. But all I do is pull it on, accept the helmet he retrieves from the storage space under his seat, and climb onto his four-wheeler. No time for romantic gestures.

He climbs on in front of me and secures his own helmet. And off we go. It's already dark and really cold and we have to go slowly to avoid the icy patches. It seems to take forever to make the trek up to the Whippets' house. But finally we arrive. Marcus pulls into the driveway and I am off and running toward the door almost before he stops.

I ring the bell and wait. As I do, I realize I still have on the helmet. I quickly take it off. The door opens, spilling warm light and the screeching laughter of a dozen girls out onto the porch. Mrs. Whippet is standing there, staring at me with a butane lighter in her hand.

"Penny?" she asks. She seems unsure, which is odd considering she just saw me only hours before, but then I realize what I must look like. Wild hair sticking up in a million directions. Eyes red and nose running from the cold ride. And wearing a frosting-streaked apron and a fleece coat at least four sizes too big.

"Don't eat the cupcakes," I blurt out. "They have peanuts in them."

She blanches and flies back into the house. I peer around the door and watch as she takes her daughter's cupcakes from the table ringed by girls just waiting to sing "Happy Birthday" and tuck into birthday cupcakes. She balances the plate in one hand and grabs the empty box with frosting still clinging to its sides with the other. She hurries to the door and thrusts the whole mess into my hands.

"I'm so sorry," I say.

She just nods. Terse. Angry. Then Daisy is at her side, eyes brimming with tears, wondering why the girl with the snotty nose and wild hair is stealing her cupcakes.

"I'm so sorry," I say again and again. Another quick nod from Mrs. Whippet. Then the door shuts, leaving me juggling a plate full of cupcakes, a helmet, and an empty box. I turn and look at Marcus standing near the four-wheeler. I don't know what to do.

What I do is burst into tears. Marcus quickly takes over, boxing up the cupcakes. He finds a hose to wash off the plate and places it on the porch. He then walks me to the four-wheeler and holds the box of cupcakes while I climb on. "We should just throw these away," I say.

"Not here," he says. And I nod at his wisdom. Better to take the death-inducing cupcakes elsewhere for disposal. I put on my helmet. Marcus replaces his own before climbing on in front of me. We have to drive even more slowly on the return trip, not only negotiating the darkness and ice, but now trying to do so while I hold a box of cupcakes and a carton of eggs. We finally arrive back at the bakery.

He helps me climb off and together we throw the cupcakes into the Dumpster behind the bakery. I take off his coat and hand it to him, and then I hand him the eggs, which are miraculously unbroken. Then for the first time, I think about him and Charity. And it hits me like an icy wave.

"Well, thanks," I say, taking a step back.

Marcus starts to hug me, but I hold out his helmet in between us. He frowns and takes it from me. The thought of him hugging me just like he hugged Charity makes me feel sick.

He stashes the helmet under his seat and climbs onto the four-wheeler. "Good night, Penny." His voice is flat and detached, and it makes my heart ache.

"Night," I say.

He starts the engine and pulls out and down the alley. I stand and watch until he turns the corner. Then the back door of the bakery whips open.

"Penny." My mom is standing in the doorway, backlit by the bright lights of the kitchen behind her. "Where on earth have you been? I've been worried sick." She doesn't wait for a response. Instead she just turns toward the kitchen. "She's here," she says. Gram joins her at the door. Both of them looking at me, anger and worry and relief etched into their faces. The fading sound of Marcus's four-wheeler makes Gram look up. Mom narrows her eyes at me. "You were with Marcus?" she asks.

"Yes," I said. "But let me explain." My eyes sting for a moment and then the tears start. In moments I'm sobbing and Mom's hugging me and smoothing my hair.

"Shh," she says. "Whatever it is—"

I cut her off, babbling about cupcakes and Tally and Marcus and peanuts. Mom keeps hugging me until I finally calm down. She leads me into the kitchen, grabbing the box of Kleenex off the desk on the way. I spend the next fifteen minutes alternating between blowing my nose and recounting everything that happened.

"Well, thank goodness for Marcus," Mom says. Then she gets on the phone. First she calls Mrs. Whippet and apologizes in ten different ways, telling her we'll issue her a full refund and bring fresh cupcakes out for the party immediately. Then she calls Mrs. Armitage, apologizing for the mix-up on her order. Then Gram drives two dozen nut-free cupcakes out to the Whippets' for Daisy's birthday while I remake cupcakes for Mrs. Armitage.

It's late by the time the three of us make it home. The chicken my mom made for dinner is cold and the rice has congealed into one giant rice ball. Mom says she can reheat the chicken and whip together a salad, but none of us is very hungry. I nibble on some cheese and crackers. Mom and Gram opt for cold chicken sandwiches and tea. I escape upstairs as soon as I can. When Mom comes up and checks on me, I pretend I'm asleep. I just don't have any more words. They've all been pressed out of me and I feel defeated.

Chapter Eighteen

Tally wasn't at school the next day. At first I thought she'd just need some space, but when she didn't show up on Wednesday, I decide to find Blake. He'd been sitting with the soccer players at lunch this week and it's obvious he's avoiding me when I see him in the hallway, which means he knows something that I don't. In between classes I spot Blake talking with some of the soccer players and head toward him. But before I can reach him, he starts walking away. I think about hurrying after him, but I know he's unlikely to tell me much of anything with his bros in tow anyway.

Art class is miserable. I feel like I'm in quarantine. With Tally gone and Charlotte back on Team Charity and Esmeralda in her old seat, I'm alone at the table. Thankfully I still have my propeller to finish, so at least I have something to keep me busy. But it still feels horrible sitting all by myself. Feeling lonely when you are alone is one thing. Feeling lonely when you're in the middle of a bunch of talking, laughing people? That's something else entirely.

"This is your last call," Miss Beans announces from the front of the room. "Tonight I'll be taking everything over to the bank where they're setting up the auction. You are welcome to work through lunch if you want, but after that, what's done is done. And what's not done? Well, it's still done." She looks around at everyone to make sure we're listening. The bell rings and everyone springs out of their seats. Everyone except me and Arthur, a guy who sits at the back with his serious gamer friends. He's building what he calls *Ode to Minecraft*.

"Bye, Penny Lame," Charity says, walking past.

"Leave me alone," I say.

Charity pauses and looks around. "Looks like you already are." The clones all think this is hilarious. Charlotte frowns and looks at the floor.

Esmeralda shakes her head and looks at me. "Don't listen to her, Penny. She's just jealous." Esmeralda pushes past Charity and her clones and out into the hall, leaving all of us stunned. Charity gives me one more withering look before heading out into the hall. The clones are close behind. Charlotte hangs back for a moment, but then she's gone, too. I might have imagined it, but it definitely looked like Charlotte smiled just a little bit when Esmeralda told Charity off.

Tally is still a no-show on Thursday. And Blake's still avoiding me. I'm actually looking forward to going to the bakery after school. In between the forty dozen cupcakes for Winter Fest and a handful of regular orders, it's more than my mom and Gram can handle alone. I'm grateful to be busy.

Unfortunately, my mom is driving me completely mental. She's double- and triple-checking everything I send out the door at the bakery, and all because I made one teeny, tiny mistake.

Okay, it wasn't that tiny, but I did catch it in time, so no harm done. Right? Wrong.

"Penny?" Mom calls from the front. "Don't forget that the Schumacher order is for blackberry with lemon, not raspberry with lemon."

"Yes," I say. "I know." I try to keep the impatience out of my voice, but I must not be successful because when Mom comes back into the kitchen to check that I'm actually following her instructions, one of her eyebrows is raised. We work in silence together. The only sounds are the mixer running constantly, trying to keep up with our frosting needs, and the oven doors opening and shutting.

"A big storm is supposed to hit right in the middle of Winter Fest," Gram says from where she's stirring a batch of lemon curd on the stove. She looks at me and I wonder if she figured out that Tally and I had no idea what we were talking about when we mentioned the upcoming sketchy weather. She narrows her eyes at me. Yep, she did. "Should make for a brisk Pudding Plunge," she says.

"How's that going?" I ask. After Tally and I convinced Gram and Dutch to take over the Pudding Plunge, we pretty much just left it up to them.

"Good," Gram says. "The pool is arriving tomorrow. Hanson's Construction is bringing their cement truck over around three. It'll take most of the night, but we'll have a pool full of chocolate pudding by morning."

"Gram," I say. "You are amazing. Thank you."

Gram shakes her head. "All I did was find the pudding mix. Dutch did all the rest." She keeps stirring the lemon curd. "Well, I did have to make a trip over to the Town Office. That Leonard Vernon wasn't going to approve the permit, but I convinced him."

"I'll bet," my mother says. She makes a face at me. Gram can be crazy intimidating when she wants to be.

"So how is it working with Dutch?" I ask.

"He seems really enthusiastic," she says.

"I'll bet," I say softly. Mom has to bite her lip to keep from laughing. I smile back at my mom and for the first time since the near cupcake catastrophe, she is finally treating me normally. Then she ruins it.

"Aren't those supposed to be pink?" she asks, nodding toward my snowflakes.

"No," I say. Because who ever heard of pink snowflakes? But also because the order clearly says blue icing with white snowflakes. Mom comes over and checks the order. Then she frowns. Because I guess when you're being hypercontrolling, you are actually hoping something will be wrong so that you can feel validated.

The front gets busy for a while, which means I can finally work in peace. I'm just tucking the last of the Schumachers' order (blackberry with lemon, not raspberry) into boxes when Gram pokes her head into the kitchen and tells me someone is there to see me. I slide the box of cupcakes into the refrigerator and wipe my hands on my apron. In my mind it's a toss-up between whether it's Tally or Marcus. At this point I'm not sure who I'd rather see. I push the swinging door and head out to the front. The person standing there makes me pause. Esmeralda.

"Hi," I say. Gram says she'll be in the kitchen and to call if I need anything. The door whooshes shut behind her. I look back at Esmeralda, who looks on the verge of tears. "What's going on?" I ask.

"Penny—" she says. A single tear slips down her cheek. "I didn't know who else to talk to."

"What happened?" I ask.

"I just need to talk to someone and you've been so nice to me." Then she glances around. "I'm sorry," she says. "You're working." She backs toward the door.

"Wait," I say. "Let me just ask my grandmother if she can watch the front." I push the door open. Gram is standing just inside the kitchen. "Well, I guess you heard," I say.

"Go ahead," Gram says. I go to the back and deposit my apron in the bin. I grab my coat and pull it on. I leave my hat in my pocket and head out to the front.

"Okay," I say to Esmeralda. "Where to?"

"Can we walk downtown?" she asks.

"Sure," I say.

We walk toward the park, where they are setting up tents and roping off event areas. Right in the middle of the park is the Ice House. They already have the first two layers in place. It's bigger than I thought it would be, almost as big as some Manhattan apartments I've seen. There are several men off-loading big blocks of ice out of the back of a truck. Several more are drilling into the blocks so they can run rebar through them to keep them in place. Mr. Fish is one of the men. He waves at us and we wave back. We watch them work for a few minutes and then head down the street.

I look over at Esmeralda. "Do you want to talk about it?" I ask.

"It's just Charity," she says. "I know I shouldn't let her get to me—"

"She can be awful," I say.

"She's just so mean," Esmeralda says.

I nod. Oh yeah. Charity is the Queen of Mean. We walk past stalls for the food vendors and a big tent where they will have the pancake breakfast in the morning and the ukulele contest in the afternoon. Along the way Esmeralda tells me all kinds of things about Charity. About how she's constantly making fun of her accent. And how she won't let Esmeralda touch any of her things even though they are sharing a room. "She got so angry when she thought I'd used her hair spray. I told her I don't use hair spray." She shakes her head, making her hair swing as if to prove her statement. "But she wouldn't believe me. And," she says, "she's constantly talking about—" Esmeralda's hand flies to her mouth.

"What?" I ask.

"Nothing," she says. But clearly it isn't nothing. We walk past where they are setting up the area for Santa. A sign states that photos are 9:00 a.m.–12:00 p.m. and 1:00–4:00 p.m. I glance over at Esmeralda, who has gone silent.

"You don't have to tell me," I say. Most of the time I couldn't care less what Charity talks about, but Esmeralda is acting so strange that I'm curious. We walk down the street toward the bank.

"She's always talking about Marcus," Esmeralda blurts out.

"What?" I ask. I stop in the middle of the sidewalk, forcing Esmeralda to stop with me.

"She told me she has a plan to get him back."

"Back?" I ask. "But they were never—"

Esmeralda shrugs. "I'm just telling you what she said."

"What did she say?" I ask.

"I'm sorry," Esmeralda says. "I've upset you. I shouldn't have said anything." She starts to walk again, forcing me to follow.

"I'm not upset," I say, although it's obvious I am. "Just tell me." The bank is in front of us. Chad Stinson's truck is parked right out front. Lights blaze in the lobby of the bank.

"Oh," Esmeralda says. "They must be setting up for the art auction." She crosses the street with me still following. I catch the sleeve of her coat just as she is starting up the steps. "Please," I say. "Just tell me."

"Well, last summer when Charity got back from staying with me in Paris—"

"Yes?" I ask. I feel like throwing up, but I want to know.

"They hung out a lot."

"As friends?" I ask. I know the answer, but it's all I have. Esmeralda looks at me with pity in her eyes. "But it's over now," I say firmly.

Esmeralda shrugs. "I think so. I mean, I've heard them talking on the phone," she says.

"What?" I ask. "When?"

"Just a couple of times," Esmeralda says. She starts up the steps toward where the front doors of the bank are propped open.

"A couple of times," I repeat.

Esmeralda stops at the top of the steps and waits for me. "Penny," she says, putting her hand on my arm. "I've seen him with you. I think he really likes you. Charity's just—"

I wait. Charity's just what? A sneak? A liar? A bully?

"Don't worry," she says. "Charity said they only kissed a few times last summer."

Her words slice through me. And suddenly all I can think of is him kissing her. And I know it was before I knew him and it shouldn't bother me, but it does. I guess I wanted my first kiss to be his first kiss, too. I wanted that one perfect moment.

Esmeralda pats my arm like that's going to make it okay. Then she turns toward the bank, where they are setting up the sculptures for the auction. "Let's go see," she says. She walks into the bank and I follow. Mostly because I'm not sure what else to do.

"*Bonjour*," Esmeralda says. Miss Beans looks up and smiles at her. But then Miss Beans spots me and her face falls.

"Oh!" she says. Rather than seeming pleased to see me or even simply surprised, she seems freaked out.

"Hi," I say. They've obviously been working all afternoon. Tables run down both sides of the lobby. Sculptures are set up every few feet with clipboards set in front of them. I spot Tally's dog right away. Beyond that are Arthur's *Ode to Minecraft* and Charity's vase of flowers made from twisted aluminum cans.

"Do you need any help?" Esmeralda asks.

"No, no," Miss Beans says. "I think we're all set." She's acting really squirrelly. Then I realize she's standing in front of something. She is clasping her hands together so tightly, her fingers are turning white.

"It looks really good," I say. I'm trying hard to act normal, but I'm not sure I'm doing a very good job. The weird thing is that Miss Beans is trying hard, too. I just can't figure out why. Esmeralda has started back toward me down the other side of the lobby. I stand there, waiting. Esmeralda finally finishes looking and joins me at the door.

"See you tomorrow," Esmeralda says.

"Okay," Miss Beans says. "Night, Esmeralda. Night, Penny." I lift my hand to say goodbye. I turn toward the door and almost run smack into Chad Stinson.

"Oh! Hey, Penny," he says. He nods at Esmeralda. He's carrying a hot glue gun in one hand and a bunch of glue sticks in the other. "What brings you two here?" he asks.

"We just wanted to peek," Esmeralda says.

"Good, good," he says. He walks past us and over to where Miss Beans is standing.

I turn toward the door again, but Esmeralda stops me. "Where is your balloon?" she asks. I scan the tables. It's not there. I look back at Miss Beans, who sighs.

"Penny," she says. "I'm so sorry. I thought we'd be able to . . ."

I walk toward her and she turns to one side so I can see what's behind her. There's a long box. But it's what's inside the box that makes me feel like throwing up. My dirigible is lying on its side. The banners are torn. The netting is tangled. The propeller is lying in pieces. But the balloon is the worst. It's broken completely in half.

Esmeralda comes up next to me and gasps. One hand flies to her mouth. The other grabs my arm as if she needs to steady herself from the shock.

"We were going to try to fix it," Chad Stinson says. He holds up the hot glue gun.

"No," I say. Because even if we can piece the balloon back together and untangle the net and rehang the banners and rebuild the propeller, it won't *fix* this.

I glance over at Miss Beans, who looks as devastated as I feel. "Maybe it just fell," she says.

"There's no way," I say. "It was way back against the wall. I made sure." I shake my head. "It was Charity," I say.

"Penny," Miss Beans says.

"It was," I insist. "It had to have been."

"Penny," Miss Beans repeats. "It couldn't have been Charity.

She left school during lunch for a dental appointment in Lancaster."

"Then she snuck back," I say.

Miss Beans just shakes her head. "She didn't." She reaches out and touches my arm. "I am so sorry."

"We can still try to fix it," Chad Stinson says. He doesn't sound that optimistic. And I don't blame him. The balloon looks like it was stepped on. For all I know, it was.

"No," I say. I walk around them and pick up the box with my broken sculpture in it. "It's okay," I say. Not because it is, but because he and Miss Beans look as miserable as I feel and, well, there's no sense in making them more so.

"Let us drive you home," Miss Beans says.

I shake my head. "I'll walk."

"I'll walk with her," Esmeralda says. We head toward the door, which is still propped open. Then we walk down the steps to the sidewalk. When we get to Main Street, Esmeralda stops. "I'm so sorry, Penny. For everything. But I must go," she says. "Mr. Wharton said I should meet him—" She nods toward the office building on the opposite side from where we're standing. She's already started back across the street. "See you," she calls when she reaches the other side.

I stand and stare after her, confused. I thought she was going to walk me home, not ditch me as soon as we got outside? I sigh and head back to the bakery, feeling as broken as my sculpture.

Chapter Nineteen

On Friday, Tally is waiting for me on the bridge where we usually meet.

"Hi," I say.

"Hi," she says back.

"Are you okay?" I ask.

"Are you?" she asks. That makes both of us smile slightly. Obviously neither of us is okay.

"Do you want to talk about it?" I ask. "About you, I mean."

Tally shakes her head. Then she pushes the sleeve of her coat up so that she can see her watch. "I'll tell you in eleven hours and seventeen minutes."

"Okay," I say. "That's very specific."

"Yep," she says. When she nods, her hair falls forward across her cheek.

"You dyed your hair," I say. She nods again, making her totally brown hair swing. It's been a while since Tally's hair has been one (normal) color. I wonder if it has anything to do with what she can't tell me for another eleven hours and seventeen minutes.

"I did," she says. "But you're changing the subject. I want to hear about you."

"Can I just tell you later?" I ask. I spent most of the night going over everything Esmeralda told me about Marcus. I don't really want to go into it all on the way to school.

"When?"

I pretend to check my watch. "Eleven hours and thirty-eight minutes from now."

She smiles and links her arm through mine. While we walk I decide to tell her about my sculpture. I finish just as we are walking up to the front doors. Tally is furious. "She's not going to get away with it," she says.

"Miss Beans said it wasn't Charity," I say.

"Of course it's Charity," Tally says. "Unless—" She narrows her eyes.

"No," I say. "I know what you're thinking. But if it was Esmeralda, why would she walk with me over to the bank?"

"Um, to see your reaction?" Tally says. I shake my head. "Then it's Charity."

"There's no proof," I say. "There's nothing we can do." At the bank I was angry. Today I just feel defeated.

"There's always something we can do," Tally says.

I pull open the front door to the school. I hold it for Tally and follow her inside. The smell hits us as soon as we walk in the lobby. Maple syrup. At first I think they must be having pancakes for lunch in the cafeteria. Okay, I know that sounds completely dumb, but what else would smell of maple syrup?

But as Tally and I make our way toward my locker, it's obvious where the smell is coming from. My locker. Syrup is oozing out of the vents and down the front of the locker below mine and making a puddle on the floor. Everyone who walks by looks horrified. A prank is one thing. I mean, you can pull toilet paper out of trees and clean shoe polish off windows and even get the stink of fish out of hair. Even the nacho cheese. It was gross and smelly, but at least it wasn't sticky. But maple syrup? I don't think you come back from maple syrup.

"Oh no she didn't," Tally says. She looks around. "Where is she?"

I wonder which *she* Tally means, but I don't see either of them.

I stop with my back against the locker directly opposite to mine. I feel heat welling up in me. Only it's not the heat of embarrassment or tears, but of anger. I say that in my head. *I am angry.* Then I say it again louder. *I AM ANGRY.* And it's not just about the ruined books and work in my locker. Although that's huge. And it's not even about my art sculpture. Or Marcus. It's just about me. I'm not going to ignore it or try to make the best of it. I'm going to—the voice in my head gets a little softer. *What?* it asks. *What are you going to do?*

"I'm going to say something," I say aloud. "In fact," I say, not caring that several people are looking at me like I've lost it. "I'm going to say a lot of things." I hear Charity before I see her. It's the disdainful *I'm better than you could ever hope to be* laugh that is the giveaway. She's walking with her minions. Charlotte is trailing a few steps behind them. They pause in front of the restroom. Charity heads inside and the minions keep walking toward us.

"Ew," Lindsey says as they pass my locker. "Is that maple syrup?" Charlotte pauses in front of us, but Tally shakes her head and she walks on past.

"Let's go," Tally says. She starts toward the restroom.

"Tally, wait," I say. "I want to do this." She nods and keeps going. "Alone," I say.

"Oh," Tally says, stopping and looking at me. "You sure?"

"Yes," I say with more confidence than I feel.

"Well, I'll go find the janitor," she says. She heads toward the office.

I walk over to the puddle. I slide my palm across the floor until it's covered in syrup and head toward the restroom. I'm not exactly sure why I want the syrup, but somehow it seems fitting. I push open the door with my clean hand and walk inside. Two girls are standing at the sinks and talking. Charity is at the far end, putting on lip gloss. The two girls look at me and my hand dripping with maple syrup and then at Charity, then back to me. Then they leave. Charity doesn't even look over. She finishes putting on her lip gloss and slides it back into her bag. Then she turns to face me.

"What?" she asks.

"Why?" I ask. I hate that my voice breaks in the middle of that one word.

"Why what?" Charity asks.

"Seriously?" I ask. "Let's see. Nacho cheese, ruining my project, and now this." I hold up the hand covered in maple syrup.

Charity laughs. It's sharp and harsh like breaking glass.

"My father did mention that the Rotary was missing a couple of jugs of maple syrup. I wondered what happened to them." She tilts her head at me. "Let me guess," she says, tapping her perfectly manicured finger against her lips. "Your locker?"

"Like you don't know," I ask.

"Wait. You think I did this?" Charity just rolls her eyes at me.

"Of course you did it," I say. "It's the same thing you were doing weeks ago."

"Like you said. That was weeks ago." Charity inspects her nails. Then she looks at me. "I didn't pour syrup into your locker," she says. "Or cheese."

"What about my sculpture?" I ask.

"Also not me," she says.

"I don't believe you," I say.

"Like I care," Charity says. "Are we done here?" She picks up her books and tries to walk past me, but I block her way.

"So that's it, then?" I ask.

"What do you want from me?" Charity asks.

"I want you to swear you didn't do this," I say. "Or at least say you'll never do it again."

"Oh, Penny, whether it's me or someone else," she says, gesturing toward my hand, "this will never stop. You're soft and weak, and you let everyone walk all over you."

"That's not true," I protest.

"Isn't it?" Charity asks.

That makes me pause for a split second. And I hate her for it. For making me doubt myself. But maybe I hate her more because I'm afraid she's right. She steps around me and moves toward the door. She turns at the last moment. "You might want to wash that hand off before you go to class."

Then she's gone.

I rinse my hand off and then push out of the restroom. I stomp down to my locker. I must look crazed because people actually step back to make room for me. I stop when I see someone standing in front of my locker with a handful of paper towels. Marcus. I don't want to see him.

"Penny?" Marcus says. "I thought you might need some help."

"I've got this," I say. I take a deep breath, then reach through the goo still oozing through the vents and dial my combination. It takes three tries before I can get it open. When I finally pull the door open, more syrup pours down my arm. I fling my hand at the lockers, sending a spattering of syrup everywhere. Then the tears come.

"Hey," Marcus says. "It's just a little syrup."

"This," I say, pointing my sticky finger toward the mess, "is not a *little* syrup."

"It's okay," Marcus says.

"No, it's not okay," I say. "None of this is okay." I glare at him.

"Let me help you," he says. I look at him, but all I can see is him with Charity.

"I know about you and Charity," I say.

"You know what about me and Charity?" he asks. It's obvious I don't mean just that she used to tutor him.

"You should have told me," I say. My eyes burn, but I refuse to cry. Not now.

"I should have told you what?" Marcus asks.

I swallow hard and say, "About last summer. And that you didn't want to go to the movies with me because you wanted to hang out with her."

"What are you talking about?" Marcus asks. "I wasn't with Charity. I was with my dad."

"I saw you," I say. I glare at him, daring him to deny it.

"Oh," he says, realizing. "It's not what you think."

I shake my head and turn away. "Forget it," I say. I slam my locker shut, sending syrup flying over everything within four feet of me. "Just leave me alone." I walk away from him and he lets me. I head toward the office. I want out. I want to be away from here. But first I want to find Tally.

Charlotte calls out to me, but I ignore her. I hurry down to the office, where Tally was headed. But the secretary tells me she sent Tally over to the gym to find the janitor. I turn to head back out into the hall and run smack into Blake. I mean, literally run into him. I bounce off and stumble backward.

"Hey," Blake says. "Where's the fire?"

"I have to find Tally," I say, my voice on the edge of panic.

"Okay," Blake says, following me. "Where are we going?"

Tally isn't in the gym. The coach tells us he sent her over to the shop to find the janitor. He sniffs the air. "Do I smell pancakes?"

Blake and I run to the shop, but she's not there either. "I sent her to the cafeteria," the shop teacher says. He sniffs. "What is that smell?" he asks.

We finally find her in the kitchen, standing in front of the sink. She's squirting soap into a bucket of water. "Where's the janitor?" I ask.

"On break," Tally explains. "Well, tell me," she says, shutting off the water. "How did it go?"

"She said it wasn't her," I say. I feel tears welling up in my eyes.

"Of course it was her," Tally says. "She's just saying that to keep from getting in trouble."

I shake my head. "She didn't care about that before. Last time she actually seemed proud of what she'd done to me."

"Well, if it wasn't her, there's only one other person it could be."

"I know you're going to tell me it was Esmeralda, but she wouldn't do this." I hold up my hand, which is still sticky from the maple syrup. "She helped me with my project—"

"Which she destroyed," Tally says.

"And she stood up for me a couple of days ago. And last night—" I take a deep breath and tell her everything that Esmeralda said. About how mean Charity is. Which both Tally and Blake say is true. And then about Charity and Marcus.

"That doesn't sound like Marcus," Tally says. She looks at Blake for confirmation. He is very engaged in reading the sign listing safety protocols for kitchen staff.

"Huh," he says. "Did you know you should wash your hands for at least sixty seconds?"

"Blake?" Tally asks.

Blake sighs. "I don't want to talk about this."

"You don't have to talk," Tally says. "Just yes or no. Do you think Marcus kissed Charity?"

"No," Blake says. Then he groans. "Can I please be excused from this conversation?"

"Yes," Tally says. Then she turns back to me. "Listen. I think Charity is the devil, but there's something a little too sneaky about all of this. This doesn't feel like Charity's brand of evil. I'm sorry, Penny, but there's only one other person it could be."

"I'm an idiot," I say.

"Why? Because you trusted that someone was who she said she was?" Tally asked. I nod. "Better that than becoming cynical." Blake leans against the wall and watches us like we're some fascinating reality show. "Besides, if Esmeralda really is evil—"

"Then she lied about Charity and Marcus." And I realize that was the real damage. Cheese and syrup can be washed out. Dirigibles can be fixed. But trust is something much harder to mend.

The door leading to the cafeteria bursts open and Charlotte comes in. "There you are," she says. "I've been looking everywhere."

"What do *you* want?" I ask. For all I know, she was in on everything. "Did Charity send you here to spy on us?"

Charlotte shakes her head and looks at Tally. "You didn't tell Penny?"

Tally's cheeks get pink. "Not exactly."

"Tell me what?" I ask.

Tally puts her hand on my arm. "Charlotte's on our side," she says. "She went in undercover."

"And it paid off," Charlotte says. She holds out her phone.

"Wait," I say, putting up my hand. I turn to Tally. "Why didn't you tell me?"

"I wasn't sure you'd go for it." Tally bites her lip. "Are you mad?"

I sigh and shake my head. "I might be later, but I'm all out of mad right now." Then I look at Charlotte. "I thought you decided to be friends with Charity again."

"No way," Charlotte says. "I'm done with her. And even more done with *Esme*." Usually Charlotte is so timid. The venom in her voice is slightly shocking. She holds her phone up again. "You have to see this."

Tally, Blake, and I all huddle around Charlotte's phone. She taps the screen and a video begins playing. It's Charity and Esmeralda. They are sitting at a table and filling gallon Ziplocs with nacho cheese from a big industrial-size can. The image is blurry and keeps cutting in and out, but it's clear who it is.

"Sorry," Charlotte says. "I know it's not the best, but I couldn't let them know I was filming them." Then she pokes the screen again. The next video is of Esmeralda stomping on my dirigible. Charity is nowhere in sight.

"Oh," I say. I cringe each time her foot crunches into my sculpture. It feels like she's kicking me as much as she's kicking my dirigible.

Charlotte looks at me. "I'm so sorry. I didn't know what she was going to do until it was too late to stop her. It was already wrecked by the time I got there. I thought I'd just better get it on film."

Tally nods. "You did the right thing." Charlotte smiles sadly at her. The video finishes with Esmeralda laughing and kicking the dirigible into the corner.

"There's one more," Charlotte says. She pokes the screen again. It's blurry at first, but then it focuses. Esmeralda is looking directly into the camera. "I got this one from Esmeralda's phone," Charlotte says.

"You can do that?" Blake asks.

"Yeah, all you have to do is—"

Tally shushes them.

"Wait, wait," the person filming says. The camera swivels and Charity's face fills the screen. She's barely able to speak, she's laughing so hard. Then it swivels back to Esmeralda. "Do that last one again." Esmeralda launches into what is obviously an impression of Tally. It's not pretty. It's mean. Really mean. Charlotte goes to stop it, but Tally shakes her head. Esmeralda goes on to imitate me and then Blake and then half a dozen other people. The last imitations are of the minions. Esmeralda uses a headband and a hair bow to differentiate which ones she's imitating. Charity almost drops the phone, she's laughing so hard. Then it's Charity's turn to do the imitations and Esmeralda's turn behind the lens. Then it's finally over.

"Well, Esmeralda's better, but Charity's meaner," Tally says. "You have to give them that much."

I think back over all of Esmeralda's schemes. Some of them are obvious. Marcus. The dirigible. The syrup. But some of them are just weird. "Charity put a note in my locker that told me to be careful. Why'd she do that?"

Charlotte shook her head. "That was me." I feel sort of dumb about that one. I had just assumed the C stood for Charity. "You wouldn't talk to me, and Tally was gone. I didn't know what else to do."

"So everything about Marcus and Charity?" I ask. I know the answer. I just want it confirmed.

Charlotte shakes her head. "There was never any Marcus and Charity. Charity wanted there to be for sure. But he was never interested." I'm beyond happy for a moment, but then I remember the hugging on the street in Lancaster. And I feel my happiness leak away. Maybe Charlotte doesn't know everything.

The door to the cafeteria swings open again and one of the lunch ladies walks in. "Out," she says.

"Yes, ma'am," Blake says. We each grab something from the pile of cleaning supplies that Tally assembled. Then we all head out through the cafeteria and into the hall.

"I hate that she's just going to get away with all of this," Charlotte says when we get to my locker.

"No one is getting away with anything," Tally says.

"That's my girl," Blake says. Then he freezes.

"What did you just say?" Tally asks.

"I said cats lie curl," he says. He looks up at the clock. "I've got to go." He's away from us and down the hall before any of us can respond.

Tally grins and does a little dance with the mop she's carrying. Happiness is pouring off of her, making both me and Charlotte smile, too. She finally stops dancing and we start toward my locker again.

"So you have a plan?" Charlotte asks.

"Not yet," Tally says. "But I will." I've seen that look on Tally's face before. If I'm right, Esmeralda and Charity are in for a big surprise.

Chapter Twenty

After school, Tally asks me if I want to walk downtown with her. The booths are all set up and some of the vendors are starting to set their things out on their tables. Winter Fest doesn't officially begin until the next morning, but the town has already started to fill up with people. The sidewalks are full with tourists going in and out of the shops and peeking into the store windows. More than a few are munching on cupcakes, which makes me glad we baked so many extra.

Tally keeps checking her watch. "You could just tell me," I say.

She shakes her head. "Not until I know for sure." Then she turns and says, "Hey, they finished the Ice House. Let's go see." We thread our way through the crowds and get in line with everyone else waiting for a chance to go inside. I spot Gram and Dutch standing together on the other side of the park. I nudge Tally and point. Then we see a big truck pulling a trailer filled with what would have to be the pieces of the pool. Gram walks over and gestures to a spot in the corner of the park well away from any of the vendors. The truck's alarm begins beeping as it backs up.

The line of people waiting to go into the Ice House is long. A volunteer tries to move people forward, but everyone wants photos of each room. Finally it's our turn. It really is amazing.

There are two big rooms, one on either side of the walk-through. One is a kitchen with ice carved to look like a table and chairs and even an ice bowl full of ice fruit. The other room is a bedroom with an ice bed, an ice dresser, and an ice rocking chair.

"Wow," I say.

"It's pretty cool," Tally says. Then she laughs at what she just said. There's a long line of people waiting so we can't linger for very long. We walk out into the park. From where we're standing, we can see the bank. A banner is hung out front advertising the art auction and inviting people to come in and see the sculptures. Tally and I stand and watch the people streaming in and out. I glance over to where Gram and Dutch are watching the workmen setting up the pool. They look like they have things handled for the moment.

"Come on," I say. "Let's go see."

Tally looks at me. "Are you sure? I mean, I completely understand if you don't want to."

I pull her sleeve. "Come on."

We walk across the grassy area in front of the Town Office. All of a sudden Tally puts up her hand. "Stop!"

I freeze. "What?" I ask. She points at the grass right where I was about to step. "Ew," I say, skirting the giant pile of dog poop.

"I hate that," Tally says. "I mean, how hard is it to just pick up after your dog?" She sighs. "I'll get a bag from inside. You stay here so no one else will step in it." She heads toward the steps of the bank. Above her the door opens and out strolls

Esmeralda, wearing a cropped winter coat over a bright green dress and tall tan suede boots. As usual she looks like she just stepped out of a magazine. She squints at the sunshine and pauses. She reaches into her purse, pulls out a pair of sunglasses, and puts them on. Then she starts forward again, the heels of her boots making ringing noises on the marble steps. When she sees us, she smiles brightly.

"Oh, hi, Tally—" she says. Then she looks at me. "Oh, Penny, I didn't expect to see you here," she says. The *seeing as how your sculpture was pulverized and therefore not part of the show* goes unsaid.

I walk over to where Tally and Esmeralda are standing. Esmeralda sniffs. "I smell maple syrup," she says. "I guess they're setting up early for the pancake breakfast."

"We know," I say.

Esmeralda tilts her head. "You know what?" she asks.

"Everything," I say.

"That's a little vague," she says. She smiles, but it's not quite as bright as it usually is. Neither Tally nor I say anything else. We just wait her out.

"Well," Esmeralda says finally. "I'm not sure what you think you *know*."

"We know it was you," I say. "The cheese, the syrup, my project. All of it."

She frowns and shakes her head. "I can't imagine what gave you that idea," she says. She smiles again, but it's no longer lovely. It's positively predatory.

I open my mouth to tell her about Charlotte's video, but Tally starts talking before I can say anything. "You don't have to admit it to us. Charity already squealed. Just how much longer do you think she'll keep your secret? Just how long until you get caught?"

"Charity wouldn't do that," Esmeralda retorts, but something flickers in her eyes. Like she might believe Tally that Charity ratted her out.

"Oh yes, she would," Tally says and then laughs coldly. "She most definitely would."

It's clear from the look that crosses Esmeralda's face that she knows Tally's right. Pressing her more, I say, "But what I don't get is why. Why me?"

She sighs, like there's no point in denying it anymore. "What else was I supposed to do? Dumped here in this horrid little town with you people while my parents travel all of China."

"So you tried to ruin my life to get back at your parents?" I ask.

Esmeralda shrugs. "You made it so easy. And I figured I'd either get caught and then my parents would have to come get me, or I wouldn't and I'd at least have fun."

"Fun," I say. Tally is almost vibrating with anger beside me. "So you trashing my locker, ruining my project, and trying to destroy my friendships was fun?"

"Yes," she says simply.

"You're not going to get away with this," Tally says.

Esmeralda laughs. It's that same melodic laugh, but now it seems cruel. "I've already gotten away with it," she says. "You have no proof. And if anyone is blamed, it'll be Charity."

"But she's your friend," I say.

"Please." She makes a face and suddenly she's not pretty at all anymore. "Just because our parents are friends doesn't mean we are. Charity might be the queen of pigs or whatever here, but in my world, she's nothing."

"You're evil," Tally says.

Esmeralda laughs again. "Well, I should really go," she says. "Maybe I'll see you tomorrow at the festival." She walks past us. The heels of her boots strike the marble with each step.

"She sounds like a horse," I say.

Tally smiles a little. "She's not getting away with this," she says.

"No," I say. "She's not. But right now there's nothing we can do." I pull her down the sidewalk and toward the bank. "Let's go in and see the sculptures."

"Wait," Tally says. "Why aren't you angrier?"

"I guess I just realized while she was talking that she's the sad one."

The scream behind us makes both of us turn. "What is this?" Esmeralda shrieks, examining the sole of her boot. She makes a face and lets loose with several French words I've never heard before. She starts furiously trying to wipe off her boot in the grass. Her heel catches and down she tumbles, landing on her hands and knees. Then she lifts her hand. It's covered in poop.

"Ew," Tally says. We turn and head into the bank.

"She really should look where she's going," I say.

"No telling what you'll step in if you don't," Tally says.

After we browse the auction, we head over to where Gram is supervising the swimming pool setup. She nods at us before striding over and telling one of the workers that he's going to get hurt holding the pipe that way.

"She seems like she's got this," Tally says. I nod. We head over to where Dutch is helping three men pour bags of powdered instant pudding into the hopper of a cement truck.

A guy with HANSON'S CONSTRUCTION written on the back of his jacket looks at us and then at Dutch. "Are these the ones?"

Dutch glances over and nods. "Yep," he says.

The construction guy turns and looks at us. "Me and the guys have got five hundred dollars if you can get Jed Hanson into that pool."

"No problem," Tally says. The construction guy picks up another giant bag of pudding mix and rips it open. We back away to avoid being covered in pudding dust.

"Do you even know who Jed Hanson is?" I ask.

"Well, I'm assuming he has something to do with Hanson's Construction," she says.

"How are you going to get him to agree to jump into the pudding?" I ask.

She shrugs. "I'll figure it out." If anyone else said something like that, I'd be skeptical, but Tally seems to have a gift for figuring things out.

Blake comes by after soccer practice and helps us unload the last of the bags of pudding. Who knew you could get fifty-pound bags of instant pudding? I look for Marcus, but he's nowhere to be seen.

At a quarter to five, Tally tells us she has to get home. "And then you'll tell me?" I ask.

"As soon as I know," she says.

"Good luck," I say.

"You don't even know what you're wishing me luck for," she says.

"Well, you can always use luck. Right?" Tally smiles, but she's nervous. She was able to forget about whatever it is while we were working, but now she's worried again. Tally checks her watch again. "Go," I say. She hugs me and Blake and then hurries away down the sidewalk. "Do you know what this is all about?" I ask.

Blake rubs the back of his neck and looks up at the sky. "Looks like snow," he says. I roll my eyes. I guess there's my answer. We help Dutch until more Hanson's Construction workers show up in their matching coats. Apparently Tally's assurance that Jed would take the plunge was enough to get all hands on deck. I tell Blake and Dutch I'll see them later and head over to the bakery.

The Cupcake Queen is slammed. The front is so full that I don't bother trying to find a way in. I decide to walk around back. Like Tally, the business of the festival was good at distracting me, but now that I'm alone again, I can't help but think about Marcus. He must hate me. Or at least think I'm completely mental. I know I need to talk to him, but what do I say? *Sorry I lost it? Sorry I didn't trust you?*

I pull open the back door to the bakery and head inside. My mom is standing at the island, piping frosting onto cupcakes. "Hi," she says. She pauses in the middle of a cupcake. "You okay?"

"I've had better days," I say.

"Me, too," she says.

"You're swamped," I say.

She nods. "I only just got here. I had a meeting in Lancaster that ran long and I only just got back."

"Was it about Tally?" I ask. She bites her lip and nods. "She told me she'd tell me everything"—I check the clock—"in two hours and seventeen minutes."

My mother nods. "Good," she says. "I'm tired of keeping things from you." She looks at the trays of cupcakes littering the kitchen. "How many cupcakes do you think you can frost in two hours and seventeen minutes?" my mother asks.

"A thousand?" I guess.

"Well, I don't think we'll need that many, but that's good to know for the future." She puts down her pastry bag and wipes her hands with a towel. "I'll be out front," Mom says. "Mrs. Hancock's been helping out." She makes a face. I'm sure Mrs. Hancock is excellent at antiques, but maybe not so much at cupcakes. I head to the sink to wash my hands and then grab an apron. I refill the pastry bag with ice-blue frosting from the mixing bowl, and then I start frosting. When I run out of blue, I switch bags and continue with white.

Mom comes in to grab a tray of cupcakes to replenish the front. She pauses next to me and sniffs. Then she leans toward me and sniffs again. "Why do you smell like maple syrup?"

"It's a long story," I say.

"I definitely want to hear it." There's a crash out front. "Later," she says, hurrying back through the door to the front.

I quit at 648 cupcakes. Then I start cleaning up. Gram shows up just as I am wiping down the counters.

"Brr," she says, rubbing her arms to get warm.

"How's the Pudding Plunge coming along?" I ask.

"The pool is almost halfway full," Gram says. "Those boys from Hanson's told me they'd finish up. They're really motivated."

"Well, that's good" is all I say. I just hope Tally can come through on her promise.

I'm standing with Gram on the back porch while Mom locks the back door. On the way to the car, Gram says she almost forgot to tell us, but we're having dinner with Dutch.

"Who's having dinner with Dutch?" Mom asks.

"All of us," Gram says.

Mom sighs. She looks exhausted. "Mom, can't we do this another night? I'm tired."

"Nope," Gram says. "I already told him we'd come. Besides, there's nothing but PB&J's waiting for us at home."

"But I need to talk to Tally," I say. *And Marcus*, I think.

"Tally will call when she's ready," Gram says. "I told him we'd be there at half past six."

"We'd better get going, then," Mom says. We head toward Gram's car. I pull open the back door and slide in. Mom and Gram get into the front seat.

Gram turns to look at both of us. "I really appreciate you coming," she says. "The truth is he asked me to dinner, but I didn't want it to seem like a date."

We head out toward the street. Gram turns right onto the county road. They already have Main Street blocked off, so we need to go the long way around. "So, Gram," I say, "when are you going to tell us about what happened between you and Dutch?" I decide to use her gratitude as a little leverage to see if I can get any information out of her.

Gram looks at me in the rearview mirror. She knows exactly what I'm doing. "It's not really that complicated," she says. "After your granddad died, Dutch started helping out. Mowing the grass. Replacing some shingles on the roof. I'd known him for years, of course, and we'd dated a few times, but nothing serious. About two years after your granddad died, he popped the question."

"He asked you to marry him?" I ask.

"He asked me to go to California with him. Marriage was mixed in there somewhere, but I didn't want to leave here. I was a single mom with a toddler and no money. I didn't want to move two thousand miles away from everything I knew."

"So you told him no," I say.

"I told him not yet," Gram says. "But he was impatient. And we fought. Then one day he said he was going and I could come or not. I chose not."

I lean forward so that I can see my mom. "And you didn't know anything about this?" I ask.

"Not a thing," she says.

"So that's it," Gram says.

"And you never spoke again?" I ask.

"There were a few letters back and forth," she says. "But eventually we didn't have much more to say to each other. The day I saw him on Main Street was the first time I'd seen him in almost thirty-five years." Gram turns left and heads back into the woods. We ride along in silence for a few minutes. Then Gram looks at me again in the mirror. "Your turn," she says.

"My turn to what?" I ask.

"Well, for starters, tell me why you smell like the International House of Pancakes."

I take a deep breath and begin. I just finish telling about Esmeralda falling in dog poop as we are pulling into Dutch's driveway.

Gram makes me tell Dutch about Esmeralda while I help her make the salad. Dutch is a good audience. He asks the right questions, has smart comments, and laughs in all the right places.

"But I'm not sure I understand why she had you so upset," Dutch says as we are sitting down to dinner. "Seems to me a little syrup, a little cheese, and a sculpture wouldn't rile you up that much."

"Well," I say, feeling my cheeks burn. "There was something else."

Dutch passes me the bowl of pasta and looks at me for a moment. "It wouldn't have anything to do with that boy I met on the beach. Would it?" I nod. "Well, from what I could see, that boy is pretty taken with you." I spoon pasta onto my plate and try not to make eye contact with anyone else at the table. "You want some advice?" Dutch asks. I look over at him. "You can say no."

"I'd like some advice," I say. Because, in truth, I really have no idea what to do.

"If he messed up, forgive him. If it was you, apologize and try to make it right. The rest is up to him." I sigh. "Hey," Dutch says, smiling around the table. "This is good stuff. I should be writing this down."

"I hate to admit it," Gram says. "But he's right." My mom nods her agreement.

"Yeah," Dutch says. "I'm a genius. Please pass the salad."

During the rest of dinner, Dutch entertains us with Joy-as-a-teenager stories. "You should have seen your grandmother," he says to me. "Pretty as a picture, but crazier than a long-tailed cat in a room full of rocking chairs."

Gram swats him with her napkin. "I was not."

"Pfft," Dutch says. "No sane person dumps a milk shake on another person's head for no reason."

"I had a reason," Gram says. "You were talking to Mary Grace."

"She was *talking* to me," Dutch says. Gram shakes her head. This is clearly not the first time they've had this conversation. Dutch looks at me. "Mary Grace just liked to stir up trouble. Plus, as far as I knew, your grandmother was only interested in me as a friend."

"Well, who gave you that idea?" Gram asks. Dutch mumbles something. "What's that?"

"Mary Grace," he says.

"So what did you do?" I ask.

Dutch shrugs. "I was sweet on your grandmother plain and simple. If she just wanted to be friends, that was fine."

"Fine?" Gram says. "You didn't talk to me for almost three years."

"We talked," Dutch protests. "Besides, by then you were going out with Charlie," he adds softly.

I glance at my mother. Charlie was her father, who was killed in a car accident when she was just a baby. Gram's green eyes are filled with sadness even after all these years. Then she smiles. "But after Charlie died, you were there." Dutch nods. "In fact, as I remember I had a hard time being rid of you."

Dutch laughs. "You loved me," he says.

Gram nods. "Maybe."

"It was the pineapple upside-down cake I made for your birthday."

Gram shakes her head. "You know what it was."

"Butterflies," he says.

She nods.

"Butterflies?" I ask.

Gram smiles. "He showed up at my door and asked me to come outside. He had this container full of butterflies he'd been raising. He released them into the air. I'll never forget those orange-and-black butterflies against the blue sky." She looks wistfully at my mom. "You already thought Dutch hung the moon, but you loved those butterflies."

I look at my mom, trying to see her as a toddler clinging to Gram and watching butterflies gliding up into the sky.

"What did you do?" I ask Gram.

"Well, I kissed him."

"Wow," I say. "And then what?"

"Well, a couple of weeks later, he left."

Dutch nods. "Biggest mistake of my life." Dutch tells us he'll be right back. He walks toward the back bedroom and returns with a box draped with a piece of fabric. He puts it on the table in front of Gram.

"What's this?" Gram asks.

He pulls off the cloth, revealing a cage full of what look like gray leaves. He grins. I lean forward and peer into the cage. What I thought were leaves are actually a dozen or more caterpillars tucked away in their cocoons. "Wrong time of year for butterflies," he says. "They'll hatch in the spring when it's warm enough. I just didn't want to wait that long." I glance over at Mom, who looks like she's about to start crying. "Joy, I was a fool not to come back. I thought I needed to find something out there, but what I really needed was right here all along."

Gram looks at the cage full of cocoons. Then at me and at my mom. She finally looks at Dutch. Then she kisses him. And I know it's all kinds of weird to see your grandmother kissing someone, even someone as awesome as Dutch, but it was nice. At least the first time. The second time after pecan pie and the third time while doing dishes was too much. And I let them know it.

Gram laughed and said I better get used to it. Dutch smiled. I can tell he liked that idea just fine.

"Thank you for dinner," I say as we're heading out. "And for the advice."

"You are mighty welcome, Miss Penny." Then he turns to Gram, who is organizing his bookcase. "Hey," he says. "I had everything just where I wanted it."

"Wouldn't be the first time you had no idea what was good for you." Then they're off again.

Mom smiles at me and I shake my head. Love can sure be weird.

Chapter Twenty-One

There's a line of cars driving past Gram's house. People are holding their phones out of their windows and snapping photos of all of the Christmas decorations. We have to wait for a gap in the line before we can pull into the driveway. The yard is so bright, it almost looks like it's the middle of the day. Gram has everything on a timer, so pretty much the minute the sun is gone, her house lights up like—well, like Christmas. The lights are blinking, the polar bears are dancing, and Tally is waiting on our front porch.

"Hi," I say. Mom and Gram both say hello to Tally before walking around us and into the house. I sit beside Tally on the porch. The wind is starting to blow, but we're protected where we're sitting.

I check my watch. Almost nine. "How long have you been here?" I ask.

She shrugs. "Not long. Ten minutes maybe."

"I thought you were going to call me," I say.

"Well, you weren't home," Tally says.

"You could have tried my mom's cell. I asked her to keep it on during dinner."

"You're right. I should have called," she says. "I'm sorry." Her sorry is very different from my dad's. His was barely an apology. I know Tally means hers. She looks at me, waiting.

"I forgive you," I say. "But next time. Call."

"Done," she says. And unlike when my father assures me of something, I believe her.

"So, what happened?" I ask.

"There was a meeting. And then Poppy and I needed to talk and then there was ice cream."

"Ice cream," I confirm.

"Mint chocolate chip."

"Nice." I shake my head. "Anyway," I prompt.

"It went well," Tally says. "Or at least it will."

"Can you please stop talking in code?" I ask, exasperated.

"I'm trying to tell you," she says.

"Well, try harder," I say.

"A few weeks ago, Poppy got the letter you saw. It was from my father's attorney." She frowns. "Basically it just meant that my father didn't want to be my father anymore."

I nod. Even though I've had days to think about it, I'm still no closer to knowing what to say. "I'm sorry," I say finally.

"Yeah," she says. "It stinks." Tally kicks the ground with her sneakers, but not in an angry way. Just a sort of sad way like she's trying to kick away the hurt. Then she looks at me. "That's why I was acting so squirrelly and angry."

"I'm pretty sure that would make anyone act squirrelly and angry," I say. "But you got ice cream," I add.

"Because there's good news," she says. "Since my dad doesn't want to be my dad any longer, it means I can be adopted."

"Oh," I say, still wondering where the ice cream is.

"Poppy wants to adopt me."

"Wow," I say.

Tally grins at me. "The other day when I wasn't in school, I had to go in front of a judge and tell her I wanted to be adopted by Poppy. Then your mom had to go and talk to her about whether she thought Poppy would be a good parent for me."

"Wow! Poppy *would* be a great parent," I say. "Holy wow!" I stare out at the dancing polar bears. Then I look back at Tally. "This is huge," I say, throwing an arm around her.

She laughs. "Yeah, I got that."

A family climbs out of their car and is taking photos in front of Gram's house. "You know," I say. "You could have talked to me about all of this."

"I guess I was embarrassed," Tally says. "I'm not sure what it says about a person when neither of her parents wants her." Then she nudges me. "Besides," she says. "It's not like you were telling me everything either."

"Mean girls and boy drama aren't in the same realm as what you've been going through," I say.

"What about your dad and Thanksgiving?" Tally asks.

"Oh," I say. "That." I sigh. "It's not the same."

Tally shakes her head. "Poppy told me that comparing pain is the old no shoes–no feet argument."

"I have no idea what that means," I say.

"It means that pain is pain. And there will always be someone hurting more and someone hurting less." Tally shoves her hands into the pockets of her jacket. "What about Marcus?" she asks.

"I don't know," I say. "Dutch says I should tell him I'm sorry."

Tally nods. "Sorry goes a long way."

"Maybe not far enough," I say.

"You know," Tally says. "This could all have been a lot easier if we had just talked to each other."

"You think?" I ask, bumping her with my shoulder. "So what now?" I ask.

"The judge said it will take a while to be official, but that she doesn't see any reason why our application will be denied."

"Wow," I say again.

"I know!" Tally says, grinning at me. The wind blows, sending the bells on the reindeer jingling. The snow globe starts playing "Jingle Bells." The lights blink in time to the music.

"My grandmother is so weird," I say.

"Not any weirder than Poppy. She said she's going to have everyone over for dinner as soon as everything is official."

"Green?" I ask. "Or purple?" I'm imagining green bread or purple cake.

"Neither," Tally says. "She wants to throw a dark dinner."

"Dark?"

"As in pitch-black."

"Well, that should be interesting," I say. Marcus's dad starts warming up on his bagpipes. I sigh. "I need to talk to Marcus. And then there's Esmeralda and Charity—"

"You worry about Marcus," Tally says. "I'll take care of Esmeralda and Charity."

"Can't you talk to Marcus?" I ask.

"Uh, no," Tally says.

"So, what did you come up with for the Evil Twins?" I ask.

"I'll tell you tomorrow at the pancake breakfast." She stands up and pulls me up with her. "I need to borrow the projector you and your grandmother made."

I go in and retrieve the camera and come out and hand it to Tally. She's off the porch and headed toward home before I can ask any more questions.

I frown at the flock of festive flamingos. As horrible as Charity and Esmeralda are, I actually would rather deal with them than talk to Marcus. But then I remember Dutch's advice. I just need to apologize and try to make it right. "Easy for you to say," I tell the nearest flamingo. He just keeps looking at me with his big goofy smile. So not helping. I decide the flamingos have helped me as much as they can and I head inside.

Gram wakes me even before it's light out. "Dutch is here. He said that people are already lining up for the Pudding Plunge."

I squint at the clock. "But it doesn't start for four hours." I sit up and swing my legs out from under the quilt. It's cold. I can't even imagine how cold the pudding is. "Is Mom still here?" I ask.

"She's already left for the bakery," she says. "Come on," she adds, handing me a sweatshirt. "I've got breakfast downstairs."

She walks to the door and then turns one last time to make sure I'm up. "You might want to brush your teeth," she says cryptically on the way out of my room.

I climb out of bed and pull on the sweatshirt. Then I creep to the top of the stairs and peer down, but I can't see anything. I tiptoe down a couple of steps and try again, but from this angle I can only see the refrigerator. Gram's suggestion that I brush my teeth hints that Dutch isn't the only one at breakfast, but from what I can see, there's no one else here. I hear Gram talking to someone in the kitchen. I step down the last few stairs. Gram walks to the dining room table carrying a plate of biscuits. Dutch is right behind her with a plate full of scrambled eggs. I shake my head. I'm sure Dutch couldn't care less what I look like first thing in the morning. On the way to the kitchen, I redo my ponytail to get my hair out of my eyes. I step into the warmth of the kitchen.

"Morning," I say.

Dutch looks up at me and smiles. "Good morning," he says.

"Hi, Penny," a voice says from behind me. I close my eyes. Are you kidding me? This is twice he's seen me in my pajamas. I open my eyes and see Gram shaking her head. She did warn me. Sort of.

"Hi, Marcus," I say, turning to look at him. He's carrying a plate full of bacon in one hand and a jug of orange juice in the other. Even though he's just wearing jeans and a flannel shirt, he looks amazing. As usual. He gives me a tentative smile. Of course he does. Last time he saw me I was covered in syrup and freaking out. Marcus walks over to the table, puts down the food he's carrying, and sits. Gram pats the bench beside her. I walk over and sit, wishing I'd taken her advice to get cleaned up a bit.

Dutch picks up a biscuit and places it on his plate. "So . . ." he says. Gram shakes her head at him. "What?" he asks. Gram passes Dutch the eggs. He spoons some onto his plate and then passes them to Marcus.

"Why don't we go eat in the living room," Gram says to Dutch.

He looks from me to Marcus and nods. "Good idea." Dutch grabs one more biscuit before they head into the living room, leaving me and Marcus alone at the table. I straighten my napkin on my lap. Then I look up.

"I'm sorry," I say. The weird thing is that Marcus says the same thing at the exact same time.

"Why are you sorry?" I ask.

"I should have told you."

I shake my head. "You don't owe me any explanation," I say.

"Well, you're going to get one anyway," Marcus says. "My mom's birthday was three days after Thanksgiving." Marcus leans back and looks out the window. "It's only the second one since she died," he said. "I thought it would be easier than last year, but it wasn't. It was harder." He frowns. "Last year I was just so angry and my dad was just, well, he was gone. This year—" He shakes his head and sighs. He doesn't say it out loud, but maybe it's sort of like how I've been feeling about my dad. I was in denial about how much he was hurting me for so long.

Now that I'm admitting it to myself, it's hard to know what to do with it all.

Marcus looks at me and I can see the pain in his eyes. Usually he seems so solid and okay that it's easy to forget how much he must be hurting. "Pat's Pizza was my mom's all-time favorite. So my dad and I decided to go there. I guess to just remember." He smiles a little, but it's sad. "We got her favorite pizza: anchovies, tomatoes, and mushrooms." I make a face, which makes him laugh. "Yeah, the pizza was gross, but it was great just being with my dad." He looks back out at the ocean just visible in the morning light. "Afterward while I was stand-ing outside waiting for my dad to pay, it just hit me that my mom's really gone." Marcus looks at me. "I ran into Charity and I guess she could tell I was off. And she gave me a hug. That was it."

"I shouldn't have doubted you," I say. *And I shouldn't have acted so mental*, I think.

"Blake told me about Esmeralda," he says. He shakes his head. "That was an awkward conversation."

"I'll bet," I say.

"She's just jealous of you."

I laugh. "I don't think so," I say.

He shrugs. I can't imagine what would make him say that. Esmeralda is sophisticated and beautiful and exotic. Every-thing that I'm not. Marcus reaches for my hand. "Are we okay?" he asks.

"We're good," I say. He gives my hand one more squeeze

and then eats a forkful of eggs. I put some jam on my biscuit and take a bite.

"Don't fill up too much," he says. "There will be pancakes later."

"A lot of them?" I ask, smiling.

"All you can eat," he says.

"As long as they don't have bananas in them," I say.

"What do you have against bananas?" he asks.

"Nothing," I say. "I just don't think they belong with pancakes."

"What about blueberries?" he asks.

I shrug. "I can take or leave blueberries," I say.

"Raisins?"

"Ew," I say. "Who puts raisins in their pancakes?"

"I've been known to put raisins in my pancakes," Marcus says.

"They're just rotten grapes," I say.

"Dried grapes," Marcus says.

"Whatever," I say. "They're still gross." Marcus laughs at the face I make. "I'm serious," I say.

"I know," Marcus says. "I've just never seen someone so passionately against raisins. What about carrot cake? Raisins or no?"

"Ew. No," I say.

"Cinnamon raisin bread?"

"No."

"I'm sensing a trend here."

"Nothing gets by you," I say.

We finish breakfast and help Gram clean up. Dutch says he's going to run down and make sure the Pudding Plunge is ready. He kisses Gram's cheek on the way out. Marcus tells me he's going home to let Sam out. "How long do you need to get ready?"

"Thirty minutes," I say. "I want to take a shower."

"Why?" Marcus asks, pulling on his coat. "You already smell like maple syrup." He's out the door and pulling it shut behind him before I can say anything.

Gram is standing at the sink looking at me. There's a blue plate on the counter beside her.

"What's that?" I ask.

"Dutch is under the impression that I ordered the blue plate special at the diner on our first date."

"Well, did you?" I ask.

"Maybe," she says. She takes a sip of her tea. "Things went well with Marcus," she says.

I nod. "Dutch was right."

"He may be right about a good many things," she says cryptically. She sips her tea again and then looks at me. "You'd better get that shower."

"Maple syrup?" I ask.

"There are worse things to smell like."

She's right, I think as I head upstairs. Unfortunately, I've smelled like a good many of them.

Chapter Twenty-Two

It takes me almost the full thirty minutes to get ready. I scrubbed with apple soap just to be sure that I don't smell like syrup anymore. There's a note from Gram pinned to the door, telling me she'll see me at the Pudding Plunge. I pull on my coat and head outside. It's cold and just starting to snow, so I dart back in and grab a hat. I pull it on and tuck my hair behind my ears. Then I head back outside. Marcus is waiting at the end of the driveway. "Hi," I say.

"Hi," he says. Then he takes my hand. We walk into town and head toward the square. There are people everywhere. Gram wasn't kidding. Hog's Hollow really does love its festivals. We make our way toward the all-you-can-eat pancakes tent near the center of town. I look in and see Blake and Tally sitting together. I wave and Tally waves back. Blake waves his fork at us.

We get into line. It's long, but it moves quickly. The guy handing out plates tells Marcus it'll be ten dollars. "Five for you and five for your girlfriend."

I startle at the words and I feel like the whole tent full of people gets quiet, waiting to see what Marcus will do, including me. Marcus just hands the man a ten and takes our plates. We move forward toward the griddle. I try to hand Marcus some money, but he waves it away. I don't want to be like

Esmeralda and just assume he's paying. Marcus gives me my plate and leans toward me. I'm not sure what to do. Do I say something? Make a joke? Or do I pretend nothing happened? But clearly something big just happened. Or it's about to.

"Is that okay?" he asks.

"Pancakes?" I ask, not sure that he's talking about anything other than breakfast foods.

"No," he says. "What he said about you being my girlfriend."

"Oh. Yes. It's okay," I say, smiling. Because I am so cool like that. But inside I'm completely freaking out. I am Marcus Fish's girlfriend. Holy wow!

Marcus grins at me and I realize I literally can't stop smiling. The line moves forward and then we're up.

"What can I get you?" the man working the griddles asks. Then he laughs. "Just kidding," he says. "All we got is pancakes."

Marcus cuts his eyes at me. I wonder how many times the cook has used that joke in the last hour. He slaps a couple of pancakes on my plate. And then a couple more onto Marcus's. They are so big, they hang off the sides. I guess Blake wasn't exaggerating about them being ginormous.

We thank him and head over to where Tally and Blake are sitting. Tally scoots over to make room beside her. Marcus sits down beside Blake. I see the light catching Tally's hair out of the corner of my eye. I turn and look at her. In addition to the icy blue stripes, she's added silver sparkle hair spray. She sees me looking and smiles at me.

"How many pancakes have you eaten?" Marcus asks Blake.

"These will make fourteen," he says. "I'm not even sure I can match last year." He shakes his head.

"Yes, you are truly a disappointment," Tally says.

Marcus reaches down the table and snags one of the syrups lined up along the center of the table. Blake's already emptied the one in front of us. Marcus hands me the syrup and I pour some on my pancakes before handing it back.

"So, you guys made up?" Blake asks. He shoves another bite of pancake into his mouth.

"Yes," I say. "Thank you for asking."

"Well, I for one am relieved. The past few days have been a little too romcom for me."

"Romcom?" I ask.

"Romantic comedy," Tally says.

Blake puts his fork down. "I'm done." I try to see what's on his shirt, but his coat is zipped up against the cold. "So when are we—" He leans forward. "You know."

"Whenever they get here," Tally says. "Charlotte's already all set up."

"Is this about Chari—"

"Shh," Blake says. "C and E."

I roll my eyes. "Okay. Is this about C and E?"

"Yep," Tally says.

"Are you going to tell me?"

"It'll be better if I don't. That way your surprise will be authentic," Tally says.

"What she means is that you're not as good of an actor as I am," Blake says.

"That's not what I mean," Tally says.

"Okay," Blake says. Tally rolls her eyes. Even over the hum of people talking and the hiss of the griddle, I hear Esmeralda's laugh.

"Let's roll," Blake says. We all get up and dump our plates into the trash can. Blake makes sure he gets his hand stamped on the way out. Apparently five dollars gets you pancakes all day long.

"Where to?" I ask.

"The Ice House," Tally says. "It's the busiest part of the festival. Also, the south wall is perfect."

"Perfect for what?" I ask.

"You'll see." Charlotte is sitting on a folding chair about fifteen feet in front of the south wall. She has my grandmother's projector in her lap. There are two wireless speakers on the ground in front of her.

"Are they here?" she asks.

"They should be heading this way any second," Tally says. She checks her watch. "We need to do this quick. The Pudding Plunge starts in half an hour."

"Here they come," Blake says. Charlotte reaches into the box and pokes the screen of her phone, and the image of Esmeralda's face is projected onto the wall of the Ice House. Several people stop in the middle of the sidewalk to watch. Charlotte pushes the screen again and you can hear Charity laughing. The video goes wonky and then Charity's face fills the screen.

"Isn't that the Hog Queen?" someone asks. More people stop. Some want to check out the projector we have, but most want to watch the show.

"Hey, Charity!" a voice calls. "You've got to see this."

"Wow," Tally says. "This is working better than I imagined."

I turn and see Charity pushing through the crowd. Esmeralda is right behind her. The video switches back to Esmeralda, who begins her imitation of Tally. A couple of people in the audience laugh. They don't know who she's imitating, just that it's funny. I glance over at Tally, but she shrugs. I grin. That's the Tally I'm used to. The confident one who just shrugs things off.

Charity pushes to the front and spots Charlotte. "You!" she says.

"That's right," Charlotte says.

"But you—you—" I've never seen Charity so flustered before. She spins and looks at Esmeralda. "That was on your phone," she says. "How did *she* get it?"

"I didn't know you could do that either," Blake says. "Turns out it's not that hard."

"Shut it," Charity says to Blake. Then she turns to Charlotte. "Turn it off."

Charlotte shakes her head.

"No way," Tally says. Charity looks at Esmeralda, who

actually seems amused by what's happening. I spot the minions on the edge of the crowd. So does Charity.

"Please turn it off," Charity says. Blake actually laughs out loud. Charity saying "please" indicates just how desperate she is. "Listen," she hisses. "I know what's in that video. Do you know what this will do to me?"

"Let's see," Tally says. "Out you as the Mean Queen in front of the whole town? Everyone already knows that." She glances over at the minions, who are edging closer. "Of course maybe they've been okay with it since you're mostly nice to them." Tally shakes her head. "If they see this? You'll lose them for sure."

"I'll do whatever you want," Charity says. She's seething, but she's also desperate. It's not a pretty combination. She looks over at the minions again. "Please," she says. "They can't know that I—"

"Why?" I ask. "Afraid you'll lose your only friends?"

Charity glares at me.

"She doesn't have friends," Tally says. "She has people who she intimidates into spending time with her."

"Tally," I say. As much as I hate Charity, I don't want to destroy her.

"Charity," Tally says. "You *could* have friends. If you'd just stop being so horrible to everyone."

Charity sneers at us. "Like I'd want friends like you losers." The video switches to Charity, who starts her imitation of Tally.

Charity closes her eyes. She knows that next is her doing an extremely cruel imitation of one of the Lindseys. "I'll do anything," she says.

"Not good enough," Tally says. She points at Esmeralda. "She has to do it, too."

"She will," Charity says.

"Oh no, I won't," Esmeralda says. She seems more amused than anything, watching Charity squirm. I guess she wasn't lying about not really being friends with Charity. Charity stomps over to Esmeralda, grabs her arm, and whispers hard and fast at her. Esmeralda's eyes get big. Whatever Charity is saying to her must be bad if it's enough to ruffle her. Esmeralda narrows her eyes as Charity finishes threatening her. "You wouldn't," she says.

"Oh, I would," Charity says.

"Would what?" Blake asks me.

"I don't know," I say. "But Charity must have something big over her."

Esmeralda is furious with Charity, but she nods. Charity turns back toward us. "Okay," she says. "We'll do it. Now shut it off."

Charlotte looks at Tally, who nods. The video goes dark and the crowd groans.

"Sorry, folks," Tally says. "But you might want to start making your way over to the Pudding Plunge. We've got a real surprise for you." Charity gasps. Esmeralda starts backing up, but Charity grabs her arm. Tally turns and looks at Charity and Esmeralda and smiles. Then she looks down at Esmeralda's feet. "You might want to take those boots off. I'm guessing pudding doesn't come out of suede very easily."

Oddly enough, watching first Esmeralda (Charity made her go first so she wouldn't chicken out) and then Charity jump into the pool of pudding was anticlimactic. The real victory was won in front of the Ice House. Seeing them both covered in chocolate goo was just the icing on the cake.

True to her word, Tally deleted the video as soon as Charity jumped. Of course we didn't delete the video of their plunge. We knew we might want to watch that one again. And again.

"The weird thing is that this might have made Charity seem more human to a lot of people," Marcus says, watching the crowd cheer as she pushes free of the pudding.

"Maybe this experience will make her nicer," Tally says.

Charity glares at us as she passes and makes a vague threat about us not hearing the last of this.

"And maybe not," Blake says.

"Either way a whole lot of people wanted to see the Hog Queen jump into pudding," Tally says. "She earned the ARK over three hundred dollars."

"What about Esmeralda?" I ask.

Blake shakes his head. "Other than the twenty bucks Marcus put in? Nothing."

I smile at Marcus, who just shrugs. I think he's going to need to find another new French tutor after this.

"Well," Tally says to Charlotte. "I'm pretty sure your cover is blown."

"Good," Charlotte says. "I couldn't stand being around them. All they talk about is their hair and whether they are getting fat and how many calories are in a serving of broccoli."

"I can assure you that we rarely talk about hair. We couldn't care less about who is fat and who isn't. As for how many calories are in a serving of broccoli?" Tally shrugs.

"But I do know. They made me look it up," Charlotte says.

"Well, don't tell us," Tally says.

After Charity and Esmeralda jump, we start working at the Pudding Plunge. Poppy is selling RPS Society and Pudding Plunge T-shirts. Blake's mom is taking donations, and Tally and I are getting people to sign the waiver before they get in line. Blake and Marcus hand out towels to people after they've taken the plunge. Monica shows up with half a dozen dogs, which bring in the donations even faster.

The line to jump in pudding continues growing all morning, snaking around the block. Just before lunch the Hanson's Construction guys gather to watch as their boss climbs the ladder. Apparently Dutch knows Jed Hanson from way back when, so he was able to convince him to take the plunge. The construction guys hoot and holler until finally Jed does a cannonball into the pudding, sending a shower of brown goo all over his men.

The Pudding Plunge slows down a little during lunch when they have to refill the pool. Gram tells us she and Dutch will mind the tables, letting us have some time to walk around. Charlotte goes to hang out with her family, leaving Blake, Tally, Marcus, and me. We spend the next hour wandering around the festival, looking at the crafts (Tally and me), eating more pancakes (Blake), and testing our skill at splitting wood (Marcus and almost Blake). Blake said he'd stick to competitive eating after watching Marcus split four logs in under ten seconds.

The art auction is busy every time we pass by. Miss Beans waves us down to tell us that every one of the sculptures has at least half a dozen bids on it. Tally's dog is the highest so far. Someone wrote *$300* at the bottom of the list of bids.

It starts snowing in earnest early in the afternoon, but rather than discourage people from jumping into pudding, it seems to have the opposite effect. It's slammed all afternoon. People pay everything from five dollars to a hundred for the chance. By five o'clock there's a layer of snow deep enough to cover my sneakers. Gram announces last call for anyone wanting to participate in the Pudding Plunge.

Tally grabs my arm. "Let's do it," she says.

"Jump in pudding?" I ask just to be sure of what the *it* is.

"It'll be epic," she says. I make a face, imagining how cold it will be. "Come on," she says. "When are you going to have another chance to jump into pudding?"

"She does have a point," Blake says. "Of course the T-shirts do read FIRST ANNUAL PUDDING PLUNGE, indicating that there will, in fact, be another opportunity."

"Why don't you do it?" I ask Blake.

He shakes his head. "Lactose intolerant."

Tally frowns at him. "Since when?"

Blake backs away.

"What about you?" I ask Marcus.

"Chocolate allergy," Marcus says. I think about all of the chocolate cupcakes he's eaten over the last few months. Marcus gives me a big smile and joins Blake at the snack table. Tally looks at me hopefully.

"Fine," I say.

"Yay!" Tally says, jumping up and down. She drags me to where Gram is calling out, "Last, last call."

"I guess we're jumping," I tell Gram. She smiles and shakes her head. But she doesn't seem surprised.

"Do you want to go first?" Tally asks.

I nod. I figure I better go before I chicken out. I climb the ladder up to the platform and walk out until I'm over the pudding. Snow has started to build up on top of the brown goo, making it look almost pretty.

"Go, Penny!" Marcus yells.

I take a big breath, close my eyes, and pinch my nose. Then I jump, tucking my knees up into my chest. When I hit, it's more of a sploosh than a splash. And I'm under. I straighten my legs. I can just touch the bottom with the tips of my sneakers. I push my head free of the pudding and take a breath. I try to wipe the pudding from my eyes, but my hands are covered, making it impossible.

"Penny!" Blake yells. "Just walk straight forward."

I step out, holding my hands in front of myself, just as I've watched everyone else do. I touch the side and feel a towel being pressed into my hands. I wipe my eyes first and start making my way toward the exit ladder. I climb out, shedding clumps of pudding from me with each step. I squeeze about a gallon of it back into the pool from my ponytail alone. I walk down the steps still wiping pudding from my eyes and my nose and my ears. My feet hit the snow just as I hear a loud sploosh behind me. I turn in time to see Tally disappearing under the pudding.

Marcus wraps a towel around me and leads me over to the heaters they have set up off to the side. "How was it?" he asks.

"Cold," I say, shivering. "And gross." I look down at myself. My clothes are heavy with pudding. Even my shoes feel full of the brown goo. "I think this beats your chum shower," I say. "Well, except for the smell."

Marcus nods. "That is a significant difference," he says. Then he bends and brushes his lips against mine. And everything falls away. All I can see is Marcus. No pudding. No snow. No crowds. And I think, *Yes!* This is my perfect moment in time. Covered in pudding and standing in ankle-deep snow, while crowds of people swirl around us. Marcus straightens and looks at me. He wipes a blob of pudding off of the corner of his mouth and smiles.

"Oh. My. God!" Tally says, sloshing over to me. "That was awesome!" She rubs her arms, sending blobs of pudding raining down onto the ground around her. I keep looking at

Marcus, who keeps looking at me. But Tally is too excited to notice that we're not saying anything. Gram and Dutch walk over to where we are. I notice they are holding hands, but I pretend not to.

"Thank you," Tally says to them. "I'd hug you, but—"

"Maybe later," Gram says, putting up her hand. Knowing Tally, she might actually hug someone. "Besides, it was surprisingly really fun."

"Next year let's do pistachio pudding," Blake says. "Or tapioca." I make a face. Chocolate pudding is bad enough. I'm not sure I want squishy blobs of tapioca sliding down my shirt. I shiver at the thought of it.

Gram sees me shiver and grabs the edge of my towel. "Come on, you two. Let's see if we can dig up some clean clothes for you before the fireworks start."

Clean clothes end up being RPS Society T-shirts and Hanson's Construction coveralls. "Maybe next time you can plan ahead and bring some extra clothes with you," Gram says.

I shake my head, thinking there's no next time. One pudding plunge is plenty. But I see Tally nodding and grinning and can't help thinking she has other plans.

Chapter Twenty-Three

Finally mostly wiped free of pudding, sort of dry, and fairly warm, we walk out onto the lawn to wait with everyone else for the fireworks. Dutch returns from helping Monica load the dogs into her car. She thought the loud noises might scare them. My mom comes over. She looks tired, but happy. She shakes her head when she sees me, but she's smiling. She puts her arm around me and sniffs my hair.

"I'm not sure if I prefer this or the maple syrup," she says. "Did you have a good day?"

I grin. Pancakes, revenge, pudding, kissing? "One of the best days ever," I say.

"So," Mom says. "Your dad called again."

"Oh," I say.

"He asked if he could come here for a day or two around Christmas. I told him that I was fine with it, but that he needed to ask you."

"I'd like to see him," I say hesitantly. I do want to see him, but I want him to do the work. No more *I'm sorry* or *Things will be different next time*. If he wants to see me, he can come here. After that? Well, I guess we'll just have to wait and see.

"Your dad could stay at the Maple Inn," Mom suggests.

I laugh thinking about him staying there. It's a great inn. It's really pretty and the food is supposed to be awesome. The only problem is the owner. Mrs. McTavish. Well, not her exactly. It's her cats. She has seventeen of them. She actually had to get a town permit allowing her to have them all. Tally told me Monica visits her every couple of months to make sure they are being well cared for. Apparently they are all happy, but Monica did cut her off. She's allowed to visit the ARK and play with the cats any time she likes. She's just not allowed to adopt any more.

"There's no hurry about talking to your dad," Mom says. "Just think about it." Mom gives me one more squeeze and then walks over to stand with Poppy, who looks tired, but happy. All of the drama around Tally and the adoption must be hard on everyone.

Marcus and Blake return with cups of hot cider for everyone. Tally shivers and looks hopefully at Blake, who takes off his coat and hands it to her.

It's the first time I've seen his shirt. THE MOST IMPORTANT THING IN LIFE IS TO BE YOURSELF. UNLESS YOU CAN BE BATMAN. ALWAYS BE BATMAN. I raise my eyebrows.

"I know," Blake says, seeing me looking at his shirt. "It's lame, but it's the last one."

"Thank goodness," Tally says.

"But hey, great news," he says, grinning at us. "I bought another dozen. So the good times are going to keep rolling into the New Year."

"Awesome," I say.

"I know," Blake says, smiling at me and then at Tally. "I know."

There's a loud boom and a streak of silver, and then a huge flower made up of silver and blue sparks blooms over our heads. Marcus slides his hand into mine. It's warm against my cold skin. There are more booms, one right after another until a huge bouquet of flowers in all different colors fills the sky. I have to keep blinking to keep the snow, which has started falling again even harder, out of my eyes.

All too soon it's over. We start making our way through the park and toward home. There's a last-minute flurry of activity around the craft stalls as people buy a few more presents. We pass the bank, which is just closing its doors, and I wonder how much money the auction raised. The Ice House is lit up with lights that change from pink to blue and back again. Hanson's has already started draining the pool. And I wonder if chocolate pudding is considered toxic waste.

We all walk toward home, following the crowds of people returning to their cars or walking toward their own houses. Tally starts teasing Dutch about his promise to consider adopting a pet.

"I'll have you know," he says, "I have already made my selection. I'm just waiting on the go-ahead from the vet."

"Which one did you pick?" Tally asks. "I'll bet it was Rufus." I'm not sure whether Rufus is the Irish setter or the Great Dane. It turns out it doesn't matter because Dutch is shaking his head. "Goldie?" Tally asks. Another shake. She frowns, thinking. But then she gives up.

"I'll give you a hint," he says. "I had to order specialty seed for him."

Tally's eyes get big. "Him? Seed? Seriously? That is so awesome!" She turns and smiles at me, actually walking backward down the sidewalk. "Isn't that awesome?"

Seed means it's one of the birds. And if it's specialty seed, it's not one of the parakeets. It's not Poe or Snowball. They're both female. Then it hits me. "You're adopting Churchill?" I ask.

Dutch nods. "I told you I go in for the hard cases."

"Thank you," I say. I feel tears welling up in my eyes. Tally spins in a circle, almost falling on the snowy sidewalk. Blake grabs her arm to keep her upright.

We all walk to the bridge that will take us toward the beach. The snow is starting to drift on the sand and the waves are silver in the moonlight. "I've got chili and corn bread in thirty minutes for anyone who wants it," Gram says.

Tally looks at Poppy, who nods. "Maybe I should go shower," Tally says. She hugs Blake and then me and then Dutch for good measure before taking Poppy's hand. They walk toward home hand in hand.

Blake's mom smiles. "Chili sounds perfect," she says.

"Well, come on," Gram says. She and Dutch head toward the house, followed by Blake's mom and mine. That leaves Marcus, me, and Blake.

Blake looks from Marcus to me and then makes a face. "Well, this is awkward," he says. "I think I'll just—" Then he turns and jogs away, heading up the hill toward Gram's house.

"I'll go get my dad," Marcus says. He squeezes my hand and starts to let go.

"Wait," I say. He looks at me. Then I do something that I wouldn't have imagined doing in a million years. I kiss him. I have to stand on my tiptoes to reach. It's fast and I might have actually missed his mouth a tiny bit, but it was a kiss. I step back and bite my lip. Marcus grins at me, which I take to be a good sign. I give his hand one last squeeze and then run after Blake.

There's pudding in my shoes and my borrowed coveralls are puddled around my ankles and I can feel my ponytail, stiff with pudding, slapping against my back with each step, but this is without a doubt the best day ever.

Acknowledgments

Thank you to Erin Murphy, my wonderful agent. I'm so grateful for your honesty, your kindness, and your willingness to plow through my first drafts. My gratitude to Jody Corbett at Scholastic is too big for this small space. Thank you for your time, for your thoughts, and for your deadlines. This story is far better than it would have been without you. And thank you to everyone at Erin Murphy Literary Agency and Scholastic for believing in this story. I'd also like to thank Anna Swenson of Scholastic Book Fairs and Ann Marie Wong of Scholastic Book Clubs for being so enthusiastic. And Ellen Duda for her beautiful artwork and vision for the cover.

Thank you to my mom and Kymberly McCuistion, who read my early drafts and encouraged me to keep digging even when I thought I wasn't getting anywhere.

My final thanks go to Harrison. I wrote this book for you. Even if it isn't at all what you'd choose to read. There are no dragons or robots or epic battles. There isn't even one explosion (unless you count the fireworks). So, I thank you for countless dinners of tomato soup and grilled cheese sandwiches, and for being my biggest fan but also my most honest critic.

Every good and perfect gift is from above, coming down from the Father of the heavenly lights, who does not change like shifting shadows. (James 1:17)

About the Author

Heather Hepler grew up an avid reader. In fourth grade, she was sent to the hall for reading instead of paying attention in class. She was almost kicked off her Little League team for hiding a novel in her glove when she was supposed to be playing right field. And more than once she missed her bus stop because she was too busy reading. And even though she's grown up now, not much has changed.

Heather is the author of several novels, including *The Cupcake Queen* and *Love? Maybe*. She currently resides in Tyler, Texas, with her son and their very spoiled pets. She can be found online at www.heatherhepler.com.